ONES SUCH AS THESE

Keith,
Here's to new
friends. It's been
a trip! Good luck
in Projects.

Al Jomme
2/3/17

ONES SUCH AS THESE

Al Fonner

Writers Club Press
San Jose New York Lincoln Shanghai

Ones Such as These

Writers Club Press
an imprint of iUniverse, Inc.

For information address:
iUniverse, Inc.
5220 S. 16th St., Suite 200
Lincoln, NE 68512
www.iuniverse.com

This is a work of fiction. The characters, dialogue and scenes are products of the authors imagination, and are not to be construed as real. Any resemblance to actual events or persons, living or dead, is purely coincidental.

ISBN: 0-595-22346-X

Printed in the United States of America

In loving memory of Patricia, Mom, and Dad.

C ONTENTS

▼

Acknowledgements

The Biblical quotations contained in this work were taken from the King James Version. A couple other interesting books I came across while writing this are *Without Moral Limits: Women, Reproduction, and the New Medical Technology*, by Debra Evans (Westchester, IL: Crossway Books, 1989); and *The World's Wisdom: Sacred Texts of the World's Religions*, by Philip Novak (New York, NY: Harper Collins, 1994).

I also want to express my appreciation for the support and encouragement received from my family, especially Ann who lent her critical eye to my effort.

EXTRACTION

The small, brightly-lit room smelled so clean, it was a wonder that any living creature could survive inside it, let alone a team of doctors and nurses. The strong smell of antiseptic permeated every corner of the place. The HVAC unit kept the space at a comfortable seventy degrees Fahrenheit, while its HEPA filters kept the air free of all but the smallest particles of dust, no bigger than a micron.

The fluorescent lamps spaced by *two*s across the ceiling hummed their eerie song, keeping a steady beat as one of the lights flickered rhythmically. The freshly waxed, marbled floor glistened under the light, and the polished ceramic-tiled walls appeared strangely luminescent.

Two doors, one marked *AUTHORIZED PERSONNEL ONLY*, allowed access into, and egress from, the room. There were no windows, which prevented curious eyes from viewing the events that unfolded within those walls.

The room itself was starkly furnished. A sink occupied one corner; fresh, white linens lay neatly folded and stacked on a shelf mounted to the wall above it. A laundry hamper conveniently stood next to the sink. An examination table was located in the center of the room. Off to the side, along one wall, was a hospital bed.

A young woman in her early twenties lay on the table. Her legs, resting on two padded supports, were spread apart with her feet held in stirrups. Even though dressed in only a hospital gown, the young woman seemed relaxed. The earphones she wore blocked out all external noise and allowed only the restful sounds of ocean waves rolling into shore to invade her consciousness. She smiled as the echo of rolling surf reverberated through her mind. She wore a virtual reality visor. It provided her with a view of an undisturbed, peaceful, sandy beach synchronized perfectly with the sounds provided by the earphones.

Ocean waves gently lapped up onto the beach as a warm, soft breeze blew in from the sea. Seagulls floated effortlessly above the water as they tirelessly searched for their next meal. Occasionally, she could hear them as they called to one another. Soft, billowy clouds danced across the sky; and the sun was just beginning to set, presenting a colorful panorama of pinks, reds, and yellows.

A screen set up across her mid-section shielded the woman's view of the procedure being performed at the other end of the table. As she lay there, an attendant gently stroked the girl's forehead and occasionally moistened her lips with a cloth soaked in ice water.

A woman dressed in putrid green pants and smock with matching booties and cap sat on a stool positioned between the young woman's legs. A surgical mask covered her mouth and nose. Goggles that protected her eyes from whatever fluids might splash on her supplemented the mask. Surgical gloves covered her slim, delicate hands as she meticulously guided her instruments through the woman's vagina. An assistant, dressed similarly, stood by to help her as necessary.

The assistant shifted feet. Her rubber-soled shoes screeched noisily across the freshly waxed floor.

Annoyed, the doctor glared at her. "Please, Ms. Jennings," she said through clenched teeth. "This is delicate work."

"I am sorry doctor," she replied.

"And can't we get someone to do something about that light?" the doctor muttered, motioning with a gloved hand toward the flickering fluorescent tube.

The assistant said nothing. She rolled her eyes as she stood by waiting for the doctor's next order.

A stainless steel cylinder mounted on a rolling cart was positioned a few feet behind and to the left of the table. Opaque windows were located on each end of the vessel, and a hinged portal allowed access to its contents. Tubes and wires exited one side of the cylinder and wound their way down to various gadgets and bottles located on the cart's shelves.

A technician, dressed in a similar outfit as the doctor's except without the mask and goggles, stood alongside the contraption. He looked rather bored as he fidgeted and shifted from side to side. Often, he would check the time on the wall clock mounted above the unmarked door.

The doctor closely observed the monitor located next to the table as she inserted an instrument into the woman's vagina. Small disks strapped to her abdomen transmitted grainy, but otherwise clear, images of her uterus, cervix, and vagina to the monitor. The grainy images provided the doctor with a surreal vantage point from which to perform the procedure.

The doctor followed her instrument's outline on the monitor as it snaked its way through the vagina until it reached the cervix. The cervical plug, still in place in the cervix, showed up clearly on the monitor. Fabricated from an absorbent material, the plug absorbed body fluids, causing it to swell and stretch the cervix. The plug had been inserted two days earlier to dilate the cervix, permitting efficient extraction of fetus from the uterus. The doctor smiled. The cervical plug was not unlike a cork stopping up a fine bottle of wine, plugging up the opening to prevent the precious contents from spilling out. The contents in this case, the doctor knew, were just as valuable as any vintage bottle of the finest wine, maybe more so.

Carefully manipulating the instrument while she watched the monitor, the doctor grabbed on to the plug with the small, cam actuated fingers protruding from the instrument. Then, she slowly removed the plug from the cervix. Finally, she guided the instrument, with the plug attached, from the woman's vagina and placed it in a tray to her left.

The doctor inserted her right hand's index and middle fingers into the vagina to perform a bi-manual exam. This allowed her to determine the dilation of the cervix. Although the images on the monitor could be used for that, she was thorough and would leave nothing to chance.

Watching the monitor, she allowed her fingers to remain in place for a few seconds. Then, when absolutely sure of the measurement, she pulled the fingers out and turned to the assisting technician. "Ten centimeters," the doctor noted pointedly. "We're good to go. Would you please…"

Before she could finish her request, the assistant took a clean towel from the instrument table and wiped the beads of perspiration from the doctor's forehead. Despite the cool climate being maintained in the room, sometimes she still broke out in a sweat—from nerves as much as anything else.

"There you go, doctor," the assistant said, as she tossed the soiled towel into a bag hanging from the table.

"Thank you. Now, let's finish this." The doctor glanced at the attendant at the head of the table. "How's she doing?"

The attendant responded succinctly. "Fine. Everything's normal."

The woman on the table continued to be hypnotized by the images implanted into her consciousness by the visor. She was oblivious to what was going on around her.

The doctor nodded in acknowledgment. Then, she looked toward the technician who'd been impatiently standing by at the stainless steel box. She frowned at his restless behavior. "Is everything ready, Mr. Shaeffly?" the doctor asked.

"Yes, doctor. It's ready." With his attention refocused by the question, the technician assumed a more rigid posture and stood by like a sentry guarding the crown jewels.

The doctor turned back towards the business at hand. She reached up with her right hand and adjusted the articulated lamp that illuminated the girl's external genitalia. She then looked at the assistant and nodded. "Ready."

The assistant handed the doctor an instrument similar to the first, except the fingers on this one were more delicate, as if used for handling fragile objects or performing sensitive operations. The doctor took the device and adjusted herself on the stool to allow a better view of the work.

With her free hand, the doctor adjusted the speculum that held the vagina open and gently inserted the instrument with her other hand. Once the head of the device was fully introduced, she switched her gaze to the monitor and slowly, stealthily snaked the tool through the vagina to the cervix.

Once at the cervix, the doctor's attention focused on the uterus and the prize it held. As she continued to insert the instrument, the membrane ruptured, and the amniotic fluid it contained gushed out. Closely observing the monitor, she paid no attention to the fluid as it fell to the floor, forming a smelly puddle whose odor she easily ignored after years of conditioning.

At this point, the doctor hesitated for a moment as she searched the screen to locate one of the fetus's lower appendages. It was essential that she locate one, lest a vital segment be latched onto by the instrument and damaged. The monitor's images were good, but if the fetus was turned just so, an arm or a leg was more difficult to find.

There! Having found one, she continued her work.

Via the monitor, the doctor closely followed the progress of the instrument as it moved along the wall of the uterus. The doctor proceeded cautiously at this point; she did not want to puncture or tear the uterine wall. After several minutes, the fingers were in place, and she carefully manipulated the device until she had a firm grip on what she believed to be a leg.

The fetus did not react. Previously administered anesthesia ensured its cooperation, and fetal monitors verified that it was still alive and suffering no trauma. If the fetus had not been incapacitated, it might have reacted unfavorably to the procedure. Vital organs could have been damaged, or the fetus killed. These were not desired outcomes.

Firmly holding on, the doctor now worked to manipulate the fetus into position for extraction with its head pointing away from the cervix.

As the doctor worked, the young woman continued to be blissfully unaware of what was happening. The paracervical block she'd been given coupled with the painkillers being pumped in intravenously, kept her ignorant of the procedure.

With the fetus finally in position, the doctor inserted the cervical guide, affectionately referred as the *shoehorn*. It aided the doctor in removing the fetus by allowing smoother passage through the cervix. The use of the guide required a little extra work for the physician, but the number of live extractions had markedly increased since its introduction.

With the guide in place, the doctor began to slowly draw the fetus out of the uterus and into the vagina, carefully guiding its progress, ensuring no damage would occur.

As the doctor shepherded the fetus along its path, the woman felt an indescribable sensation in her pelvis. Startled, she tried to look down, but the attendant reassuringly steadied her, gently stroking the woman's forehead.

On the monitor, the doctor could see that the fetus had passed through the cervix. Now, she focused her attention once more on the vagina's opening as she continued the extraction. After a few seconds, a tiny foot popped from the vaginal opening along with the attached tool. Then a leg appeared, and then a torso. Finally, the head slid out as she caught the small body in her hand.

The doctor held the tiny, unmoving, blue-tinted mass of tissue in one hand.

"It's perfect, doctor," noted the assistant.

"Yes," the doctor replied while turning it over to examine it more closely. "It is a fine specimen. Good color, no deformities, and I would estimate it at about one and a half kilograms. It will do quite nicely." Of course, the doctor had no idea which purpose this one was destined for. Seeing that it was female, she knew that however it was employed, when its tissues were no longer useful, the ovaries could be removed and the eggs harvested for use in other applications.

By this time, the technician had already wheeled the stainless steel box over to the doctor and had the portal opened. The technician held two small tubes in readiness for the doctor. The assisting nurse took the fetus and held it while the doctor cut the umbilical cord. The doctor took the tubes from the technician, checking them to ensure they were primed. Then, she attached the tubes to the fetus. The procedure took a few minutes.

When the doctor had finished, the technician touched a button on the cart's control panel. A soft hum came from one of the cart's gadgets, and fluid in the tubes began to flow into and out of the fetus. Digital readouts came alive as the technician made some entries on the input pad.

The assistant placed the fetus in the box, which contained a fluid of its own. Then the technician attached several sensors to the fetus's head and torso. After he'd completed his work, he closed the lid and fastened it.

As the doctor looked on, the technician checked the readings on the panel. "Everything's normal, Doctor. Blood pressure, pulse, temperature, brain activity...everything."

"Excellent," replied the doctor, smiling under her mask. "Now, take it to the nursery."

The technician wheeled the cart through the door marked *AUTHO-RIZED PERSONNEL ONLY*. The final application for this fetus didn't matter to the doctor, or her staff. It could wind up in a dozen different places: organ renewal, pharmaceuticals testing, experimental medicine, cancer research, AIDS research, cosmetics, etc…The list went on and on.

"Doctor."

The doctor looked over at the attendant.

Motioning to the girl, the attendant said, "She's restless and wants to know how much longer."

The doctor walked over to the table and took the young woman's hand, as if she were trying to convey some feeling of compassion. She looked into the girl's eyes and, pulling her mask down, said, "We'll be done very soon. All that's left for us is to get you cleaned up."

The woman smiled and nodded.

Letting go of her hand, the doctor turned to the assistant. "All right, you know what to do. Any questions?"

"No questions," the assistant replied immediately. "Ensure all of the placenta is expelled, clean her up, and get her into recovery."

"Yes, that's correct." The doctor replied. Then, she hesitated for a moment as she quickly went through the procedure in her mind. "Well, I can't think of anything else. If there are any problems, let me know."

As the doctor started for the restricted door, the assistant called out, "By the way, that was beautiful work, doctor."

Without looking back, or missing a step, the doctor answered, "Thank you. It's been a pleasure." And she was gone.

JENNA

Jenna's peaceful slumber was shattered by the piercing wail of the alarm. The sound drove through her psyche like a train thundering through a tunnel. She moaned as she fumbled for the snooze button. Just a few more minutes of sleep, she thought. But Sleep was a creature not likely to come so easily to her. Like a fickle feline, it mocked her from a distance, balancing its tail at half-mast as it stole surreptitiously past the nick-knacks perched precariously upon the mantle. Sleep had become an elusive thing—not easy to catch, and even more difficult to hold on to.

The alarm sounded its reveille once again. With eyes shut tight, Jenna resisted the alarm's call. After another restless night, she had fought too hard to finally doze off. She was not yet ready to give up her warm place for the perils of the living. Groaning, she reached for the alarm clock and fumbled for the "snooze" button in hopes of claiming a few minutes more rest. She found the switch at last, and the alarm died away as suddenly as it had begun.

With eyes closed, Jenna lay in silence. She longed for sleep to return and cover her with its aura of forgetfulness. The stillness was penetrated by her soft breathing and, upon occasion, the jagged snore of her love, Joe, who lay next to her. She remained motionless as the minutes passed slowly by, but the anxiety that dogged her spirit would not release her from its cold grasp. A relentless tormentor, it caused her heart to pound a fitful cadence, awakening her inner fear with its cease-less drumming.

Again, the abrupt triggering of the alarm shattered the silence. And again, she reached over to shut it off. After the wailing had stopped, Jenna looked at the time through bleary eyes. "5:30" glared at her in large red numbers from the clock's display. It was time to get up. No use staying in bed anyway. It would do her no good. She grudgingly pulled herself up from the comfort of her nest. She did not want to leave its security but knew she must.

Groaning, she rubbed her eyes. Another day, she thought. And how many days had it been now—seven, eight? Her menstrual cycles always began promptly with the first quarter of the moon. It was one of the few constants in life that she could count on. But this cycle was late, and she was concerned. God, she thought, let it begin this day.

Jenna stood beside the bed for a moment, gazing at Joe as he slept. His tall, slender form was barely recognizable under the covers. With rough, CroMagnon features crowned by a dark patch of tightly curled hair, he wasn't much to look at. She loved him, however, in spite of that. Despite his coarse appearance, he was a gentle and soft-spoken. He was creative, smart, and witty. Most important, he was loving; and he made her feel important. But as Jenna looked upon his shadowed form, she wondered if love would be enough to hold their fifteen-month marriage together through the ordeal that she suspected was about to change their life together.

Jenna left the bedroom and went into the bathroom. She touched the light switch. A soft, rose tinted glow illuminated the room. Leaning on the sink, she stared into the mirror as the lighting program slowly brightened the room. Gazing into its reflective surface, she was dismayed by what she saw.

Surely this was not herself looking back from the glass. The woman in the mirror looked much older, aged by too little sleep and too much anxiety. The careworn features stared back at Jenna from the mirror, reminding her of a grizzly, old hag she'd seen in a childhood dream.

Her eyes were jaded and red. A frown adorned the woman's face and her hair was unkempt. How very sad, Jenna thought, until she realized that it was herself staring back from the mirror. Feeling a strange sense of foreboding, she shuddered.

Jenna reached into the shower and started the water. She stepped back and pulled the old, faded nightshirt she wore off over her head. She caught a glimpse of herself in the mirror and stopped to look at her body. She turned from one side to the other, studying the shape of her form. She had a slim physique, but not skeletal. Her small breasts hung firmly above a flat stomach; and the gentle curve of her derriere created a smooth, flowing transition between her legs and lower back.

Jenna sighed. She watched her diet, staying mostly with fresh vegetables and fruit. She rarely ate red meat; and she took time each day to exercise and meditate, giving thanks to the Blessed One for her good fortune. But for what purpose, Jenna wondered. Physical beauty was transient and at the mercies of time and circumstance. It could be betrayed by the ravages of time or destroyed by an untimely accident

"Damn," she muttered as she stepped out of her panties. Her period was still delayed. It was true, she thought bitterly, biting her lower lip. She was pregnant. Jenna's mind filled with images of children climbing all over her, clinging to her, suffocating her with their incessant pleading for more attention, more of her time, more of everything. There would be no end to their incessant demands. She picked up her panties and threw them into the hamper. Why was this happening? What message was the blessed Mother trying to convey?

She entered the shower and rested her head on the wall while the hot, pulsating stream cascaded down her back. What was she going to do? She couldn't have a baby. She wasn't ready to be a mother. She and Joe had discussed having a family one day. But they'd agreed to wait a couple of years before they would give it any serious consideration. And now it looked as if their whole scheme was about to crumble. A baby was about to be dropped into their laps, and she didn't know what to do.

Her mind raced. What were her options? She could give the baby over to an adoption agency, but then she would have to muddle through another eight months of morning sickness, cramps, weight gain, and depression. She could keep the baby; but that would disrupt her plans, thrusting her into circumstances she wasn't prepared for. She could abort it, a guaranteed solution. But at what cost?

Of course, she wasn't even sure that she was pregnant. She had to be rational about it. She could do a home test and have a more definite indication of her condition. Then she would be able to think more clearly about what had to be done, enabling her to make an informed choice. If she wasn't pregnant, she could relax. If she was, though, she could have an abortion. Either way, Joe would never have to know. She smiled at that thought.

Jenna finished her shower and stepped out onto the turquoise bath mat. She dried off with a large, beige bath towel that was nearly as big as she and dropped it on the floor. Then she ran a brush through her dark, bobbed hair, leaving it to dry in the open air. She looked at herself in the mirror. She felt better, now. And she looked better, too, she decided. Her skin tone looked healthier, and her hair no longer resembled a home for some little furry creature.

She went back into the bedroom and quietly opened the closet door. A light inside came on as the door opened, creating a soft white glow. Jenna sorted through the collection of outfits hanging from the rod and selected a teal jump suit. She picked a bra, panties, and a pair of socks from one of the drawers, and gathered up her things.

Exiting the closet, she unintentionally closed the door with a sharp bang. The sound it made shook the room, and she feared that she'd aroused Joe from his slumber. She stopped in her tracks and looked toward the bed. He was barely visible in the dark and only stirred, remaining absent to the world, Jenna returned to the bathroom and dressed.

Breakfast that morning consisted of half a grapefruit and decaffeinated coffee. Jenna carefully peeled the skin off of the fruit, leaving the rind on the table for the time being. She tore the grapefruit into two roughly equal halves and consumed the sour fruit one section at a time. The bitterness of the first piece made her grimace, and she was certain that her face was about to cave in. The feeling, however, quickly subsided as she continued to eat.

From the radio, the gentle sound of music filled the kitchen. Jenna wasn't sure what the name of the song was, but its melody touched her spirit in a way that was pleasant to her. The tempo was easy, and the tune had a gentle quality—cyclical and effortless. She closed her eyes and allowed the music to carry her away from the distress that had invaded her world.

Jenna picked up the coffee cup and took a sip. She frowned at its bitterness. Setting the cup back on the table, she watched the wisps of vapor rising up from the cup, marveling at the way they moved. So beautiful, she thought. Gracefully rising up and dissipating, blending with the One. Even when separated, all things eventually return to the unity of the Universe.

Jenna glanced at her watch. It was 05:52 AM. She popped the last section of grapefruit into her mouth, swallowing before it was completely chewed. She quickly downed the remains of the coffee and placed the cup in the sink. In the living room, she hurriedly pulled a wind breaker from the closet, and slipped it on. She left the apartment, stopping for a moment to make sure the door was locked behind her. Then she headed for the basement garage where her electric car waited on its charger.

Jenna didn't care for the garage. She thought it a dreadful place—dreary, like a dark, damp cavern formed in the bosom of the Earth. Its walls were a depressing gray, and exposed pipes and conduit criss-crossed throughout the ceiling like a web spun by a huge spider.

The garage existed, she felt, as a supernatural black hole, absorbing the life force from everything that entered therein. It was an anomaly of the Universal Mind set upon the Earth to maintain the celestial balance between the living and the dead. If she lingered there, she was sure that its gray walls and cold floor would suck the essence from her soul.

She hurried to the safety of her car as soon as she reached the basement. Once inside the vehicle, Jenna breathed a sigh of relief. She flipped on the power switch. The battery meter pegged to the right, indicating a full charge. She carefully backed the car away from its charging stabs and guided it toward the garage door and the street beyond.

The commute to the Nockamixon Nuclear Power Station where she worked as a health physicist took between thirty and fortyfive minutes, depending on the weather and traffic. She looked forward to the drive every time she made it. The early trip gave her time to prepare herself, mind and soul, for the coming day. And in the evening it allowed her time to let go of the troubles that had attached themselves to her during the day.

The scenery was gorgeous. The road followed a ridge, which gave her a good view of the river below, and the rolling hills rising up from the opposite bank. In summer, the treecovered hills provided a living tapestry of greens. The land seemed alive as the wind moved the trees to and fro. Come October, the hills took on a new life as the trees went through their annual transformation. The land exploded with color, reds, yellows, and oranges, as far as the eye could see. It reminded her of wonderfully decorated pillows upon which she could curl up and go to sleep.

If summer embodied life, and winter most certainly represented death, then autumn was like the twilight years of life. The irreversible changes it brought signaled that the end was near. And spring, of course, meant renewal and rebirth as the succession of time continued unabated. It was a cycle that had endured from the beginning, representing in some small way the intricacies of the Universal Mind

Once she'd left town, Jenna rested her head back against the driver's seat. She focussed her attention on the road ahead; and, for a few moments, her mind remained cluttered. The apparent pregnancy she faced was unsettling. Her whole future as she had envisioned it was nonexistent. Even now, the invader controlled her thoughts. She could not escape it.

These troubles, though, left her as she focussed on the road ahead, pouring all of her energy into the drive. The anxiety that dogged her faded away. The things that she held dear appeared before her mind's eye: friends, family, her own personage, Mother Earth. All of these, like a kaleidoscope, danced through her consciousness.

Slowly, the tension departed from her body, starting with her face and working its way out through her fingers and toes. Tension, care, anxiety, all exorcised like demons that had possessed her spirit until, at last, she was able to touch the Goddess within.

Jenna's thoughts wandered into the recesses of her mind. She recalled one encounter she had had with a small number of her sisters. They had gone out to a wooded hilltop one warm summer's evening and found the biggest tree there. It had been a gnarled, old oak towering fifty feet above them. The nine of them had stood in a circle around the tree and shed their clothes. After disrobing, they each had set down, some on pillows they'd brought, the rest on their neatly stacked garments.

There had been no shame, no guilt, no giggling, only reverence. Standing before one so magnificent, so connected with the blessed Mother, had been a solemn occasion. It had been an event not to be taken lightly.

Jenna recalled meditating on the tree as, one by one, each woman had stood up and put her arms around the tree, hugging it. Some had done so for a few seconds; others, minutes. When Jenna's turn had come, she recalled feeling odd hugging a tree. But how else was she to come to understand such a magnificent creature as this? She remembered standing up and putting her arms around the tree.

The sensation of her flesh coming in contact with the rough, cool bark of the Woodland Goddess had caused her to tremble. The only thing she recalled feeling at first was the tingling of her smooth skin against the tree's rough, gnarled exterior. But as she remained still with her flesh pressed against the tree's cool, coarse bark, the sensation had taken on a whole new meaning. She had become part of the tree—roots, trunk, branches, leaves, bark, all of it.

She remembered the sensations clearly: the warm, moist soil around her roots providing the tree with nutrients she needed to live; the refreshing wind blowing through her leaves, gently swaying her limbs; the birds nesting in her branches singing their beautiful songs; the insects living in her bark, tickling her skin as they scurried here and there. It had been incredible! Jenna had never felt anything like it before. It had been all she could do to let go and sit back down.

After they'd each had a turn, everyone had stood up and took their neighbors' hands, forming a circle around the tree. Jenna remembered dancing around the tree, chanting. She couldn't recall the exact words, but she could remember their essence: reverence for the Eternal Mother, and respect for the Woodland Goddess.

The chanting had gone on for about ten minutes. How many times they went around that tree, she couldn't recall; she'd lost count. It had all been very hypnotic, and wonderful.

Still in a circle, they had set back down with their backs resting against the trunk of the tree. She remembered each one extended her legs to the front so that her feet touched her neighbors'. It had been a little uncomfortable at first; but after her flesh had melded with the tree's coarse, outer skin, Jenna recalled entering a euphoric state.

Using a fallen branch as a talking stick, they had passed it around; and whoever wanted could share her thoughts or feelings on the experience. Jenna remembered that one of her friends, Joan, asked why they had to do it in the nude. It had been an honest question, one that was greeted with chuckles from some of the others.

Their master, Roxanne, had quieted them down like a mother quiets her baby. She had then explained to the group that nudity was important because clothing interfered with the exchange of life forces between the tree and the women, as individuals and as a group. She had likened it to the leaves of the tree blocking out the sun's rays. Everyone had been enlightened and nodded in approval towards Roxanne and Joan for her insightful question.

Jenna smiled as she remembered. The experience had been one of the most rewarding of her life. She had connected with the tree and allowed the forest guardian to share with her its wisdom. True, it had been only for a moment; but that moment had let Jenna glimpse into the mind of the Mother experiencing more truth than she could learn in a lifetime.

The car smoothly glided along the ridge as Jenna effortlessly maneuvered it along the twisting rode. Rounding a turn, a valley opened up before her. Lake Nockamixon extended away from her, and the sun was barely sitting on the ridge to the east. As Jenna guided the car down the slope, she could see the power plant on the near shore. The domes of its containment buildings gleamed in the morning sun. These cylindrical giants dwarfed the surrounding buildings.

The sign at the plant's main gate flashed its messages as Jenna approached. "…Day 45 without a disabling injury…Unit 2 enters day 405 of record run…Unit 1 refueling outage begins 10/10/32…Congratulations to Maria Sharpton on the birth of her 9 lb., 7 oz baby girl…"

In a sudden moment of realization, Jenna's lips parted as she took in a quick, sharp breath. She could be like Maria in nine months—on a delivery table in a hospital, struggling to keep her sanity as she labored to force an invader from her body. Looking over her shoulder, she knew the she could not allow it to get that far. She would have to know for sure. A sick feeling welled up in her stomach. How was she going to get through this day?

THE TEST

At 7:05 PM, the sun was dipping behind the ridge west of the power plant. The eastern sky was a dark blue accented by puffs of somber clouds hanging easily in the sky. Jenna watched the clouds as she walked through the parking lot. She envied their isolation and wished that she could approach life with the same indifference as they did. After a day fraught with anxiety, she was glad when she reached the solitude of her car, and even happier to be leaving the main gate onto the access road and heading back to town.

At the end of the access road, she made a right turn onto the main road. The car crept as it climbed the hill up to the ridge above the valley. Barely reaching fifty miles per hour on the steep grade, its motor whined like a crying baby. "C'mon," she mumbled to herself.

Navigating the gentle curves of the road as it wound its way along the ridgeline, Jenna's thoughts turned to her immediate problem. She needed to swing by the pharmacy on the way home to pick up a home pregnancy test. The stop wouldn't add too much time since she passed it on her way to and from work anyway. Just a minor inconvenience, albeit a necessary one.

Jenna sat back in the seat, glad to have a moment to relax. The day had been especially taxing, even more than usual. She enjoyed her work as a health physicist and got along well with her coworkers. The job was usually interesting, although there was way too much paper-work for her enjoyment.

She'd spent a lot of her time this day in meetings as the station pre-pared for the upcoming Unit 1 refueling outage, for which she was the Lead Health Physicist. A fuel load was good for two years. So, each year one of the two reactor plants would shutdown for refueling while the other stayed on line. An outage generally ran for four weeks, bar-ring no unexpected surprises.

Nockamixon had first come on line twenty years ago. The station had two reactor plants, each capable of generating fifteen hundred megawatts of electricity, for a total of three thousand megawatts. They were among the first in a new generation of inherently safe reactor plant designs built in the early twenty first century.

Jenna's mind slipped back to the present. Her period still was still absent. Each time she went to the restroom, she would anxiously lower her panties, afraid of what she may not find. Was she pregnant? She had to know. She wished that the road were straight so she could make the commute at top speed. The quicker she got there, the sooner she could do the test.

The anticipation gnawed at her relentlessly. She wasn't ready for children, not yet. And what would Joe say? She wasn't sure. She'd only known him a year before they got married. And although she felt close to him, lately she'd sensed a void developing between them that con-cerned her greatly. Was it his work? Was it some awful thing she'd unknowingly done? She wasn't sure, and it made predicting his reac-tion dubious at best. She decided not to say anything until she was sure, if she said anything at all. That was the safest thing to do. No point in getting Joe upset.

The car strained to hold on to the road as Jenna rounded the last turn outside of town. She sped past the "Welcome" sign that marked the city limit and soon found herself parked in front of King's Phar-macy. The thought of someone seeing her in the store buying a pregnancy test didn't sit too well. The last thing she needed was to have a nosy neighbor tell Joe what she'd bought.

Of course, she knew that she was being foolish. So what if someone saw her? It was none of their business. Besides, in this day and age, not too many people were concerned about what other people were doing.

Jenna walked into the store. She wasn't sure where to find the tests, and she wasn't about to ask anyone either. So, she walked quietly along one end of the store, trying to be as inconspicuous as possible. She glanced up each aisle as she passed them one by one, studying the directory the hung from the ceiling. Finally, she stumbled onto the feminine hygiene products. She walked slowly along the shelves, carefully examining the packages as she went by.

At last, she located the pregnancy tests. There were several brands to choose from, in all prices. Accuracy was important, but so was convenience. She didn't want to choose the cheapest, or the most expensive. One titled "Posi-Sure" was moderately priced and assured ease of use. It also had an attractive box with a picture of a field in full bloom that she found amusing—a field in full bloom could be interpreted as a sign of fertility. After several moments of indecision, she picked up the "Posi-Sure" test and headed for the front of the store.

As she neared the registers, Jenna remembered that she needed shampoo. She turned crisply and made her way to the hair care products. The shampoo she'd been using was causing her scalp to itch terribly. As a matter of fact, she had scratched so forthrightly at one point in the day that a coworker had made some crack about the benefits of a flea collar. Well, that did it; she was determined to make a change.

A friend had told her about a new shampoo that was guaranteed to add body to her hair and revitalize her scalp; Feta 5000, Jenna thought it was called. The shelves were heavily laden with all manner of shampoos and conditioners, each one promising body and shine. After quickly scanning through the bottles and boxes, she spotted the item in question.

"FETA 5000." The name was emblazoned on the bottle for all to see. Jenna picked up a bottle and examined the front. "FETA 5000, Guaranteed to rejuvenate and revitalize your hair…right down to the roots!" Just like her friend had said. "Made with allnatural humanoorganic compounds to infuse rich proteins directly into tired hair and scalp." Sounded like just what she needed, although she did wonder what humanoorganic compounds were. Oh well, no matter. As long as it stopped that itch.

There were four checkouts at the store's front. One was out of order and two of the others were being used. Jenna walked to the open register. She passed the bar codes of the shampoo and pregnancy test past the checkout station's reader and placed the items in one of the small bags located on a rack next to the register. A small screen located across from her displayed the items' names, codes, and prices, including tax.

Jenna passed her hand over the reader to conclude the transaction. Her name, social security number, and employer code appeared on the screen. A fraction of a second later, information appeared on the screen indicating that the cost of the item would be deducted from her account. The transaction was complete.

"Thank you, Jenna Kelemen." Jenna shook her head. The voice sounded suspiciously like the one she heard in almost every other business she patronized.

She picked up the bag and turned to leave the store when a familiar voice behind her said, "Jen, dear. How have you been?"

She turned to face a man who was at least twice her age. Henry Philips was an elderly man of medium build with silver hair and quick, brown eyes that disappeared into two narrow slits as his mouth curled up into a broad smile. As a retired U.S. Marine, he maintained his trim, physique; so his body barely showed its eightytwo years.

Jenna had first met him in front of her apartment building a couple of years earlier. She had been struggling with an unwieldy package, trying to get it up the front steps when this elderly gentleman offered to help. She had gladly accepted his assistance and discovered that he lived on the first floor of her flat. She had been immediately drawn to the man; he was so much like her grandfather had been before he died. Good natured, gentle, and compassionate, he was always there to lend an ear and more than eager to share his thoughts.

"Fine, Hank," she answered, with a smile, glad to see her old friend. He had all but vanished a couple of weeks ago. She had missed him very much. Jenna forgot about her problem for a moment. "What brings you out this late?"

"Just picking up some medication," he answered, momentarily lifting one hand with a package in it. He coughed into his clenched hand. It was a labored cough, like something blocked the passage between his lungs and mouth.

She was struck by the sound. The man was the picture of health for someone his age. Then she noticed the cane he carried. It was new. He'd never used one before, not that she'd noticed, anyway.

"Oh, Hank," she said, "are you okay? I haven't seen you for a couple of weeks."

"I haven't been feeling well," he answered. "Been having trouble breathing…never had trouble before," he said painfully. "My doctor thought it was asthma, but she's not too sure now. I'm going to see a specialist tomorrow."

"Oh, Hank," Jenna said in disbelief. "Does your doctor think it's cancer? Does she have any idea?"

"No, no. She doesn't think it's cancer," Hank replied reassuringly, yet unconvincingly.

"Thank god," Jenna sighed with relief.

"But, being a primary care physician, my doctor also said that she can't be positive. So, she wants me to see this other doctor, a Dr. Molotov."

"Well then, let me know how it turns out," she said. "Can I give you a lift home?"

A big grin came across his face. "Yes. I'd appreciate that very much."

They left the store and got into Jenna's car. The ride home was made mostly in silence. Down Central Avenue to Hawthorne Street. At one point Hank asked, "What about you? Anything new in your life?"

"No," Jenna said. "Nothing new."

"You sure?" he asked with a grin. "You wouldn't be hiding something from me, would you?"

"No. Of course not." Then she remembered the home test. Had he seen it?

"Suit yourself," he said with a sigh.

When they reached the apartment building, Jenna drove the car into the garage and carefully guided it onto its charging stabs. The two got out of the car and silently walked to the elevator. Hank pressed the call button. Then he turned to Jenna and winked one eye, smiling all the while. She returned the smile.

The elevator doors slid open. Jenna got in first, followed by Henry. "One," Henry said. The doors closed and the box began it assent.

Jenna glanced at Henry. He was looking back at her. An intense frown highlighted his face. What was he thinking, she wondered. Had he seen the test? At last, she said, "You be sure to let me know how the tests come out. All right?"

"Sure I will, miss," he answered. The elevator's doors slid open as they reached the first floor. "As soon as I know anything, I'll let you know." Then he left the elevator, walking slowly down the hallway to his own apartment.

"Three," Jenna instructed the elevator as she watched him out of the corner of her eye. The doors silently closed, and the elevator placidly began its ascent to the third floor. Coming to an abrupt stop, the elevator's doors opened on to the third floor's hallway that led past several apartments.

The hallway itself was plain. The walls were dirty cream, and worn brown carpet covered the length of the floor. Jenna's apartment was the last one on the left. She stepped out of the elevator and began what seemed like one of the longest walks of her life. Finally, she stood in front of her door. She dreaded going in, anxious of what she might discover, afraid of what Joe might do.

Jenna slowly opened the door, hoping to enter without being noticed. Gently stepping inside, she could see Joe busy in the kitchen. He hadn't noticed her yet. Good! She turned towards the bedroom; but before she got very far, she heard his feet shuffling out of the kitchen.

"Hey, Jen!" Hurrying over to her, he took her in his arms before she had a chance to turn around and planted a very passionate, wet kiss right on her mouth!

"Mmmm, I'm glad you're home," he purred, all the while gazing into her eyes.

"Uh…well, I'm glad to be home," she replied. Jenna was evasive.

"Hey, are you all right?" Joe asked. His face twisted up into a worried look, and his eyes searched hers for some clue as to her condition.

"All right? Well, uh, I guess so." Jenna paused for a second, trying to collect her thoughts. "Look, I'm sorry, Joe, I've just got a lot on my mind right now."

"Well, if you say so." His voice registered with just a hint of disbelief. "Anyway, I've prepared something special for dinner. We're going to have a little celebration." Joe's eyes brightened up again, and the tone of his voice became animated.

"Celebration? What are we celebrating?" Jenna's interest was aroused. She hadn't a clue as to what there was to celebrate.

"I can't say just yet," he replied. "You'll have to wait until after dinner." Joe's face beamed. For some reason, he was obviously very happy about something.

He gave her a hug. As they separated, he looked down. Something caught his attention. Reaching for her hand, he asked, "What's in the bag?"

Jenna looked down in horror! Her pregnancy test, he mustn't know. When he straightened up, she snatched the package from his hand.

Joe was stunned. In utter amazement, he exclaimed, "God, Jen! What the hell's a matter with you?"

Jenna was backed into a corner. She didn't know what to do. Thinking quickly, she came up with a good story he wouldn't question. "I think I have yeast infection. So, I stopped at the pharmacy and picked up a tube of vaginal cream. It's just…well, it's embarrassing."

"Yeast infection, huh? Nothin' serious, I hope." Joe sounded really concerned, although she wasn't sure if his distress was meant for her or for himself.

"Well, Joe, no one's gonna die from it," she replied sarcastically.

Joe hugged her and said, "Ah, I'm sorry, Jen. I didn't mean to be cruel. I love you, Jen, and I don't want anything to happen to you." He sighed. "I guess I'm just a big, dumb jerk."

"Yeah, well, maybe you are." Her heart beat a little slower now. She'd narrowly avoided what could have been a very ugly scene.

Looking into her eyes, and cupping her chin in his right hand, Joe softly said, "Now, go get ready for dinner." Then, he gently kissed her on the forehead.

Joe turned and headed back toward the kitchen. Jenna watched him for a moment. She noticed a slight bounce in his walk that she hadn't seen for some time now. Something really had him excited. She was thankful that he didn't discover her little secret; and hopefully, he never would.

Jenna didn't stop when she entered the bedroom. She continued on to the bathroom. Turning the lights on as she entered, she fumbled to remove the box from the bag.

The test was simple. Hold the strip in the urine stream, just enough to moisten it, not soak it. Remove the strip and wait 10 seconds. If a large, blue dot appeared, she was pregnant. If it didn't, then she wasn't.

Jenna anxiously opened the box and nervously removed the test strip from its sealed, plastic wrapper. It was no bigger than her little finger. A small, oval hole containing the test agent was located at one end of the strip. No moving parts, just a spot of chemicals. It was so simple, a child could use it. She set the strip on the counter next to the toilet.

About three hours had passed since Jenna last relieved herself. The urge to urinate was almost unbearable. Was it due to the lapsed time since her last visit, or was it the desire to get this over with? She wasn't sure, and really didn't care. With the pressure building, she positioned herself on the seat. She shuddered slightly when the stream finally commenced.

As she rose to her feet, Jenna pulled her pants back up and fastened them in place. Nervous, she impatiently counted the seconds. As they slowly ticked by, her mind was tormented by what she might find. If the test was positive, she would terminate; there was no question about that. She wasn't ready for motherhood. She wasn't even sure if she ever wanted children. Besides, the world could barely support the current, exploding population as it was.

Seven…eight…nine…ten. Time was up. Jenna was afraid to look. She didn't want this. She never asked for this. It just wasn't fair! She knew, however, that she had to face up to reality. So, summoning up her courage, she hesitantly cast her gaze upon the oval.

"Shit," she whispered to herself in disbelief. The dot did appear. She was pregnant after all. The thing she had wanted to avoid most was right now staring her in the face, laughing at her, and making a mockery of her life. Her mind raced as she thought about what to do next. She would have to see her doctor for verification and termination. And Joe, well, maybe he would never have to find out. If she could abort the fetus before she got very far along, he would be none the wiser. Besides, whatever reason he had for celebrating, she didn't want to ruin it.

The evening had been a pleasant one. Before dinner, Jenna had changed into a brightly colored, shear body suit with matching spike-heeled boots. The blues, greens, and oranges of the outfit swirled together obscuring the details of her body that otherwise would have been clearly visible. The effect was erotic. The outfit was one of Joe's favorites. She felt sexy knowing that it aroused him so, which allowed her to forget the unpleasantness of her reality—at least for the moment.

Dinner was one of the best Joe had ever made. The bread, the salad, the soup, all were perfect. And the lasagna! Joe'd really outdone himself this time. The sauce was a delight and the noodles were cooked just right: tender yet firm.

The end of dinner, though, had been the climax. Joe offered a toast to their health and happiness, and their continued love for each other. When he'd finished, he broke the news that he'd been holding in all evening. The proposal that he'd submitted to Akagi Enterprises had been selected. He was very excited, like a little boy at Christmas; and Jenna, too, was excited and proud.

Work for Joe had been scarce these last few months. There had been the occasional odd job such as remodeling projects for offices and homes, but nothing like this. Designing Akagi's new regional head-quarters would be a real challenge for his talents and a much-needed stretch for his imagination. It also meant a significant boost for their income.

Now, reclining on the sofa with soft, relaxing music playing in the background, Jenna felt warm and secure. Fortune really was smiling on her. The pregnancy was an inconvenience that could be easily eradi-cated. She enjoyed her work, for the most part. Joe's career was getting a much needed, and well-deserved, boost. It just didn't get better than this, she was certain.

Joe had gone into the bedroom to get something. What it was, she couldn't guess. Perhaps he'd bought her a gift as part of the celebra-tion, or perhaps he was slipping into something more comfortable. It didn't matter. She would find out soon enough.

Taking a sip from the wineglass she'd been fondling, Jenna could hear Joe coming back into the room. She set the glass on the coffee table and struck her sexiest pose.

"God, Jen!" Joe's voice dripped with disappointment as Jenna felt something drop on her hip and fall to the sofa. "When you said you were having female troubles, you weren't kidding."

He came around to the front of the sofa and, pointing to the small box he'd just dropped on her, said, "I found that in the bathroom."

Jenna was speechless. She'd neglected to destroy the box. She'd never intended for him to find out this way. Now, he was aware that something was going on. How far would he press it?

Jenna sat up and looked at him. Towering over her, he seemed like a giant. He didn't look angry, though. His face revealed something else. Sorrow, worry, she couldn't be sure.

"Look, Joe…"

"I want the truth, Jen," he said, cutting her off. "No games. Are you pregnant, or not?"

"Look, the test was positive, but…"

"But what? Those tests are almost foolproof." His eyes narrowed. "How could you do this to me?" he asked, throwing his arms in the air.

You son of a bitch! she thought to herself. Jumping to her feet, she looked him in the eye. "How could I do this to you? Hey! You're not the one pregnant, here, pal!"

Caught off guard, he exclaimed, "Don't raise your voice at me, damnit!"

"I'll raise my voice if I want to!"

They stood there, staring at each other, toe to toe. He looked down at her, his eyes filled with sorrow and hurt. The silence seemed to last forever as they both searched for the right words to say. He shifted his weight to his left and sighed. She crossed her arms in defiance.

Finally, Joe broke in. "Look, Jen. This isn't gonna get us anywhere. I'm sorry I was insensitive. This must be hard on you." He gestured towards the sofa. "Can't we sit down and discuss it?"

Jenna studied him for a moment. She knew he was right. "Okay," she softly replied.

They both sat down on the sofa, leaving a little space between them to emphasize the current mood.

"Now, what can you tell me?" Joe sounded businesslike, efficient.

"Well, my period's about two weeks late." She tried to match his nononsense demeanor, but it wasn't part of her psyche. "So, I figure I'm about six weeks along."

"All right." He took her hand and asked, "What do you plan to do next?"

"I'm going to make an appointment with my gynecologist to verify the test, and then…"

"And then what?"

"And then I'll abort it, if it's confirmed."

He sighed. "Okay. Good."

"That's it?" she said. "Okay? Good? I would have thought that you'd be a little more concerned."

"Well, I am, Jen," he said. "You know I want to have children some-day. We've discussed this many times before. This just isn't the time. You hadn't thought of keeping it, had you?"

"No," she replied. "That thought never even entered my mind. I just thought that you'd be a little more concerned."

"I'm sorry, Jen. I didn't mean to hurt you." He leaned over and kissed her. At the same time, his hand snaked its way from her knee up her thigh and to her pubic region.

"No…stop, Joe," she said as she resisted his advances, pushing him away. "I…I can't. Not right now, okay?"

He stroked her hair and sighed. "Okay. I guess this evening hasn't been as perfect as either of us hoped," he said. He sat back with a disappointed look on his face.

She cuddled up next to him. "Just hold me right now. That's all I want."

He put his arm around her, and she cuddled up next to him. The soft rhythm of the music continued in the background as they both remained still, each one lost in the solitude of their own contempla-tion.

DR. KUMAN

After a short drive across town, Jenna arrived at the medical center where her gynecologist, Dr. Kuman, had her office. The building itself was rather plain. It was pale gray with neatly trimmed shrubbery lining the structure at ground level and along the concrete sidewalk leading up to the entrance. The outside wall of the first floor was all glass, except for supporting columns evenly spaced around the building. Sunlight glaring off the windows hid the lobby from outside viewing. The building was not as tall as the other buildings in the vicinity, but it still blended in perfectly with the surrounding structures.

She entered the north side of the building through one of the lobby's two revolving doors and proceeded to the elevators. The lobby was desolate, having no furnishings to speak of. Two drab, contemporary prints of cityscapes hung on the south wall. The place was dreadful, Jenna thought. It was wasted space, obviously never intended for anything other than a passageway.

Dr. Kuman's office was on the fourth floor of the building. Jenna touched the up arrow located next to the elevator nearest the lobby. She could hear a faint whir as it made its descent from the third floor.

Approximately ten seconds passed before the doors opened. When they did, a woman about forty and very trim stepped out without acknowledging Jenna's presence. Jenna didn't give it any thought and walked into the elevator. "Four," she commanded, and the doors closed in front of her. The elevator began its ascent.

As the elevator made its way to the fourth floor, Jenna had a few seconds to reflect on her predicament. Five days had passed since she had performed the home test. That had given her a lot of time to think. Did she ever want to have children? Was there really some biological instinct common to all women that made them want to experience the joys of motherhood?

Perhaps as a child, when Jenna was more idealistic and sure that there was a difference between right and wrong, that desire had existed for her. Childhood had been a world of absolutes, an exercise in simplicity; and it was easy to see things in black and white. Jenna vaguely remembered playing at being a mother to an inanimate piece of plastic that resembled a baby. The experience hadn't been real, but it was somehow satisfying for the young girl.

More certain was the wonderment she experienced at her grandfather's farm when a new calf came into the world and bonded with its mother. The helpless newborn would struggle to stand on spindly legs, all the while its mother carefully, lovingly nudging it with her nose. This was a miracle she'd seen many times.

But eventually the miracles lost their luster, and things weren't so simple. Jenna and her mother had moved in with her mother's boyfriend soon after her parents' separation. In her new environment, Jenna found herself thrust into a world of relativity. She learned to interpret her environment based only on how she perceived her surroundings. Objectivity was discarded in favor of subjectivity. Never mind that the fire was hot and could scar you for life; if you liked the pain, put your hand in it. And truth? Truth was just another casualty in a painful childhood.

There was nothing special about motherhood, anyway. Anyone could do it. In their effort to be natural mothers, lesbians had for decades been undergoing artificial insemination, and some had even gone so far as to clone themselves in an effort to procreate without the need for a man. Homosexual men adopted children regularly. There were even experiments under way where a man would attempt to bring a fetus to viability by carrying it in his abdominal cavity until it was sufficiently developed to be removed surgically and maintained in an artificial womb.

Children had become a commodity. For decades, they'd been referred to as a resource, like coal or oil. They were bought, sold, and traded much like a fine wine, or a champion racehorse. Even egg and sperm cells suspended in a frozen state in some cryogenics lab were hot items. From where she stood, Jenna just didn't see any advantage in it.

Joe had been such a child. For months after she and Joe had first met, he wouldn't talk about his family. Then one day, after gaining his trust, he opened up to her.

His mother had been married once but was divorced before there were any children. During the marriage, she discovered that she was homosexual which eventually led to the breakup. She moved in with her lover after leaving her husband. Eventually, the two decided that they wanted to have a family of their own.

But how do two woman make a baby? In and of themselves, it was impossible. However, medical technology permitted an egg taken from his mother to be fertilized in a lab with the sperm of an anonymous man who was nothing more than a set of favorable characteristics that the women had agreed upon. The fertilized egg, one of several, was implanted into his mother's womb; and nine months later, Joe was born.

Joe never knew the truth until he was seventeen. He'd always wondered who his father was. All his friends knew who their fathers were, but his mother continued to avoid the subject. Eventually she broke down and told him, feeling that he was ready to know.

His first reaction was disbelief, then denial. He felt robbed of his personhood, existing but not fully human. Jenna could remember him laughing as he told her that his father was a sperm cocktail, a semen milk shake. Joe never hated his mother because of it, but his trust became an asset that she would no longer possess.

Reaching the fourth floor, the elevator came to an abrupt stop. The doors opened on to a long, brightly-lit hallway that passed a dozen doors before sharply turning to the right. She left the elevator and started off down the hall. Her gynecologist's office was the fifth one on the right. She stopped for a moment at a water fountain to get a sip of water. Then, she quickly walked the last few steps to the door.

Jenna opened the door and entered the reception room. It was small, with ten chairs lined up, five on opposite walls, and a magazine rack mounted to the wall just inside the door. As she went in, she noted that the only other person there was a man involved in some novel. She continued on to the receptionist's window.

The face behind the window was a familiar one. Jackie Walker had been a receptionist here for as long as Jenna could remember. She was an older woman, about fifty, and on the heavy side. The tight curls of her short, dark hair framed her full, round face perfectly and accented her dark, friendly eyes.

"Good morning, Jackie." Jenna smiled.

Jackie looked up from her work, and smiling, returned the greeting. "Why, good morning, Ms. Kelemen. How are you today?" It was a canned response, but Jenna appreciated the civility behind it.

"Oh, I'm fine, Jackie. Ah, I've an appointment with Dr. Kuman?" Jenna was nervous, and the statement seemed more like a question rather than a fact.

Jackie turned to her monitor to check the appointment list. "Yes. Yes, you do." She then looked at the clock. "Hmm, the doctor's with a patient right now, but she should be done soon. So, if you'll just have a seat."

"Oh," Jenna said, "all right." She turned around and took a seat across from the man reading.

Alone with a strange man in a gynecologist's waiting room, she felt a little awkward. For the life of her, she couldn't figure out why a man would be here by himself. She studied him for a moment. He was about 30 and boyishly attractive. He was casually dressed and clean cut. Nothing unusual to speak of. As he turned the page of his book, she noticed that he was wearing a gold wedding band. She decided that he must have brought his wife for an appointment.

Looking over at the magazine rack, she saw a copy of one of the more popular new age magazines, Celebrate!. She leaned over and noticed that it was the current edition, which was unusual for a doctor's office. With nothing else to do but wait, she pulled the magazine out of the rack.

Paging through it, she didn't see anything that interested her. There were the usual fare about yoga techniques and meditation. One article did catch her eye, though. It was titled, "Jesus of Nazareth: Shaman to the World." The author, Dr. James Emerson, was a renowned New Testament scholar and spiritualist. Jenna had read many of his articles and found him fascinating. This was one man, she felt, who really knew how to help people unlock the christ-consciousness in themselves.

Before she could really begin the article, the door next to the receptionist's window opened and a woman entered the waiting room. She looked to be about five months pregnant. The man got up to meet her, and they left the room hand in hand.

After a few moments, the door opened again. A short, thin nurse stood in the doorway and said, "Ms. Kelemen?"

"Yes," Jenna answered as she stood up.

"If you'll follow me." He held the door open until she was inside.

Jenna followed the nurse down a short, plain hallway that led to another door that was already open. As she entered the examining room, she observed that it was a little cooler in there than in the waiting room.

The examining room was about ten feet by eight feet. The walls were painted a light shade of blue, and the floor had an offwhite tile covering. At the center of the far wall, an examining table protruded

out into the room. To the right of the table was a door that opened
into a small restroom. Along the wall to her right was a counter with
cabinets above and below it, and a sink in the center of its top. A cur-
tain running along a track mounted on the ceiling could be pulled
around the table. To the left was a door that went into the doctor's
office.

"Would you please hop up on the table?" The nurse motioned
towards the table. Jenna sat on the table, studying the nurse for a
moment. He did not look familiar.

The nurse pulled a small instrument from one pocket and inserted it
into her ear. She heard several clicks followed by a beep. The nurse
removed the instrument from her ear and discarded its plastic cover.
"Temperature, thirtyseven. That's normal. Your pulse is a little high,
though," he said.

"Well, I'm a little nervous," she assured him.

Unmoved by her admission, he grunted. Next, he took the blood
pressure cuff off of the hook at the end of the table. Taking her right
hand, he wrapped the cuff around her upper arm. He then reached
over and touched the start button on the wall panel. The cuff was
tight; and as the pressure built up, it constricted her arm until Jenna
thought it would burst.

A few seconds later, a beeping sound came from the panel. The
nurse removed the cuff from her arm and returned it to its hook. He
looked at the readout. "One thirtyfive over ninety. That, too, is high
for you. I guess you are nervous." He shook his head.

Jenna sheepishly smiled at him.

The nurse entered the data into Jenna's file. Then he said, "The
doctor will be with you shortly."

Jenna thanked the nurse as he left, but he didn't acknowledge it.

She hadn't waited long before Dr. Kuman entered the room from
her office with a file in hand. She was a petite, middleaged woman,
about fortyfive, with black hair highlighted by streaks of gray. Jenna

liked her very much. She was firm, yet gentle. And she had a good spirit.

Dr. Kuman walked over to Jenna and said. "Good morning, Jenna. How are you today?"

"Oh, I'm okay, Dr. Kuman. You're looking good."

"Well, thank you. I'm feeling well, too." She glanced at the file. "Now…What can I do for you. You're not due for a checkup for another six months. Is something wrong?" Dr. Kuman looked concerned.

"Yes, there is. I think I may be pregnant."

"And what makes you think that? Is your period late?"

Feeling anxious, she replied, "Well…yes. About two weeks late now." After a moment's hesitation, she continued, "And I did a home test, too. It was positive."

"Hmm," Dr. Kuman ran her long, slender fingers through her thick, dark hair. "Two weeks late…and a positive home test. Possible, but inconclusive."

Jenna wanted to protest, but Dr. Kuman continued, "You know, home tests are only about ninetyeight percent accurate. There are many factors in an uncontrolled environment that can alter the result; and a late period…well, there could be several reasons for an abnormal menstrual cycle."

She looked at the file again. "I see in your record that we changed your birth control medication. Have you noticed any unusual responses to it?"

Jenna shifted her weight on the table. The paper covering the table underneath her rustled as she moved. "No, nothing unusual…except for this late period."

Dr. Kuman put her left hand on the table and leaned into it. "Yes, well, a change in medication can result in an aberrant menstrual cycle." She thought for a moment; then, she said, "All right, then, let's check you out!"

The doctor walked over to the counter area and took a cup out of one of the cabinets above it. She handed it to Jenna and said, "Now, Jenna, please fill this for me…at least half way."

Jenna took the cup and hopped down. She walked around the table and into the restroom, closing the door behind her. Pulling her pants down, Jenna considered just how ridiculous this was. She had to urinate in a cup, without missing it!

She recalled a story that Hank had told her many times before about his days in the U.S. Marines in the late twentieth century. He had told her how the marines and sailors had a fierce rivalry between them, and how they used to ridicule each other. One of the jokes was about how only sailors washed their hands after taking a piss because they always got some on themselves. It made her laugh, jiggling the cup and splashing some urine on her hand. "Oh, shoot," she whispered to herself. "This'll make a good one to tell Hank."

After she'd washed her hands, she returned to the examining room and handed the cup back to Dr. Kuman. "Here you are," she said.

"Thank you." Dr. Kuman had set up her equipment on the counter while Jenna had been in the restroom. The test was done electronically using a small device that had a mathematical keyboard on the front with an L.C.D. readout next to it. A small, jointed arm protruded from the top, to the right and down. Two small fingers held an even smaller tube in place that disappeared back inside the arm.

The doctor took the cup and measured its temperature and pH with a small probe connected to the computer by a wire. This data was entered into the computer so that it could make adjustments for these parameters, ensuring the test's accuracy. Having done that, she placed the cup next to the computer and touched the start button on the keyboard.

Jenna watched as a small motor inside the device moved the arm over and down into the specimen. Then, through a differential pressure, a predetermined quantity of the urine was pulled up into the tube and transferred to the device's analyzer. After about thirty seconds, a green light on the keyboard illuminated and a soft, pulsating beep was emitted from the device.

"All right, Jenna," Dr. Kuman said, "let's see how it came out." She stepped over to the counter from the examining table and looked down at the keyboard. Her face tightened a little, then loosened. "I don't know if I should congratulate you or not." She looked over at Jenna. "It is positive."

"What?" Although she'd been expecting the worst, Jenna was still caught off guard by her announcement. She, too, looked down. The letters *POS* appeared on the readout.

Wanting to confirm her observation, Dr. Kuman concluded, "You see?"

"Just great." Jenna was beginning to feel the pressure, now. She looked at the doctor and asked, "How far along am I?"

Dr. Kuman turned around and leaned back onto the counter. Looking up, she closed her eyes for a second. "Well, if you are two weeks late," she opened her eyes and looked at Jenna, "I would estimate four to six weeks. Now, the next…"

"Wait a minute." Jenna's face had tightened, and she clenched her fists. "I can't have a baby. I'm not ready! My husband isn't ready! He doesn't even know…" Her words trailed off in a sigh.

Dr. Kuman reached over and took her hands. "All right, all right, Jenna." Speaking softly, she continued, "We can take care of this. I think it's obvious you want to terminate the pregnancy."

Calmer, now, Jenna answered, "Yes. That's right. I do."

"Well, then, that's definitely within your rights." Dr. Kuman paused for a moment, then continued, "Let's go into my office where we can discuss your options, alright?"

"All right," she replied.

Dr. Kuman led Jenna into her office. The office, larger than the examining room, was decorated more liberally. A window in the wall to the right allowed a view of the hillside. A door to the left led into the receptionist's area. Several colorful, bright contemporary prints hung on the walls, along with the doctor's diplomas. Below the window was a love seat with tables at each end. Several plants were positioned throughout the office. The doctor's desk was located across from the door that they had come through. Dr. Kuman directed her to the love seat while she sat at the desk.

Dr. Kuman turned towards Jenna. Putting her left hand on the desk, she haphazardly thumbed through some papers. She scratched her head and cleared her throat. Obviously, she had something in mind but was just trying to think of the best way to say it. "Jenna, are you positive that you want to terminate?"

"Absolutely!" The question irritated Jenna to no end. She was a wonderful doctor, but who did she think she was making Jenna account for her decision?

She leaned forward. "Very well, then. As I see it, you have two options."

Two options? What was Dr. Kuman talking about? The only option Jenna felt she had, that she *wanted*, was to rid her body of the cancerous growth developing inside her womb.

"One, I could prescribe an abortifacient, enabling you to expel the fetus in the privacy of your own home. Or..."

"Or what?" Jenna was beginning to feel a little disturbed by her debating the issue.

"Or, I could refer you to an institute that specializes in cases such as yours." She leaned back in the chair.

"What do you mean?" Her voice echoed the doubts in her mind. "Why would I want to go to some institute?"

Dr. Kuman looked at Jenna. With a serious tone, she continued, "Jenna, you may not realize it, but you have a real opportunity, here. There is a big demand for fetal tissue..."

"There is? Well, what does that have to do with me?"

"Let me finish." Dr. Kuman leaned forward again. "You see, recent Supreme Court decisions, oh, within the past decade or so, have opened up whole new research opportunities for science and industry:

research that was unheard of before, research that may change the fate of humankind."

"So?" Her tone was skeptical.

"Don't you see? This is a chance for you to profit from this unfortunate event?"

"Profit? How? What do you mean?" She was still skeptical, but the doctor had struck a chord that made her want to hear more.

"Let me explain." She pulled her chair a little closer. "As I said, research of all kinds that use fetal tissue has really taken off. Now, some companies out there are willing to pay quite well for this material..." She leaned a little closer. "...but they won't accept material that wasn't collected in a controlled fashion. The majority of the material harvested comes from cloned embryos. But that doesn't preclude them from harvesting from other sources."

"So?"

"So, if you abort this fetus using an abortifacient, at home, as far as they are concerned, it is useless." She sat up straight. "That's where this institute comes in."

"Really? And how so?" Now, her curiosity was building.

"This group I speak of is very involved in all areas of bio-medical research. Among the things they do is oversee the collection and distribution of fetal tissue. I could give you their number."

"Well...wait a minute." Jenna was somewhat overwhelmed by the proposition. "Why would I want to go through this any longer than I have to?"

"That's a fair question, and one that I really can't answer. I can tell you, though, that they pay up to fifty thousand dollars, depending on the quantity and quality of the tissue that you provide to them."

Quantity? Quality? She wasn't sure that she heard that right. What was Dr. Kuman talking about?

"Look, you call and they can tell you more than I can. So..."

"Um, I don't know," Jenna said.

"Listen, we have at least two weeks before you absolutely have to decide. Any longer, and it may be too late to terminate via an abortifacient. So, why don't you take a couple of days to think about it. Then you can call me back. All right?"

Jenna thought for a moment and then said, "Well, I'll think about it. But I really don't know. I mean, I just want to get rid of it."

"Yes, I know you do," Dr. Kuman said, "and let me assure you that I have only your best interests in mind. You have nothing to lose, and much to gain. So, think it over. If you decide not to call them, then we'll abort it. But remember, if you're going to terminate, why not profit from it?"

"Well...I don't know. You do have a point though." She sat back. "Are you sure about these two weeks?"

"Absolutely."

Jenna sighed. "All right, I'll think about it." Why not? It was a compelling proposition.

Dr. Kuman's eyes brightened, and she smiled. "Very well, then, Jenna. Let me know your decision as soon as you make it."

"Okay."

"Good." She stood up and took Jenna's hand to help her up. "Well, I hope to hear from you soon."

"Oh, you will. Goodbye, Dr. Kuman."

"Goodbye, Jenna."

Dr. Kuman walked Jenna out through the examining room and into the hall. Jenna continued on, alone, down the hall and into the waiting room. By this time, two other women were there. She must have been with the doctor a long time, or so it seemed. She said goodbye to Jackie and politely greeted the other two women on her way out despite the sick feeling in the pit of her stomach. Dr. Kuman's proposition seemed innocent enough. Would it open up a whole new set of problems? She would have to give it some serious consideration.

Either way, she would be rid of the fetus. Aborting now would be quicker, with little risk to herself. Dr. Kuman's suggestion required that she wait some unspecified period of time, not to mention the uncertainty. What did she mean by quantity and quality, and how would it affect her physically, as well as emotionally?

Ending the pregnancy was still what she wanted. Now, the question was how?

TEAM PLAYERS

Dark, dreary clouds filled the sky in all directions. The late afternoon's chill seemed even more miserable, thanks to a constant, numbing drizzle. On an empty street, Jenna walked home from a convenience store that was down the street from her flat. The stress that day had been particularly numbing causing her to develop a skull splitting headache. Discovering that she and Joe were out, she'd been forced to make the journey to buy a bottle of pain reliever.

The raincoat Jenna wore did little to keep her warm, and its small hood failed to prevent the rain from striking her face, causing sharp points of irritation with each drop. She shivered uncontrollably in the cold, wet day.

Alone with her thoughts, Jenna began to consider her dilemma. She was definitely pregnant, which was easily reconciled. Dr. Kuman's proposal, however, had something that she found to be both intriguing and disturbing. Not only could the pregnancy be terminated, but she could profit from it as well. But how long would she have to carry the fetus? How would she explain it if and when her condition became obvious? How would it affect her mentally, physically, and spiritually? Could any amount of money adequately compensate for the inconvenience that she was sure to experience?

Jenna reached the apartment building and went inside, glad to be out of the foul weather. To her surprise, and satisfaction, Henry Philips was standing outside his door with his back to her. She hadn't seen him since the evening he told her about his health problem. She had been wondering how it went with the specialist. What was his name? Molotor, Moloshor, Molotov? Well, it didn't matter. She proceeded back to where he was and stopped beside him.

Hank had been fumbling with his combination; but he looked away from it as Jenna approached him. Seeing that it was Jenna, smiling and brighteyed, coming toward him, Henry smiled a big, toothy grin.

"Jenna, darling," he said as he leaned over and gave her a big hug. "Oh, it's been too long."

"Hi, Hank," she responded warmly. "How've you been?"

With his eyes avoiding hers, he leaned back and said, "Oh, pretty well for an old man, I guess. And how have you been?"

"Good, good," she answered.

From the way his eyes darted around, she could tell that something was up. It wasn't like Hank. He always looked her in the eye when he was speaking, unless they were exchanging jokes or he was relating one of his stories. No, something was wrong. So, she asked, "Hank, are you alright?"

"Why, of course. I'm fine," he said, trying to reassure her. "Don't worry about me. I…I'm just an old man…you have your whole life ahead of you."

There was a hesitation in his words that did nothing to ease her mind. Remembering his visit to the doctor, she asked, "How was your visit with Dr. Molotor?"

"Molotov," he corrected her. Hank looked down the hall toward the front doors for a moment. Then he continued, "Well, I'm still here, which isn't saying much." His voice was distant, and he spoke with an uncertain hesitation that didn't escape Jenna's ear.

Jenna asked, "What do you mean, you're still here?"

He huffed and said, "Just that, I'm still here."

Putting her hand on his, she said, "Now, Hank, something's wrong. I can tell. You're just not yourself today. Tell me what's bothering you, please?"

He looked at her and turned to his door. He unlocked it and motioned for her to follow him in which she did. He closed the door behind her. "Please, sit down," he said.

Jenna sat down on the sofa. This wasn't the first time she'd visited his apartment. Over the years, she'd stopped by many times to visit or drop off some homemade bread. It was a warm place, filled with memories of a full and exceptional lifetime. Family photos, marine corps memorabilia, state penal system awards. All gave testament to a man who'd lived a full and productive life.

Hank sat down beside her. Jenna took his hand and said, "Now, tell me what's up."

Shaking his head, he looked down at the floor. "It's my lungs, Jenna. Dr. Molotov told me I've got a condition called…" he hesitated for a moment, searching for the words, "…pulmonary alveolar proteinosis."

Pulmonary alveolar proteinosis? Jenna had never heard of that one before. It sounded terrible, and she wanted to comfort him. She squeezed his hand more tightly and said, "Oh, Hank. That sounds serious. What else did he tell you?"

Hank pulled his hand from hers and picked up a pamphlet that was lying on the end table next to the sofa. On the page he turned to, there was a diagram of a set of lungs with Pulmonary Alveolar Proteinosis printed in bold letters at the top. He fumbled with it for a moment and then handed it to her, all the while gazing at the floor.

Jenna looked at Hank for a second or two after taking the pamphlet from him. He sat next to her motionless, his hands clasped, staring at the floor. This was not the strong, confident man she'd come to love and respect. The muscles in his lean face were tight, and his lips were pinched so that she could hardly see them anymore. She'd never seen him look so weak.

Taking a minute or so to read what was on the page he'd opened to, she tried to absorb as much as possible. Alveolar proteinosis is a condition where the spaces between the lung's alveoli fill with a granular material consisting mostly of fat and protein from the blood. It occurs in previously healthy people, mostly men between the ages of twenty and fifty. It may progress, remain stable, or clear up spontaneously. The condition can be localized, or spread throughout one or both lungs. In some cases, there aren't any symptoms and the patient can live out his whole life without knowing the condition exists. In severe cases, though, breathing difficulties can result during physical activity. The page she was on made no mention of treatments available.

Having finished reading that page, she thumbed through the pamphlet but found nothing else on alveolar proteinosis. She closed the pamphlet and thought for a moment. What could she say? How could she comfort him? He was obviously distressed over the matter. If she could draw him out, perhaps he would reveal more of the condition, and then she could respond more assuredly.

Putting her hand on his knee, she asked, "Are you in any pain?"

He shook his head and answered, "No...not really." He sat up, turned his head to the side, covering his mouth, and coughed. He breathed in deeply, held it for a moment, and exhaled. It sounded like a sigh.

Looking at her, he continued, "When I'm doing something that requires any amount of effort, like...well, like walking farther than two or three blocks, breathing becomes especially difficult. It's almost as if someone's put a load of bricks on my chest. Pain's not the word for it. Pressure, maybe, but not pain. And it's very uncomfortable. Sometimes I just have to stop and rest for a moment. I tell you, I've never experienced anything so damned debilitating."

"Oh, Hank," she said, softly touching his cheek. "Is there anything they can do about it?"

He looked away for a moment. She was certain that there was a tear in his eye, but he wiped it before she was sure.

Looking back at her, he spoke. "Yes, well, the good doctor indicated that sometimes it does clear up on its own; but he added that, at my age, that wasn't very likely."

"Is there anything else?" she asked.

"Yes, he also mentioned something called bronchopulmonary lavage. I believe that's what he called it."

"What's that?" she wondered aloud.

"Well, as he explained it, it's some kind of procedure where they flush out your lungs, like we used to do to radiators in those gasoline powered cars years ago."

Jenna thought back for a moment to when she was a little girl. The automobile her mother had at that time had a gasoline engine. She could remember her mother taking it to a garage every so often for routine maintenance. She'd never seen it done, but she guessed that flushing the radiator was something performed during one of those visits.

"Did the doctor seem to think that this might help you?" she asked.

He didn't answer. He just sat there, staring into space. His body was shaking, like he was cold or frightened. A single tear rolled from one eye, leaving a wet trail down his left cheek.

Putting a hand on his shoulder, she asked again, "Hank, did you hear me? Does the doctor think that this procedure will help you?"

He blinked and wiped the moisture from his eyes. "You know, I've been healthy all my life. Hardly ever been sick. The sickest time I can recall was when my brother, Bob, and I got into the neighbor's watermelon patch."

Hank smiled as he continued, "It was late, and we were supposed to be asleep. But we snuck out and over to old Mister Manson's place, and we each found the biggest melon we could carry back to our barn. When we got back, we spent the next couple o' hours eating those melons. Well, we never did finish. What we didn't eat, we threw to the hogs."

He started to chuckle. "Boy, you never saw two sicker boys than the two of us the next morning. We had the shits the rest of the day! Our folks never did figure out why we were so sick."

Hank started to laugh. Jenna joined in. For the next couple of minutes, they couldn't stop.

When he finally regained some composure, Hank sighed and said, "No, Jen. Don't worry about me. I'm an old man. I've had a lot of years, most of them good. I've got children, and grandchildren, and even a couple of great grandchildren. The Lord's truly blessed me, and if He's gonna call me home, well, I'm ready."

Jenna was taken aback by what he'd just said. Was he going to die? She didn't see anything in that pamphlet about alveolar proteinosis being terminal. As a matter of fact, sometimes it clears up on its own; and, if nothing else, this bronchopulmonary lavage sounded promising. Why, then, was he talking like a man on his deathbed?

She sat back on the sofa and stretched her legs. Jenna recalled the time her grandfather died. Cancer had taken him from her, and there was nothing she could do. Now, she felt just as powerless.

She looked at Hank. A moment ago, he had been quite animated and full of life. Now, he rested his head in his aged hands, his gaze fixed on the floor. His frail, tired body barely moved as he drew in shallow, rapid breaths. Every once in a while, his tongue darted out and moistened his thin, cracked lips. He said nothing, but his form spoke volumes. He looked like a beaten man.

Jenna was stymied. This was not the same man who volunteered at the youth center, helping young adolescents realize their potential. Nor was he the lively, charismatic individual who Jenna had spent many Saturdays with at the senior citizens' center playing cards or pool, or just talking. She wanted to cry but fought back the tears.

Jenna gently rested her hand on his withered shoulder. "Hank, I don't know what I can do to help you; but if there's anything, anything at all, call me."

"Yes," he muttered. "All right."

"I better get home, Hank. Are you going to be okay?"

"Yes. I'll be fine."

"All right, Hank. I'll see you later."

As she walked towards the door, Jenna glanced back at Hank. He was still sitting on the sofa, motionless. She thought that he looked like a man in prayer. There was more to this than he'd told her; she was sure of that.

But, she had her own obstacles to overcome. A part of her hoped that he wouldn't trouble her any longer with his problems. Another part wanted very much to be there for him. A third part was torn between the other two, trying to maintain some semblance of continuity.

After leaving his apartment, Jenna got on the elevator. A woman carrying a baby followed her. The infant couldn't have been more than six months old; and the woman looked tired but content. There was a certain glow about her.

Jenna was reminded of the Mothergoddess and her child. The woman gave life to the child just as Mother Earth had brought all things into existence. All creation is alive through Her spirit, and this mother and child are part of the community that was the Universal Consciousness.

Jenna began to wonder how this related to her. Wouldn't the thing growing inside her be part of the cosmic consciousness as well? All her life she'd been led to believe that the fetus wasn't a person until it was actually born. Before that, while still in the mother's womb, it was nothing more than a glob of tissue, part of the mother's body like the liver or the appendix.

If that was the case, then that would imply that the child did not actually become part of the whole until after it was born and independent of its mother's body. While in the womb, then, does it draw its existence from the mother? It was a perplexing question, fraught with far reaching ramifications. But how could it be otherwise?

The individual never really joined with the One until after he has passed through Death's Portal, leaving the physical womb of the Blessed Mother, no matter how high a level of consciousness he has attained. In the same way, the unborn child could not be a person until after it emerges from the womb, departing the woman's body. This must be the case, she thought; but she still wondered if her logic made sense.

Jenna got off the elevator when it reached her floor. The apartment seemed empty when she entered it. She glanced around the room, but there was no sign of Joe. From the looks of his work center, he must have been hard at it for most of the day. A pencil stub lay carelessly on a writing pad filled with notes. A half-empty glass sat perched on some papers. The wastebasket was full. Even the computer was still running with a variety of geometric figures floating across the screen.

Jenna supported herself on the door jam as she removed the soaked shoes and socks. The chill had numbed her feet, and they throbbed slightly. She took off her raincoat and threw it on the floor. Then, she dragged herself over to the easy chair that beckoned to her and plopped down, sinking into its plush cushions.

The chair felt warm and secure. She crossed her legs and began to gently massage her aching feet, each hand kneading a foot. As she sat alone and rhythmically rubbed her feet, the life began to creep back into them, tingling as if bathed by a thousand needles. She wiggled her toes.

Then, she heard the toilet flush and the bathroom door open. It was Joe. He walked into the living room, hair messed up and a shadow of stubble darkened his face. He noticed Jenna curled up in the chair and walked over to her.

"Hi!" He bent down and kissed her. "What's it like outside, cold?"

She looked up at him and sighed. "Yes, and miserable."

"Are you okay?" he asked.

She looked away and pushed back her hair with one hand. "Yeah, I'm fine. Just tired." She looked into his eyes and took his hand. "So how about you? Been busy?"

He knelt down on the floor next to her. "Yes, very busy. The Akagi project is really shaping up nicely. Hey. Are you hungry? I can get you something, if you'd like."

Shaking her head, she sighed, "No, I'm not hungry. Joe, can we talk?"

"Well, sure. We can talk," he said.

She took a deep breath and closed her eyes for a second. "Joe, I saw my gynecologist yesterday…"

"Yes. I meant to ask you about that."

"Please, let me finish."

"All right, all right," he murmured apologetically. "Don't get your bowels in an uproar."

She glared at him for a moment. Satisfied that she'd cowed him, she continued. "Anyway, she confirmed my pregnancy." She hesitated, then impatiently asked, "You know I just wanted to abort it, don't you?"

He nodded.

"It should have been a simple thing, but…"

"But what?" he asked. "Did she try to talk you out of aborting it?"

"No."

"Well, then what?"

She sighed. "She wants me to see another doctor."

"Another doctor, huh. Why? Is there something wrong?"

"No, there's nothing wrong," she mumbled. Staring blankly, she remarked, almost under her breath, "They'll pay me to abort."

"What?" Joe said.

She looked at him. "They'll buy the fetus. All I have to do is call this institute?"

"Let me get this straight," Joe uttered in disbelief. "They'll pay you to have an abortion…as long as they can keep the leftovers."

"Crudely put, but yes. They'll pay me to have the abortion."

"Oh, that's incredible." he said. "How much?"

"Well, it depends," she said uneasily.

"Depends on what?" he asked.

"Well, if I understood Dr. Kuman correctly, the bigger the fetus is, the more they'll, uh, compensate me."

"Did she give you a dollar figure?"

"No…no, she didn't. That's why I have to call this institute."

"Are you going to call them?"

"I don't know. That's why I wanted to talk to you tonight. Dr. Kuman said I'd have to decide soon."

Joe took a deep breath and let it out slowly. "Okay, Jen," he said after a few moments contemplation. "Let's look at your situation logically, all right?"

"All right."

Joe stood up and stroked his chin for a second. Then, he looked at her and said, "You're thirty-two years old with a good job, a career woman."

"Yeah, so."

"Having a child would drastically alter your plans, right?"

"Well, yes. But what's your point? I've already decided to abort."

"You're a college graduate, aren't you?"

"You know I am, Joe."

"Aren't you still paying off student loans? Wouldn't you like to move on to graduate school?"

She smiled and answered, "Yes…to both questions."

"All right then." He leaned forward. "You could sell that fetus and use the money to pay off your outstanding student loans. If there's anything left, you could put it toward that Master's degree, or you could buy yourself something you need, or want. Either way, having those loans paid off will make getting loans to finance a Master's degree program a lot easier."

For the next few minutes, Jenna thought about what he'd said. As she did, Joe went into the kitchen. Deep in thought, she paid him no mind. Joe made a good point. Jenna did have some debts she'd like to get out from under, and grad. school was one of her ambitions. Since she was going to abort anyway, why not further her own cause?

When he came back out, he was carrying two glasses. He sat down and handed her one.

"Thank you," she said, more out of habit than gratitude.

"It's sparkling water…and I put dinner on." He leaned over. "So, what have you decided?"

"You're right, Joe, but don't you think I haven't thought about all that already?" She took a drink from the glass and set it in the coffee table. "I'm just not sure that I want to have this…this tumor growing inside me for any longer than I have to."

"Now, Jen, I know how you feel…"

"No…no, you don't! You can't possibly know how I feel!" She stood up and began to pace. "You're not the one who'll have morning sickness. You're not the one who'll gain weight and have to buy maternity clothes. You're not the one whose body will suffer from a cancerous growth wreaking havoc with your internals."

She stopped and, looking down on him, asked, "And what about us, Joe? What will it do to us when I start getting bigger? What will you think when it's over and my body still bears the marks left by the experience?"

Joe laughed, and his eyes twinkled. "Is that what's bothering you, that I still won't love you should your body bear the signs of pregnancy?" He stood up and took her in his arms.

Gazing into her eyes, he softly said, "Jen, I love you. You're the best thing that's ever happened to me. You're supportive, caring, interesting, smart, fun. You don't crowd me, or try to change me. Why, I've never known a woman quite like you before. When they made you, they broke the mold." He hesitated. "No. I'll never stop loving you."

Tears filled her eyes as he spoke. It was a tender, honest moment, one she needed very badly. "Oh, Joe. I love you so much."

They held each other tight for a few minutes. Neither one spoke. The only sound was that of their breathing. At last, Joe stepped back and pulled her down on the sofa next to him.

Jenna wiped her eyes. "I guess it wouldn't hurt to at least call this place."

"No. No, it wouldn't," Joe agreed. "Find out what they have to say. Then you can make an informed choice. And whatever you decide, I'm behind you all the way."

She sighed and rested her head back for a second. "Okay, I'll call tomorrow and see what I can find out."

"Good," Joe said. "Now, why don't you get cleaned up, and I'll go check dinner." He leaned over and gave her a quick peck on the cheek. Then he got up and started for the kitchen.

Before he got there, Jenna called out, "Joe!"

He stopped and looked back.

Smiling, she said, "Thanks, Joe. You've made this so much easier for me, being supportive and all."

"Hey! We're a team, right?" he replied. Then, he went into the kitchen.

Jenna got up and headed for the bathroom. Knowing what Joe thought had been crucial in her decision. It affected him, too. Maybe not as much as her, or not in the same way. Nonetheless, she felt obliged to get his input. They were a team, after all. He'd said so himself. And being married, there was more truth in that than words could express.

THE REFERRAL

Jenna felt more certain about what had to be done following her conversation with Joe. It was clear that neither one of them wanted to become parents right at that moment. And Joe's support in the decision to carry the fetus to an indeterminate stage of development was crucial, as far as Jenna was concerned. The ordeal would affect him as well as her, albeit indirectly; and she had to know that he would not turn away from her.

Jenna sat at her desk waiting for someone to answer the call she'd placed. The vidphone rang once, then twice. "Good morning. Dr. Kuman's office...Oh. Hi, Ms. Kelemen. How can I help you?" Jackie was always pleasant on the phone, one mark of an outstanding receptionist.

"I'd like to speak to Dr. Kuman, if she's available," Jenna said. She still felt unsure about waiting to abort, but the discussion with Joe had quelled her doubts to some extent. She was reassured to know that he cared about more than just her physical attributes. He would stick it out, or so she thought.

"Let me check. Would you please hold?"

"Yes, I'll hold."

The screen switched from Jackie at her receptionist's station to a beautiful sunset on some tropical island with soft, soothing music playing in the background. Elevator music, Jenna thought to herself: soft, easy, and relaxing.

A few seconds later, the image changed again. This time, it was Dr. Kuman.

"Well, hello, Jenna," she cheerfully said.

"Good morning, Dr. Kuman."

"I didn't expect to hear from you so soon. I'm glad you called. What can I do for you?"

"I've made my decision…about what we discussed the other day?" she hesitantly replied, even asked.

"Excellent. And your decision?"

Suddenly, there was a knock at Jenna's office door: not a respectable rapping, but a heavy thumping. "Could you hold, please, Dr. Kuman?" she asked. "There's someone at the door."

"Yes, Jenna. I'll hold," Dr. Kuman answered.

Jenna switched her vidphone to hold, leaving the good doctor to languish in a similar state of limbo to which she'd been subjected.

"Come in," she called out.

The door opened and one of the maintenance supervisors, Bob Rizhowski stuck his head in. "Good morning, Jenna."

"Yes, Bob, what can I do for you?" Despite her irritation at the intrusion, she maintained a level of civility.

Bob entered the office and sat down in one of the chairs facing her desk. "Well, it's about this containment spray valve job. I really think that if we do the work with the valve in place, the added dose won't be all that unreasonable. Removing the valve will…"

"Hold on, Bob." Jenna leaned forward with both elbows resting on the desk. Angling into the wind was natural, and she often found Bob to be a big windbag, anyway. "I've been over that survey data myself, and I think that removing the valve first is the way to go. However, I'm not unreasonable." She momentarily studied the outage schedule posted on the wall across from her desk. "Now, that job is next week, right?"

"Yeah, next week."

"I'll meet with you this afternoon." Glancing at her vidphone, she added, "But I've got a call on hold right now."

"Oh, I'm sorry. I didn't mean to interrupt." He checked his wrist-watch's calendar. "This afternoon will be fine. Around one o'clock?"

"One o'clock will be alright."

"Good. I'll see you then," he noted as he stood up. Without saying goodbye, he hurried out, closing the door behind him.

With that done she switched the call back on.

"I'm so sorry, Dr. Kuman. I…"

"That's all right, Jenna. Now, back to your decision."

"Yes, well…" She cleared her throat and took a sip from the mug on her desk. "I've decided that it wouldn't hurt to at least talk to these people you mentioned…you know, to see what they have to say."

"Excellent, excellent. Let me give you the number." Dr. Kuman pressed some keys on her desk, and a phone number appeared on Jenna's screen. "Are you getting it?"

"Yes," Jenna answered as she noted the number in her personal ledger.

Dr. Kuman continued, "You call them as soon as you can. They can answer all of your questions."

"Well, do you think there'll be any delay? I mean, I don't want to wait too long."

"Oh, Jenna. I wouldn't be too concerned about that," she said. "Just mention me when you call, and they'll get you in."

"Um, okay, Dr. Kuman. I'll call today."

"Excellent," she replied. "And if there are any problems, let me know, all right?"

"All right. I will." She checked her watch. "I gotta go now. Thanks for all your help."

"Well, I'm here to help, Jenna. I only have your best interests in mind. Goodbye for now." The screen went to a test pattern. She'd switched off.

Jenna turned off her vidphone. She swung the chair around and gazed out her office window. The hillside that her office faced was alive with autumn hues: browns, reds, and oranges. In a few weeks, it would all be gone. The dying leaves, no longer able to hold on to the trees from which they sprouted, would fall to the ground.

All of those trees, she thought to herself. The hillside was covered with them; and each year, thousands upon thousands of leaves fell, covering the earth in a dry carpet of decaying vegetable matter. As the leaves decomposed, new soil would form: soil rich in nutrients that would feed the new life brought forth in an ever-continuing cycle of life and death. Mother Earth wasted nothing.

One o'clock came much too soon for Jenna. She sat quietly in the meeting as Bob Rizhowski droned on, hardly able to stay focused on what he was saying. Her thoughts were fixed on the phone call that she would make after the meeting ended and the uncertainty that it held. After forty minutes, the meeting was over. Nothing had changed.

Jenna stopped in the rest room on the way back to her office. For some reason, meetings always left her with the urge to urinate. She didn't understand it, but it was true. She ran into an acquaintance of hers, Sharon Fordyce, who had stopped in the restroom, too.

Sharon was a financial analyst in the station's budget office. She and Jenna had started working at the station on the same day. So, they'd been through a lot of the general employee training and orientation sessions together which added up to more than just a few shared lunches.

Through it all, Sharon had shown herself to be pleasant enough; but she and Jenna just never quite clicked. Jenna thought that Sharon was too absorbed in her husband. "Sean this," or "Sean that," She talked about him almost constantly. It was like he was the lord and she his servant.

Sharon was beaming at this particular encounter. Her smile was exceptionally bright and her eyes twinkled. At five feet, four inches, and one hundred thirtyfive pounds, she was an average woman. Nevertheless, Jenna thought that she may have put on a few pounds. Of course, she wasn't about to say so. That would be a social faux pas, not to mention an affront to Sharon's womanhood. Although Sharon didn't share Jenna's paradigm of the universe, Jenna had to at least respect the woman's goddess-head.

"Jenna! It's so good to see you," Sharon exclaimed as she warmly embraced her. "It's been so long!"

That was true, Jenna thought. She had been on vacation. She learned, upon returning to work, that Sharon had been temporarily assigned to the Corporate Office. That had been about two months ago.

"It's good to see you too, Sharon," she replied. "And you look so radiant!"

"Why, thank you, Jenna." Sharon smiled and blushed, her face turning a rosy hue. Regaining her composure, she proclaimed, "I've got some good news."

"Really? Well, tell me before you burst," Jenna politely prodded.

"Sean and I are going to have a baby!"

"That's great, Sharon. When're you due?" True, they weren't the best of friends; but that didn't stop Jenna from being excited for her. She knew that Sean and Sharon had been trying to have a baby for a couple of years now. For a moment, she forgot about her own pregnancy.

"May thirteenth," Sharon proudly responded. "We're so excited. There's so much to do."

"Oh, that's terrific, Sharon. I'm so happy for you both."

Sharon continued on, and the minutes slipped by like hours. She talked about how much she and Sean wanted this baby, how they'd visited fertility specialists, and how they'd almost given up. She described their quest for just the right name and explained why they decided on Theodore Andrew for a boy and Alexandra Anne for a girl.

Jenna nodded and smiled all the while, trying to at least appear like she really gave a damn. Then, Sharon got around to the cost of baby furniture. "Excuse me, Sharon," Jenna politely interrupted. "I really have to go. Perhaps we could have lunch sometime soon, and you could tell me more then."

A baffled look crossed Sharon's face. "Oh, all right."

"I am sorry," Jenna said as she checked her watch. "Look, ah, I'll call you later to set something up, okay?"

"Yes. That...that would be fine," Sharon said.

"Great," Jenna said. "Talk to you later, then." She turned and left the restroom.

Jenna was seated at her desk a few minutes later. Uncertainty gnawed at her. The palms of her hands were moist with sweat. She nervously chewed on a piece of gum as she punched in the phone number that Dr. Kuman had given her. The discussion she'd had with Joe the night before cut away much of the doubt and fear, but the roots were still there.

To have Dr. Kuman prescribe an abortifacient would be so much simpler. She could take the drug and it would all be over in a couple of days. The tumorous growth would be flushed down the toilet to float along with all of the other human refuse on its way to the nearby sewage treatment plant where it would be made into fertilizer.

She was about to disconnect when the other party answered.

"Good morning. This is the ASAMAR Corporation, LifeScience Research. How may I help you." The man who answered had a round face with a thin, dark mustache decorating his upper lip. His hair was short, thick, and wavy; and his eyes were clear green. Jenna thought him attractive.

"Yes," she replied. "My name is Jenna Kelemen, and, ah, I was referred to you by my gynecologist?"

"I see," the man noted. "And what is your doctor's name?"

"Dr. Kuman." Dr. Kuman had said to mention her name, Jenna suddenly recalled, which eased her mind.

"If you'll wait a moment, I'll connect with one of our counselors.

Before Jenna could respond, the picture switched from the man to a holding tape. Unlike the tranquil ocean view at Dr. Kuman's office, she was forced to watch an advertisement for ASAMAR Corporation. Various scenes of ground breaking discoveries and cutting edge technology all brought to her by the wonderful people at ASAMAR. All the while, the voice of a woman who sounded as if she'd rehearsed one too many times, accompanied by upbeat music, droned on. Jenna wanted to laugh at the absurdity.

After about a minute, the advertisement was replaced by the image of a woman of African descent. She had an oval face accented by full lips and a prominent nose. Her hazel eyes were warm and friendly, and her head was shaved, revealing a perfectly round dome with a small birthmark on the left side.

"Hello," the woman stated cheerfully. "My name is Mandisa Zambezi. Can I help you?

"Well, I don't know," Jenna said. She was unsure. "My gynecologist, Dr. Kuman, referred me to you."

"Oh, yes." Ms. Zambezi appeared to be pleased at the sound of her name. "We've been expecting to hear from you, Ms. Kelemen."

Jenna was baffled. How did this woman know her name? Why would they be expecting her call? What else did they know about her? She didn't get a chance to ask these questions.

"Dr. Kuman called about your case earlier today," Ms. Zambezi noted. "It's common practice when we get referrals for the primary physician to notify us before we see the patient."

"Oh, well, that explains it." Jenna was relieved. "What else do you know?"

"We have your case file already, Ms. Kelemen," Ms. Zambezi explained. "We know that you are in excellent health and that you are at the fifth or sixth week of gestation."

"All right. So…" Before she could say anything else, Ms. Zambezi interrupted.

"Now, Ms. Kelemen, it's important that we see you as soon as possible. We know how important this is to you and that you have only a limited amount of time. We want to help you make an informed choice. Can you come in tomorrow?"

"Tomorrow? Why so soon?"

Ms. Zambezi cleared her throat and looked intently at Jenna. "We must accurately determine the week of gestation you're in and the condition of the fetus. Then, and only then, can we explain your options, enabling you to make a choice that's right for you, you understand."

"I see," Jenna uttered. "Let me check my calendar."

"Please."

Jenna opened up her compucal. She saw no special meetings or appointments that would require her presence. She also noted that she had a few vacation days left for the year. The practice was uncommon and generally frowned upon, but she was sure that her supervisor would let her take the day off for medical purposes.

"All right, Ms. Zambezi. Tomorrow will be fine."

"Good. Now, you'll need to be here by 8:00 AM. There is a whole battery of tests we need to run, not to mention the consultation. Do you have any questions?"

"Well, yes," she replied. "How do I get to your office?"

"Oh, I'm sorry," Ms. Zambezi confessed. "Here. Let me send you a map.

A map showing shuttle routes and times appeared on Jenna's screen.

"I've got it," Jenna said.

"Good," Ms. Zambezi answered. "We're in the LifeScience Research Building on the second floor. Just ask for me when you get here."

"Okay."

"Anything else?"

"No, I guess not," Jenna replied, still unsure.

"Well, then, I'll see you tomorrow."

"Okay. Goodbye." Jenna switched her vidphone off before Ms. Zambezi could return the farewell.

The time was 3:10 PM. Jenna had been at her desk since talking with Mandisa Zambezi. She spent the intervening period mindlessly thumbing through some reports on the station's compnet. Data for the accumulated radiation dose for the outage showed that they were within the estimated personrem to date. She took particular notice of the 2B primary coolant pump overhaul; the project was well within the allotted dose estimate. The extra shielding and time spent on additional training for the maintenance crews had not been a wasted effort. When she'd grown tired of this, she decided it was time to see her supervisor about taking tomorrow off. So, she left her office and headed for Maurice Winans'.

Maurice was a soft spoken, honest man who didn't mince words. He was tall, thin, muscular man of African descent. His strong features stood out against his light skin, and his close cropped hair had short, tight curls. He had been hired from another utility to replace the previous Radiological Controls Supervisor who had moved on a couple of years ago. Jenna liked him very much, although they didn't associate much away from work.

Since his office door was open, Jenna poked her head around the frame. He was sitting at his computer diligently working the time away. His office was rather plain, which was unusual for one of the department heads. Even the people he supervised had more nick nacks, pictures, and other paraphernalia crammed into their small cubicles. All he had was his desk, computer center, a couple of chairs, a large schedule board on one wall, and some family photos on his desk.

"Excuse me, Maurice?" she interrupted.

He looked towards her. "Jenna...come on in," he called while motioning to her. "Please, have a seat."

Jenna seated herself in one of the chairs. "I don't want to take up too much of your time. So, let me get right to it."

"Very well, then. Go ahead."

Jenna cleared her throat. "I have a few vacation days left, and I'd like to take one tomorrow. I know it's highly irregular, but…"

"That's fine, Jenna," he cut in. "If you say you need tomorrow off, it must be important."

"Well, it is, Maurice, and I appreciate you letting me take it off on such short notice."

"Don't mention it. Is there anything else?"

"No, no, that's it," she said. "Thanks again."

She left his office relieved and started for the cafeteria to get a chilled beverage. She walked a little more energetically now that one more obstacle had been hurdled. The ball was rolling, and Joe would be placated. Jenna herself was feeling somewhat alleviated as well, like one brick out of the whole load she'd been carrying had been removed.

She got home at 6:30 PM. Joe wasn't there since he'd gone to Philadelphia for a few days to meet with representatives from Akagi Enterprises to go over his plans for their new regional headquarters. He'd left the phone number of the hotel where he was staying, and Jenna thought about calling him. She eventually decided against it. There was no point in disturbing him until she knew something more. Besides, she knew how he felt about being smothered.

On the way home, Jenna hadn't thought that she was hungry; but now her stomach was grumbling. She went into the kitchen and rummaged through the refrigerator for something to eat. She found a bowl with some leftover casserole from the previous night and popped it in the microwave.

While dinner heated, she turned on the TV to the allnews station. She was really only interested in the weather, but that wouldn't come for a few minutes. So, she went back into the kitchen and waited for her food. Even there, Jenna could still hear the TV.

The anchor's voice was deep, clear, and well articulated. "…On the national scene, today, the U.S. Supreme Court upheld a lower court decision that found that the parents of a thirteen year old male had violated his Fourth Amendment right against unreasonable searches and seizures, and his Fifth Amendment right regarding deprivation of liberty. The drama began when the boy's mother found a small amount of an illegal drug in his room, and the parents confined him to their home, except during school hours, for a period of one month.

"When asked to comment, the boy's father said this, 'The damned state holds us responsible when our kids screw up, but they take away our ability to discipline our own children. What the hell are we supposed to do, anyway?'

"In a related story, the parents are still awaiting trial for the possession of illegal narcotics…"

Jenna laughed when she heard that. It was sad, yet comical. A child suing his own parents because they'd tried to discipline him. Of course, grounded for a whole month was excessive. Two weeks would have been more appropriate, she was certain. And why was the boy's mother going through his personal things to begin with? As a member of the Universal Consciousness, the boy was entitled to the same respect as any other of the Mother's creatures. Jenna shook her head.

She returned to the living room with her food and plopped down on the sofa. The weather report still wasn't up yet. So, she muted the sound.

The casserole hadn't lost any of its flavor while it languished in the refrigerator overnight, and the microwave had warmed it to just the right temperature.

Sitting in the quiet of the apartment with soundless images unfolding on the TV screen, she sat back and began to eat. From time to time, she glanced at the TV to see if they'd gotten to the weather segment.

The scenes often depicted violence or misery. People in less developed areas of the world were starving. Brush wars that had erupted on different continents still raged. Third world countries demanded a larger piece of the global pie under threat of widening terrorist activities. One scene showed a commuter train near Buffalo, N.Y., which had been attacked by rocket fire that very day. They were still pulling bodies from the wreckage.

The images sickened Jenna. Why did humanity go on treating each other so horribly, she wondered. In the past few decades, the world had turned in ever increasing numbers to pantheistic monism of one form or another: all is One, and the One is God. Therefore, everyone and everything was a part of God, or a manifestation of the One. If more and more people have realized this truth, she pondered, why, then, do we continue to destroy each other?

It was a question not easily answered. Homo sapiens throughout history had been a very cruel and deceptive entity, often preying on the weaknesses of its own kind. No other creature is like us, she mused. We alone of all creation possess the ability to do good, yet we are so drawn to evil and self-destruction.

After dinner, Jenna cleaned up the kitchen, more to keep busy than anything else. She dutifully scrubbed by hand the dishes she'd dirt-ied—no use in running the dishwasher for so small a load.

Jenna went to bed early that night. She was tired and would have to get up early to catch the shuttle. She lay in bed, thinking of Joe. How she wished he were here. How she wished she could see her grandfather again; he would make everything all right.

Sacrifice for Mother

The alarm went off at 5:00 AM, rousing Jenna from a sound, restful sleep. After silencing the interloper, she dreamily reached over to caress Joe's arm but found him absent. At first, she was surprised; but, as her mind cleared, she recalled that he had gone to Philadelphia.

She rolled back and stared vacantly into the darkness, wondering if Joe had spent the night alone. It was a silly notion, and she hated herself for having even entertained it. Of course he had spent the night alone. She was only being paranoid. Her mind was so occupied with the pregnancy that her subconscious was running unfettered allowing all manner of beast to rise up within her psyche.

She closed her eyes, focusing on the Goddess, and began to chant, "Gratitude to Mother Earth, sailing through the night and day; from Her loins I did spring, beautiful and complete; from her mouth do I take the nectar of life; I suckle at Her breasts the life sustaining milk of the Universe; blessed are you, oh, Mother Earth." Several minutes later, Jenna arose from her nest to begin her day.

Jenna went into the bathroom and hit the light switch. She didn't bother to wait for the illumination to reach its full intensity before she had the shower going and her nightgown off. She stepped carefully into the shower and stood motionless for a few seconds as the warm water sprayed onto her face and cascaded down her body, falling from her breasts and splattering onto her feet. She turned around and let the water run down her back and buttocks. Then, she tilted her head back and allowed the warm, massaging spray to drench her hair and scalp.

Jenna held the soap firmly, so it wouldn't slip from her fingers, as it often did, and faithfully lathered every part of her body. She slowly turned to permit the spray to liberally rinse the cleansing residue from her skin. She poured a small amount of shampoo into one hand and methodically worked it into her hair. Then she tossed her head under the shower and ran her hands over her scalp as she rinsed the suds out.

Jenna turned the water off and stepped onto the shag rug next to the tub. She took one of the towels from the bar and carefully dried the moist, little domes of water from her skin that had adhered there. Then, she dried her hair as well as she could and threw the towel in the corner.

Back in the bedroom, Jenna pulled a pair of green slacks and matching blouse out of the closet. She fumbled around in one of her drawers until she managed to retrieve a bra, a pair of underwear, and stockings. She quickly put on the underthings and the blouse.

As she pulled the slacks up around her hips, she wondered how much longer she'd be able to wear normal clothes. How long would it be until she would have to buy maternity clothes? The thought of it sickened her. When she'd finished dressing, she ran a brush through her hair a few times to get the tangles out. She didn't see any need to put a lot of makeup on either; so, she dispensed with it.

It was 5:32 AM when she entered the kitchen, which didn't leave much time. Jenna quickly ate a breakfast bar consisting of whole grains and nuts packed together, fortified with vitamins, and covered with honey to give it flavor. She washed breakfast down with a glass of grapefruit juice that left a sour taste in her mouth that she grimaced at. Not too satisfying but nutritional.

She dashed back to the bathroom and hastily brushed her teeth. When she'd finished, she grinned and examined her handiwork. Her teeth were not quite perfect, slightly crooked and uneven. Mother never saw fit to get her braces when she was younger.

Jenna checked the clock. It read 5:58 AM. She hurried to the door, slipped on a pair of casual shoes and threw on her coat. She slammed the door behind her as she rushed out. The sound reverberated down the empty hall, and the walls shook from the concussion. If the sound woke anyone, she wasn't concerned. It was their problem. They probably needed to get up soon, anyway.

She dashed to the elevators and, thankfully, found one on her floor, doors open. Jenna got in and directed it to the lobby. The doors slid shut, and the elevator suddenly dropped as it began its descent. The sensation it caused made Jenna think she would lose the breakfast bar she'd hastily consumed. Soon, to her relief, the elevator came to a smooth stop, and the doors slid open. Jenna passed quickly through the lobby and down the front steps to the street.

The day was going to be sunny. The eastern sky was brilliant yellow with the sun just peeking over the hilltops; while to the west, progressively darker shades of blue engulfed the horizon. The air felt cool against her face but not frigid, with a gentle breeze blowing in from the southwest. She walked four blocks to the train station. She didn't want to miss the train and be late for her appointment.

The commuter train was the logical choice for this trip since the Life Science Research Facility was within easy walking distance of a station and it was much faster than driving. After a brisk ten-minute walk, Jenna arrived at the station just in time. The train had just pulled in as she hurried through the building. She hopped on to one of the cars in the middle of the string, let out a sigh of relief, and walked into the passenger compartment.

About a dozen people occupied the car. Some slept while others read or vacantly stared out the window. A couple of them glanced up when the door slid open and she entered. Both were men. One was older, probably in his fifties, and dressed in a dark gray business suit with a gray overcoat draped over the back of the seat. The other man was younger, about Jenna's age. He was dressed in dark blue coveralls with a dungaree jacket like someone who worked with machines, possibly maintenance. For a few moments, the two men regarded Jenna through longing eyes. Her eyes met theirs, first the older man's, then the younger's. An uneasy chill ran the length of her back. She felt naked.

The train effortlessly glided away from the station. Jenna walked to the other end of the car and seated herself in a place at the rear of the compartment. She rested her head on the back of the seat and closed her eyes hoping the nausea that had suddenly come upon her would leave her to her peace. Jenna emptied her mind and allowed her muscles to relax. Rhythmic, repetitious muses that echoed the tempo of the wheels against the rail drifted through her consciousness, penetrating her psyche. She lost all sense of her surroundings as she slipped into a trancelike state. To the other passengers, she must have appeared to be asleep; but she was really in paradise.

Some time later, Jenna woke to find the train had made a routine stop about thirty minutes from her destination. The nausea had left, and her mind was refreshed. Since there had been three other stops before this one, the car was about half full. People of all races and social status were scattered throughout the compartment. Like those who were there when she got on, the new riders slept, read, caught up on paperwork, or stared hypnotically out the windows.

The train was a unique environment, she thought, where people of all nationalities and differing levels of wealth came together in peace. Of course, it was a peace more out of mutual distrust than anything else. Any other place, and these same people who coexisted for the moment in harmony would not even share the same neighborhood.

As the train started off again, Jenna noticed that someone had left a newspaper on the seat across from hers. With time to kill, she reached over and grabbed it, hoping that no one would return to reclaim it.

Page one had a story about one of the Martian colonies' ecodomes being breached. Over two hundred people were killed as the dome's atmosphere was sucked out. Another two hundred were still alive, trapped in sealed buildings, awaiting the rescue effort that had been recently organized. A large, color picture of the colony, taken from an orbiting station, accompanied the story. The North American and the European Alliances had established four colonies so far under a joint effort.

Another story on the front page had a picture of the President signing a document. The caption read, "President Signs 'Population Management Act of 2032'". The story didn't go into too much detail, although it did say something about more efficient use of Federal resources in slowing population growth. It seemed that the whole basis for the "Act" was a decision handed down by the U.S. Supreme Court in 2020 that clarified what *person* meant when used in the "U.S. Constitution".

Jenna thought about the story. For years, many, including psychologists, theologians, lawyers, scientists, ethicists, as well as laymen, had argued that personhood should be based on one's ability to rationalize his or her being, that to be a person, one had to be aware of one's existence in relation to the environment. Therefore, grounded on this premise, a small child could not be defined as a person, nor a feeble-minded elder, nor a lunatic, etc...

The debate continued until a man was put on trial for the murder of his six-month-old daughter. He had killed the child while she slept. The mother had died soon after giving birth, and he blamed the child for her demise. As a single parent, he claimed she was an undue burden. As an atheist, he claimed that a creator had endowed no one, least of all a six-month-old child, with any inalienable rights, since there was no creator. The man declared that the act was no worse than having an unwanted dog destroyed; the child was asleep when he killed her, anyway. So, the end was swift and merciful; and she felt no pain.

After a string of appeals, the case eventually reached the U.S. Supreme Court. In a six to three decision, the Court decided that, indeed, any reference to a creator, a god, or any other spiritual entity, when applying the "Constitution" violated the "First Amendment"; and therefore, individual rights come within the jurisdiction of the governing body. Subsequently, a person, as referred to in the "Constitution", could be defined as someone who is able to rationalize their own existence; and that people who do not meet this criterion shall be granted such rights as the State deems appropriate and expedient.

Jenna remembered the uproar that caused. Many religious fundamentalists and conservatives protested vehemently, some even went to prison. But the media and the politicians largely ignored their plea.

What followed was like dominoes. First, the more liberal states, like California and New York, followed the Court's lead and began to legislatively define "person." Through the years, other states followed suit until only a handful remained, like Iowa, who had not seen fit to narrowly define personhood.

Jenna was eighteen when that decision was handed down. She could remember bits and pieces of the story. One thing she recalled was one side arguing that the "Constitution" was a living document, always evolving to meet the needs of society as society itself changed. But she was just eighteen and unimpressed by the affairs of government. Now, however, she wondered how this definition of "person" would affect her and how it was viewed by the Universal Mind.

As she turned the pages, another story briefly grabbed her attention. It involved a religious sect in Louisiana that had recently begun the practice of annual human sacrifice. The group had been charged with first degree murder for sacrificing one of its members. The leaders were convicted; but they appealed saying that they were well within their "First Amendment" right of freedom of religion. The victim had also signed a statement indicating his desire to be their offering.

The appeal eventually reached the Supreme Court where it was decided that as long as the person sacrificed agreed to do so voluntarily and signed a statement attesting to that desire, then the sect was indeed within its rights. According to the article, they were celebrating the fifth anniversary of that landmark decision with, what else, a human sacrifice.

Jenna thought about that story for a moment. To give one's life in honor of the One was a supreme sacrifice. Few ever gave themselves over so completely. She wondered, though, if the Mother wanted Her children to throw themselves onto a knife in Her honor. Better to give one's life in service to the Mother, Jenna felt, than to throw it away in a useless gesture.

Turning to the horoscope, Jenna anxiously read hers, Taurus. For today, it read, "Be alert for opportunities. Listen to the advice of others as today marks the beginning of a new and better life for yourself." Amazing, she thought. Perhaps this whole thing would turn out for the best, anyway. It was written in the stars.

She put the paper down and gazed out the window. The day was beautiful with puffy clouds dotting a clear blue sky. She watched as the train's shadow raced along the tracks, cutting through poles and bridges like a ghost through a solid wall.

As the train sped along, a rabbit darted into some nearby brush. How sad, she thought, that the poor creature had to leave its breakfast in such a hurry.

Farther on, she spotted a deer drinking from a stream that ran through a nearby field. It looked up as the train passed, but she wasn't able to determine if it was a buck or a doe because the train moved so quickly. Either way, it was a magnificent creature; she felt lucky for having seen it.

Soon, the train was rolling through an urban area once more. Houses and storefronts whisked by. As they approached Jenna's destination, an announcement was made alerting the passengers that the next stop was just ahead. Jenna sat in silence while some around her wrestled their coats back on, put down the paper or book they'd been reading, or stretched after the snooze they'd taken. The train smoothly coasted into the station and came to a stop. Jenna waited for those impatient few who'd already been standing to pass before she got up and stepped through the door.

Hopping down onto the pavement, Jenna found that the air was cooler and the breeze stronger than it had been when she'd left home. She checked her watch; the time was 7:43 AM. She hurried out to the street and examined the signs to get her bearings. Satisfied that she knew which way to go, she started off.

The first part of the walk took her up a gentle slope alongside a vacant lot. Tracks from heavy machines crisscrossed the black, muddy ground. A surveying team was busy shooting lines along one side of the lot with a laser transit. Several men in hard hats and coveralls stood nearby, patiently waiting for the team to finish. Two machines, an earthmover and a grader, had been started up. The engines idled loudly, making a deafening roar, and black diesel fumes spewed from their exhaust.

Jenna was saddened by the sight, and sickened by the fumes blowing towards her. Instead of a building, she wondered, why couldn't they turn this into a park with a playground for the children? Squirrels and rabbits could live there, and birds would fill the trees saturating the air with their songs. Perhaps a pond could be placed in one corner and stocked with fish, and a fountain erected in the center would add sparkle and elegance. It would be a beautiful place for commuters to wait for their train, she thought.

She continued on her way, picking up the pace. Some of the men were looking over toward her, but she paid them no mind. As long as they didn't get obnoxious, it mattered little if they watched her. On the train, she'd felt exposed when those two men gawked at her. Here, it wasn't so bad. She was out in the open and didn't feel trapped. These men were also on the other side of the lot, at least one hundred yards away, not within arm's reach. The fear of being accosted by strangers in tight quarters had haunted her ever since she was a child when her mother warned her again and again to be careful around strangers on their apartment building's elevator.

Soon, Jenna reached the top of the rise up which she'd been walking. The air moved more quickly there, and it seemed colder. The sun had risen well into the sky by then. The clouds drifted lazily through the sky. Far to the west, a line of shadows rose from the Earth, and it looked as if a cold front was moving in.

She strode along quickly now with a slight bounce in her steps. The sound of her feet striking the pavement created a steady rapping noise. The rhythm made her recall one of her favorite tunes. It was an old song that her mother used to sing to her when she was younger, and still did sometimes. She couldn't remember the words, but the melody was tattooed into her brain. Jenna began to hum as she walked on.

Before long, she stood at the parking lot of ASAMAR Corp.'s Life Science Research Facility. It was a large, redbrick building stretching at least two hundred yards in front. There were three floors above ground, and who knew how many below. Each floor had a line of windows that ran the length of the building. On the first floor, located at the center, was a spacious, glassenclosed entrance. The driveway branched off of the main road and right up to the door. The grounds in front were well-kept, with neat hedges and well-maintained flowerbeds. From this side, it was magnificent; she had no idea as to what awaited her behind the facade.

Jenna checked the time. Her watch indicated 8:03 AM. She almost dreaded going in, meeting Ms. Zambezi face to face, and delaying the inevitable. But she'd come this far. If she didn't care for what they had to say, it wasn't too late to have Dr. Kuman administer the required drug. So, she pushed her doubt aside and swiftly passed through the lot, heading straight for the entrance.

Jenna noticed a middle aged woman as she approached the building also heading there. The woman, who wore a long, heavy, beige overcoat, walked erect with long strides. She was purposeful and commanding. They arrived at the door simultaneously, and Jenna saw that the woman was shorter than she, about five feet tall with a medium build. Her blond, graying hair was pulled back, revealing a pleasant, oval face with full lips and a strong chin. Jenna was taken by her piercing blue eyes and prominent nose. The woman smiled, showing a mouth full of perfect teeth. Jenna courteously gestured to allow the woman to enter the building first.

"Thank you," the woman said.

The doors automatically opened as the woman approached. Jenna fell in behind and followed her in. They passed through the set of double glass doors into a sprawling lobby. The furnishings and potted plants were tastefully arranged, creating a natural path through the foyer.

Jenna followed the woman to the elevators. When they arrived, the woman touched the up arrow. The two of them waited patiently, pretending not to be aware of the other's presence. Jenna looked back towards the doors. Traffic outside was beginning to pick up now, and more people were coming into the building. Was it too late to go back? A soft ding caught Jenna's attention. She looked around and saw that the elevator doors were opened. The other woman was just stepping in. Jenna followed.

After they were both in, a voice from above asked, "What floor, please." Although computeraudio technology had made tremendous advances, it still sounded mechanical.

"Three," the woman ordered.

Jenna cleared her throat and said, "Two, please," as if the ride would be smoother if she were a little more courteous to the elevator's control program.

The doors quietly slid closed, and the elevator smoothly began its ascent. Jenna nervously fondled one of the buttons on her coat. She didn't know what to expect. Dr. Kuman was only able to give her a clouded idea of what she was getting herself into, and Ms. Zambezi was even less revealing.

Jenna looked around the box she'd found herself in as if looking for an escape. Her eyes met those of the other woman; and, for an instant, she believed there was a kind of telepathy between her and this stranger. Before she could be sure, the elevator halted its ascent, and the doors opened.

Jenna left the elevator without looking back. The doors slid shut behind her. On the facing wall was a placard showing room numbers and the direction to go. She examined it carefully until she located the right office: Fetal Research, Room 220. The arrow pointed to the right. Jenna looked at her watch; it read 8:10 AM. She turned and swiftly walked down the hall.

Several people passed her in the hallway. Some dressed casually like they were here for the same reason she was. The rest, though, wore lab coats or business suits. They all passed in silence, not making eye contact, as if they were all filing past a coffin for one last look at the deceased. Jenna was glad that they didn't notice her, or acknowledge her if they did.

Eventually, she reached room 220 and hesitantly opened the door. The room she entered was about fifteen feet by ten feet. Comfortable chairs and love seats lined the walls to her left and right, with a few chairs situated in the center of the room. Two other people, a man and a woman, occupied the room. Holograms of ocean views adorned the walls above the chairs.

At the end of the room was a counter with doors on either end. Jenna walked up to the counter. An attractive woman of African descent was seated behind the counter. The woman's red tinted hair reached to her shoulders. She wore a stylish, floral printed blouse; and a single, gold chain with a cross dangling from it graced her neckline.

The woman smiled when Jenna reached the counter. "Good morning. How may I help you?"

Jenna was nervous and fidgeted some. "Ah, I'm Jenna Kelemen; I'm supposed to see a Mandisa Zambezi?"

"Oh, yes, Ms. Kelemen," the woman cheerfully replied. "Ms. Zambezi said to expect you. If you'll have a seat, I'll let her know you're here."

"Okay, thanks," Jenna muttered.

She turned around and headed for the seat that was farthest from the other two people. Jenna sat down and sighed, relieved to have come this far. She looked around for something to read but saw that all of the reading material was in a rack up by the counter. She didn't feel motivated enough to get up.

A television monitor in the opposite corner, mounted to the wall, was on. The program appeared to be one of those moronic talk shows. Sometimes Jenna thought that those shows had interesting guests; but that was the exception, not the rule. The rest of the time, it was all useless hype. She couldn't hear it, anyway.

Jenna glanced at the man and woman who were there when she arrived. She wondered why they were here. Was that woman in the same predicament that she was in, or did they have some other business to conduct? The man looked to be considerably older than the woman. Was he her father?

Jenna shook her head and sighed. She didn't know how long it would be before Ms. Zambezi made an appearance. With nothing else to do, she put her head back against the wall, closed her eyes, and drifted off into another dimension.

THE SNAIL

Hearing a door, Jenna opened her eyes and looked towards the receptionist's station. A tall woman of African heritage was speaking to the receptionist. The woman's scalp was shaved clean. She wore a royal blue blazer with a matching knee-length skirt and a white ruffled blouse. The woman had a noble quality about her, like a painting on the walls of an Egyptian tomb. Jenna instantly recognized her from the vid-phone: Mandisa Zambezi.

When Ms. Zambezi had finished conferring with the receptionist, she approached Jenna. "Good morning. I'm Mandisa Zambezi, but you may call me Mandy, if you like. And you must be Ms. Kelemen." She extended her hand.

Jenna stood up and accepted Ms. Zambezi's hand. It was slender and warm. "Hi, Ms. Zamb…uh, Mandy. You can call me Jen, or Jenna"

Ms. Zambezi said, "I hope you haven't been waiting long. If you'll follow me, we'll get started." And with that, Ms. Zambezi hurried out of the room with Jenna close behind.

They left the reception room through the door on the right of the receptionist's counter. Jenna followed Ms. Zambezi down a hallway, and into a small office. The nameplate on the desk had *Mandisa Zambezi* engraved on it in bold text. The office was small, with the desk, a computer, a couple of chairs, and some plants.

Ms. Zambezi seated herself behind the desk and motioned for Jenna to sit down. "Now, Jenna, as I told you yesterday when we spoke, we've had an opportunity to review your file. We know that you are about six weeks along in your pregnancy, and healthy. Tell me, why have you decided to consult with us?"

Jenna shifted in the chair. She was nervous "Well, this is an unplanned pregnancy; and I want to abort it. I mean, that's why I went to Dr. Kuman in the first place, to abort it. But then she told me about how you would pay me if I let you have the fetus." Jenna sat back.

"Well, believe me," Jen continued, "I just wasn't sure; but after I talked to my husband, well, we decided it would be all right, just to look into it, you know?"

"So, then, this was never a planned pregnancy to begin with?" Ms. Zambezi asked.

"No, never," Jenna firmly answered. "I'm just not ready for motherhood yet."

"And you said that you're married, correct?" Ms. Zambezi asked.

"Yes. That's right," Jenna answered.

"You realize, then," Ms. Zambezi said, "that your husband will have to sign a waiver releasing all claims to the fetus, assuming that he is the father."

"Oh," Jenna stammered. "I didn't know that."

"Yes," Ms. Zambezi said. "The legal ramifications are staggering. If it were just an egg cell, then there would be no question of ownership. But once the egg is fertilized, then the law requires that the rights of the father be considered as well."

"Well, I don't think that'll be a problem," Jenna said. "I mean, we've discussed this, and we're both in agreement. We don't want a baby."

"All right, then," Ms. Zambezi said. "That will make this so much simpler. But before we can discuss the details, we have to run some tests."

"What kind of tests?" Jenna asked. She was worried, as well as curious, about what invasions of her body there might be.

Ms. Zambezi made several entries on the keyboard and turned the monitor so Jenna could see. A computer model of a transparent female body appeared on the screen. The internal organs were clearly visible through the translucent skin. She then made a key stroke and the view zoomed in on the abdomen. As it did, the uterus and ovaries became obvious.

"There are two tests we do," Ms. Zambezi began. "First, we perform an ultrasound to give us a general indication of the fetus' condition. We also determine its maturity at this time."

While she described this, three discs appeared on the model's abdomen. Simulated sound waves emanating from them bounced off the organs and returned to the sensors. As this occurred, the uterus opened up revealing a nondescript mass.

"The second test is what's called amniocentesis. During this test, a small sample of the amniotic fluid is removed. The sample is analyzed to determine any abnormalities in the fetus. We get the results back in three to four days. It is usually important that the fetus not have any defects, which this test should tell us."

The image rotated slightly and a device resembling a needle was introduced through the abdomen and into the uterus. The presentation continued until the needle had been removed; then, Ms. Zambezi turned the screen away from Jenna.

Jenna stared blankly as Ms. Zambezi turned the monitor back around. This was something she hadn't expected. It seemed like a lot of effort was spent in removing a blob of tissue.

Before Jenna could react, Ms. Zambezi said, "Well, then, if there's nothing else, let's get started." She touched a button on her desk.

"Exam analysis." The voice sounded detached, and Jenna wasn't sure if it was a man or a woman.

"Yes, this is Ms. Zambezi…"

"Good morning, Ms. Zambezi," the voice interrupted. "How can I help you?

"Could you send a technician to my office. I have a young lady here who needs pictures and fluid."

"Someone will be right up."

"Thank you."

Ms. Zambezi turned her attention back to Jenna. "A technician will be right up. He will take you down to *Exams* where they'll do the tests we talked about. It shouldn't take very long. Then, you'll come back here and we can discuss the terms."

"Oh. All right," Jenna said

Soon, there was a knock at the door.

"Come in," Ms. Zambezi said.

An attractive, sandy-haired man wearing white pants, shirt, and shoes entered the office. "Ms. Zambezi? I'm Brandon Irons. I was sent up from *Exams*." His voice was high, almost feminine, but otherwise clear and well articulated.

Ms. Zambezi smiled and gestured towards Jenna. "Yes, Brandon. This is Ms. Kelemen. You'll be escorting her down for testing, and bring her back to my office when you're finished."

"Yes, ma'am." He looked at Jenna. "If you'll come this way, please."

Jenna glanced at Ms. Zambezi who smiled reassuringly. Then, Jenna got up and followed the technician out of the office.

Jenna stepped into the elevator with the technician. As yet, neither one had spoken; and she was beginning to feel uncomfortable.

"Sub one," he commanded, after they were both inside the elevator car.

"Sub one?" Jenna uttered, stupidly.

The technician looked at her. "Yes, ma'am. This building has six levels. Three above ground and three below. The offices and common areas are above ground. The labs, operating rooms, and nurseries are below."

Nurseries? What were those? But before she could ask, the elevator stopped and the doors opened.

Jenna followed Mr. Nepal down a long, wide, immaculate corridor. With each step, his shoes squeaked obtrusively on the shiny floor tiles making Jenna believe she would go out of her mind. They passed many doors with electronic key-locks marked *AUTHORIZED PERSONNEL ONLY* and *DO NOT ENTER* before they stopped at one.

The technician put his hand to the pad; and a second later, the door opened. They stepped into another, shorter hallway with a desk just inside the door. A plain looking Euro-American woman with graying hair, wearing a white outfit similar to Mr. Iron's sat at the desk.

Mr. Irons stopped at the desk and gestured towards Jenna. "This is Ms. Kelemen. Ms. Zambezi sent her down for pictures and fluid. I'm going to take her to number three."

The woman looked up, unconcerned. "Okay, Brandon…No, wait. You better use number four. Number three's computer panel's been removed for repairs."

"Oh, shoot," he whined. "That's right. I completely forgot. Okay, number four it is."

He looked at Jenna. "Right this way, ma'am."

Jenna dutifully followed him down the hall, his shoes making that same irritating noise the had out in the main hallway. She wondered if he was doing it on purpose, just to annoy her. At last, he turned into a small room. She followed him in, and he closed the door.

The room was small, with an examining table protruding from one wall. Above the table was a shroud and above that, a monitor built into the wall. A counter with some cabinets below it ran along one side of the room. It looked very sterile.

"All right, if you'll pull your shirt up to your chest and lie down on the table, we'll get started." Mr. Irons turned his attention to a drawer under the counter.

Jenna sat on the table and pulled her blouse up to just below her breasts. A chill ran up her spine, and she shivered. Then, she did as the technician instructed and laid back on the table.

The table was hard. The thin piece of foam rubber padding failed to make it any more comfortable, and the disposable cover on the table-top did nothing to ease her discomfort.

As she lay there, Jenna watched the technician. His back was to her, and he was fumbling with something. What it could be, she didn't know. His body effectively blocked her line of sight.

She lay back and closed her eyes. How did she let herself get talked into this? It was crazy. All she wanted was to be free of the pregnancy. Such a little thing; but now, she found herself in a compromising position, at the mercy of a man she didn't know, in a place she didn't really want to be.

Jenna heard the drawer slide closed. She opened her eyes and saw Mr. Irons walking towards the table carrying a syringe that had a needle the she was sure was the size of a small sapling.

She nervously watched as he pulled up a stool and set the syringe on a small stand next to the table. He looked indifferent, like it didn't matter to him what happened. It was just a job.

He reached over to a small panel in the wall next to the exam table and flipped a switch. The monitor above the table came on, showing some sort of test pattern. The technician visually scanned the panel and the monitor. Satisfied that all was functioning properly, he took three small disks attached to the panel by wires from hooks that were next to the panel.

Mr. Irons looked at Jenna. "All right, now. So as there's no alarm, let me describe the procedure. First, I'm going to attach these sensors…" He held up the disks for her to see. "…to your abdomen using a jelly compound. The sensors will emit and receive sound waves which will allow me to see the fetus on the monitor."

Of course, she couldn't see the monitor. The shroud effectively block her vision.

"Based on the image, we will be able to determine the age of the fetus. Then, I will use the monitor to aid me in sampling the amniotic fluid."

"How?" Jenna nervously asked. "I mean, will it hurt?"

Mr. Irons chuckled. "Goodness, no. True enough, the needle looks ferocious; but really, you won't feel a thing. I will apply a numbing compound to the point of insertion before I take the sample. Believe me. You will feel nothing."

Uh huh. Right. As sincere as the technician sounded, Jenna didn't quite believe him.

"Now, let us get started." He smiled reassuringly.

Despite his smile, Jenna was finding the prospect of the needle a little unnerving. She wanted to escape, to run away. But there was no place to go, at least not physically.

She closed her eyes and relaxed her body as much as she could. Then, she opened them again to see Mr. Irons take a tube from one of the drawers. He removed the cap and squeezed out a small amount of the goo at three locations on Jenna's abdomen. The cream was cold, and she wanted to squirm from the sensation it caused. But she didn't.

Next, he attached the sensors by placing them on the spots of jelly and sliding them back and forth. When the disks were in place, Mr. Irons stated Jenna's name, social security number, and date. The computer picked up the audible input and automatically prepared a file for her tests.

Jenna closed her eyes and wished herself in another place. This was not where she wanted to be. These were not the circumstances that she wanted her life to be in. She tried her best to will the anxiety away, but she wasn't practiced enough in the technique to make her escape absolute under these conditions. Soon, she found herself in a place she'd been many years ago.

She was thirteen and pregnant. By the time she was certain, it was too late to use an abortifacient. So, she endured all of the humiliation, pain, and loneliness that accompanied a surgical abortion.

Jenna recalled the experience as if it happened yesterday. Greeted by an overly pleasant counselor, she was escorted into a drab, starkly furnished room that included a strange looking table, among other things. The table had stirrups at one end, not unlike the pedals on her bicycle. The counselor gave her a paper gown to change into and told her to have a seat on the table after she had changed. A short time later, a doctor and two nurses came in. All three were dressed in green suits made out of the same material as her gown. The most startling thing she remembered about them, though, were the smiles that adorned their faces. It all seemed so normal for them, like they'd done this a thousand times before.

Speaking to her in a calm, soothing voice, the doctor introduced himself and the team. He then briefly told her about the procedure. The next thing she knew, she was lying back on the table with her feet in the stirrups and her legs firmly strapped in place. One of the nurses assisted the doctor while the other gently stroked Jenna's forehead and spoke to her in a soft tone.

Jenna felt a slight pinch as the doctor administered a local anesthetic. A few minutes later, she heard what sounded like a vacuum cleaner. She tried to look, but the nurse stroking her head wouldn't let her. She wanted to scream; but somehow, she couldn't. She felt alone, isolated, friendless. And then, it was over.

The counselor returned, and the doctor, along with the nurse that assisted her, left. The other nurse, the one who attended to Jenna, stayed to help her cleanup and dress. The counselor gave her a half dozen or so *industrial-sized* feminine pads. The nurse told her that there may be some bleeding for a few days, which was normal, and to use the pads as long as necessary. Then, the counselor escorted her out to the lobby where her mother was waiting.

"Ms. Kelemen," she heard a voice say, "we're finished."

Jenna opened her eyes and blinked for a moment. The light was bright and irritated her eyes. She looked down as Mr. Irons detached the sensors and cleaned the jelly compound from her abdomen.

He smiled. "All done. You can get off the table now."

She lay on the table, motionless, unsure of where she was.

"Are you all right, ma'am?" he asked.

Jenna blinked and looked at him. "Yes. I'm all right." She hopped down onto the floor, glad to realize that it had been only a dream. Realizing that her blouse was still hiked up to her chest, she pulled it back down and smoothed it out.

The whole procedure couldn't have taken that long. She looked around the room for a clock, but didn't see one. "How long…"

"Twenty minutes. If you'll follow me, I'll take you back to Ms. Zambezi's office."

Jenna followed the technician as he left the room. They stopped at the desk at the end of the hall just long enough for Mr. Irons to leave the syringe with the technician on duty. Then it was down the hall to the elevator.

After a quiet ride on the elevator and a short walk, Jenna found herself at Ms. Zambezi's office. The door was opened and she could see the woman diligently working on the computer. Mr. Irons knocked.

Ms. Zambezi looked away from the console and smiled. "Come in, come in. How'd it go, Brandon."

"Just fine," he said, confidently. "The data should be in file now."

"Good, good." She glanced at Jenna. "All right. Thank you, Brandon."

Mr. Irons nodded and left.

"Please, sit down," Ms. Zambezi said. "I trust it wasn't as, ah, painful as you'd expected."

"No," Jenna said, "it really wasn't."

Ms. Zambezi smiled approvingly. "Good; I'm glad. Now, let's pull up your file."

Jenna watched as Ms. Zambezi made some entries on the console.

"Ah, here it is."

Jenna couldn't see the screen as Ms. Zambezi reviewed whatever was on it. Occasionally, she would stop and utter a satisfied sound as if she was pleased with the report.

Jenna was curious. She tried to crane her neck so as to give her at least a partial view of the monitor, but to no avail. "Can I see?" she asked.

Ms. Zambezi looked at her through piercing eyes. "Yes," she said. She turned the monitor so Jenna could see. A three-dimensional image glared at her from the screen. Ms. Zambezi pointed to a nondescript mass just to the right side of the screen and said, "That's the fetus."

Jenna squinted but saw nothing that would indicate to her anything special.

"At this point in development," Ms. Zambezi said, "the fetus is little more than a sliver of tissue. It is approximately fifteen hundredths of an inch long, and there is little to distinguish it as potentially human. This knob here," she said, pointing at the lower part of the object, "would one day be the head. And that section in the middle that looks like it is throbbing is the heart bulge. With its tail like section, it resembles, if anything, a snail."

Jenna stared at the image for several minutes. It did look like a snail. It couldn't possibly be human, could it?

"This is excellent, Jenna," Ms. Zambezi said. "The fetus is developing perfectly. No abnormalities that could be detected by an ultrasound; of course, we'll have to wait for the lab to finish analyzing the fluid to make a final determination. But, it looks good. And the computer gives the fetus an age of four weeks."

"Four weeks?" Jenna was just a little confused. She thought that she was at least five weeks along.

"Yes, four weeks." Sensing Jenna's disbelief, Ms. Zambezi continued, "Of course, that doesn't count the two weeks of its embryo stage. So, really, you are six weeks pregnant."

"That's what I thought," Jenna noted. "But now what?"

Ms. Zambezi punched some keys on the console and glanced at the monitor before continuing. "First, let me tell you about the procedures we use to remove the fetus…"

Jenna listened and watched intently as Ms. Zambezi described the various techniques used to harvest the fetus. There were two primary types; and neither had really changed that much since the twentieth century.

Dilatation and evacuation, or the vacuum method, was still used during the first trimester, since the condition of the fetus wasn't particularly important. It was the tissue they were after.

For later abortions, when the fetus could be maintained outside the womb and its organs were more fully developed, the extraction method was preferred. First introduced in the late twentieth century, it was most effective for removing live, undamaged fetuses.

When Ms. Zambezi had finished, she asked, "Do you have any questions?"

Jenna blinked and shook her head. What could she ask? "No…no questions."

"Very well, then." Ms. Zambezi made some more entries on the console.

"Now, about compensation," Ms. Zambezi began, "you will be paid on a sliding scale as determined by the usefulness of the fetus and its stage of development." She stopped and thought for a moment. "For example, if you gave us the fetus right now, it would be worth no more than $500…because its applications are limited. But, if you were to, say, carry it into the third trimester, well, it would be worth at least $50,000. One reason is that we save the expense of maintaining it in a nursery for those additional weeks. That in itself saves us tens of thousands of dollars.

"But beyond the savings is a whole range of applications available for a more fully developed fetus. They provide a ready reserve of organs for life saving transplants. They make perfect laboratory specimens on which to test drugs and other medical procedures. They are larger, which means more material for tissue research and other industrial use.

"I don't know," Jenna said. "I mean, I just want to get rid of it…and I don't want to wreck my body doing it, either."

Ms. Zambezi said nothing as she looked at Jenna. The woman's eyes seemed to penetrate deep into Jenna's thoughts, and Jenna became anxious.

"Yes, I can see your dilemma," Ms. Zambezi said at last. "You are a very attractive woman…bright, athletic. You, know, most women can go into the twenty-fourth or twenty-fifth week with little or no adverse effects. Sure, they put on some weight, but usually no more than ten or fifteen pounds. A woman with your obvious athleticism should have no trouble getting back into shape after twenty-four weeks.

"So, let's say you carry the fetus into the twenty-fourth week. Then, we will extract it."

Jenna felt unsure. She looked at Ms. Zambezi and said, unconvinced, "Well…I don't know."

"It would be worth $35,000 to you," Ms. Zambezi said. "Now, who couldn't use $35,000?"

Jenna looked around the room, searching for an escape. Ms. Zambezi reminded her of a sales person: they always had the best deal and could make anything sound good.

She thought about Joe and the discussion they'd had. She could pay off her loans and still have some left. And most importantly, she would be rid of it, one way or another.

After several minutes of considering her options, Jenna said, "Well, what's fifteen pounds, right? And it's only a few more months. I mean, it's not like I'd be spending a lifetime raising a child."

Ms. Zambezi smiled. "Excellent, Jenna. Now, I have some papers for you and your husband to sign and a schedule of appointments for you…"

Jenna only half listened as Ms. Zambezi continued to tell her about what would be occurring over the next few months. In a way, she was relieved. Another hurdle in the quest to terminate the pregnancy had been jumped. Now, it was just a matter of time.

THE DREAM

Jenna walked along the dried creek bed. The scorching sun sitting upon its throne in the early afternoon sky laughed at her from upon high. Bits of dried earth and stone scurried away from her across the bleak, hard ground as she mindlessly shuffled one foot in front of the other. The air, hot and smothering, burned her lungs with each breath. A scorching wind blew out of the southwest pasting her face with gritty bits of sand and dirt.

In the creek bed, a small whirlwind gyrated and spun, forming a cone out of the loose dirt and small stones. The small tempest moved to and fro as if by its own volition. The gyrating funnel stayed just out of reach as it continued its macabre dance, seemingly leading her forward.

She saw a house in the distance. It was big, like a mansion. The sunlight reflected off its white exterior, almost blinding her. She shielded her eyes with one hand to lessen its glare. The house's trim was gold, and the columns supporting its facade glittered with precious stones. The front displayed no windows, although a large door flanked by marble columns was positioned in the center. An arch rose from above the door, providing a Romanesque effect. Around the house stood a multitude of people, all dressed in white. Above the house, a great beast with the head of a lion and the wings of an eagle drifted effortlessly through the sky, circling the mansion below.

She trudged on, cumbersomely shifting one foot in front of the other. The blisters on her feet were unbearable. Her throat was parched, and her lips dry and cracked. Sweat soaked Jenna's shirt; it adhered uncomfortably to her skin. Perspiration trickled down her forehead, stinging her eyes. She truly wanted to give in and let the scorching sun dry her bones, but she couldn't. She knew that relief waited for her in that mansion.

The winged beast continued to float easily in the sky. She thought, if only it would come and carry me the rest of the way. She tried to signal it but didn't have the strength to lift her arms. She opened her mouth to call to it, but her throat was dry and no sound could be made.

Full of despair, she began to run towards the house. Hot air filled her lungs as she breathed heavier and more rapidly. The murderous sun beat down upon her, robbing her body of its remaining strength. As each blistered foot pounded the ground, terrific pain shot into her brain; and she moaned in agony as tears welled up in her eyes.

As she got closer and closer to the house, the despair began to vanish, replaced by hope. Despite the pain, the thirst, and the exhaustion, she could feel herself getting stronger and running faster as the house grew bigger and bigger. In the multitude, she saw one man, his robe crimson as if it had been dipped in blood. He lifted his hand and beckoned her onward. Drawing closer to the figure, she perceived a sympathetic, gentle gaze originating from his dirty, blood streaked face. He started to walk toward her, almost floating, to meet her.

Jenna awoke with a start! She was in her own bed, but something had grabbed her leg under the covers. She looked and saw Joe sleeping soundly beside her. The thing held tightly to her ankle and was pulling on it! It felt cold and clammy, like steel.

The room was pitch black. She couldn't see what it was. She became panicky. Breathing faster, she tried to scream but couldn't. She tried to fight it off, but didn't have the strength. It kept pulling and pulling and pulling. Paralyzed with fear, she broke out in a cold sweat.

She struggled, tried to grab on to something, anything; but there was nothing to hold on to. It pulled her farther and farther down the mattress. Her leg throbbed with pain, like something was crushing it. She tried to kick it off with her other foot, but its grip was too tight. She struggled against it with all her strength. She contorted her body, tried to scream, tried to get free from it!

"Jen! Jen!" Joe called as he shook her. "Wake up! You're having a nightmare."

Jenna opened her eyes. She and the bed were soaked with sweat, and her leg ached as if it had been twisted off. She threw off the covers and stared. Yes, the leg was still attached to her hip, and there was no blood. She wiggled her toes; they responded. She flexed the muscles, and they responded. Her leg tingled a little, like it had been asleep; but it still functioned. It had only been a dream.

Joe studied her in the soft glow of the reading lamp he'd turned on. Jenna's face was pale in the light, like she'd died for just one moment. Her eyes were glazed and empty. Her breathing, rapid and shallow. Jenna's whole body trembled, and her skin felt clammy when he touched her cheek.

"Jen, are you all right?" Joe asked hesitantly as he studied her expressionless face. She did not respond; so, he gently shook her again. "Jen! Answer me."

She blinked and slowly turned her gaze towards him. The color was beginning to return to her face, and tears pooled in her eyes. She stared at him for a moment and then began to sob.

Joe reached over and pulled her close. Stroking her hair, he said, "Jen, it's all right. You were just having a bad dream. Everything's fine now."

"Oh, god, Joe," Jenna mumbled through the sniffling. "It was horrible. I've never experienced such terror in a dream before."

"Do you want to tell me about it?" he asked as she rested her head against his shoulder and he tenderly rubbed her back.

She sat up, wiped the tears from her eyes, and snuffed her nose. Choking on the words at first, she related the dream to him and how it was really a dream within a dream. She told him of the dry heat, the parched land and creek bed, and the whirlwind that danced before her, leading her on along the bed. She described the white house and how it was magnificently adorned with gold and jewels. She painfully spoke of her walk, her blistered feet, and her aching body. Then she recounted the winged beast, illustrating its motion though the sky above the house. Finally, she told him about the great host of people that stood before the house and the man who stood in their midst.

Then, as Jenna described the second part of the dream, she spoke more urgently, breathed more rapidly, and gestured more frantically She recalled in detail how the thing grabbed her foot, how it felt as it held on, and how she struggled against it. She articulated, then demonstrated, how she tried to scream but couldn't, and the way she tried to seize on to anything but found nothing. She told him about the way it felt as she was being torn from her sanctuary, and the shock when she woke to find that she was in her own bed, safe.

When she'd finished, Joe shook his head and sighed. "Jesus christ, Jen. That was one hell of a dream."

Jenna stared blankly for a few moments. Then she bit her lip and looked at him. "Yeah, it was one hell of a dream. Oh, god, I don't know if I can go back to sleep after that. What time is it?"

Joe glanced at the clock. "It's almost four o'clock."

"Oh," she groaned. "There's no way I'm going back to sleep."

"Well, what are you going to do, then?" he asked. "You could just stay in bed with me, and we'll cuddle. It's really too early to get up anyway, especially since it's Saturday."

She smiled. "Yeah, you're right. It is too early." She leaned over and gently kissed him. "Just hold me, then, okay?"

Jenna curled up on her side facing away from Joe. He in turn cuddled up next to her, getting as close as two people could. He wrapped his arms around her, and she rested her hands on them. Jenna dozed off some time later, feeling secure in his embrace.

Several hours passed before Jenna woke up. She opened her eyes and found that Joe was already out of bed. Sunlight leaked into the room through the window blind cutting a swath across the dust that floated freely in the air. She glanced at the clock. It was 8:15 AM. She hadn't thought it possible, but she managed to sleep another four hours. She sat up and stretched her arms towards the ceiling, pulling the muscles in her torso until she thought they'd snap. Then, she got out of bed and slipped her nightgown over her head.

Looking at herself in the mirror, Jenna turned left and then right to examine her profile. Eleven weeks. She was in week eleven of the gestation period. She couldn't really see any difference in her body, although she thought her pants had been a little tighter yesterday. She'd noticed a little more hair coming out into her brush lately, too.

Soon enough it would become obvious to anyone who saw her that she was pregnant, although Ms. Zambezi had told her that she needn't worry about that before the twentyfourth week, which was when she'd agreed to have the little cancerous growth removed, anyway. If she began to show conspicuously before then, Ms. Zambezi had told her, wear loose clothes and eat a lot: people will just think you've gone on an eating binge.

Jenna opened a bureau drawer and rifled through it searching for something to wear. She pulled out a lavender, stirruped jumpsuit with a single lilac embroidered upon the left breast. She slipped her trim body into the suit and fastened the shoulder snaps. The outfit fit more snugly than she remembered.

She regarded herself in the mirror for a moment. The suit hugged her body, and her breasts stood out like pillows on a well made bed. She was certain that her stomach was a little more pronounced, too. She ran a brush through her hair a few times and counted the strands entangled in the bristles when she was done. Then, she left the bedroom.

Joe sat at the computer with a mug in one hand and a pencil in the other. As he stared at the screen, the pencil wove in and out through his fingers. Setting the mug down, he stuck one end of the pencil in his mouth and aggressively chewed on it. Deciding that it had lost its flavor, he put it down, folded his arms, and sighed.

Jenna scrutinized him for a moment. He was still wearing his pajamas, and he'd put those horrible, ratty slippers on. Joe said they were comfortable; Jenna thought they should be disposed of. He hadn't shaved yet, as evidenced by the dark shadow covering the lower portion of his face. He must have sensed her presence because he looked up, lifted his eyebrows, and smirked at her.

She walked over to him and rested her hands on his shoulders. Looking past him, she asked, "What are you reading?"

"Just catchin' up on the news," he huffed.

Jenna searched the screen to see what was causing his frustration. The image on the monitor revealed a ransacked room with overturned tables, broken cabinets, and smashed equipment strewn throughout the scene. Scrawled on one wall in red was "MURDERERS". The headline above the picture read, "CHRISTIAN EXTREMISTS SABOTAGE LOCAL SCHOOL BASED CLINIC."

She went on to read that a clinic in a Philadelphia high school had been ransacked. Based on some tracts that had been left behind at the scene, local officials believed that a radical Christian Fundamentalist organization known as the Apocalypse Revolutionary Front was responsible. The tracts called for an end to the wanton destruction of human life and the servitude of the nation's adolescent girls in filling the coffers of the abortion industry. The police considered this to be an inside job since there was no sign of forced entry. Local parents were concerned that there might be a fundamentalist working at the school, coming into contact with the children, and spreading his twisted beliefs.

"Wow!" Jenna exclaimed.

"Incredible, isn't it?" Joe asked rhetorically. "Ignorant fundamentalist shit heads!"

She rubbed his shoulders as they tensed up. "Well, Joe, they're entitled to their opinion. I mean..."

"Opinion, my ass." Pointing at the image, he declared sarcastically, "These concerned citizens are nothing but a god damned bunch of radical fascists! They ought to be locked up, and each one forced to choke down a copy of their socalled "Word of God," page by page."

Joe always made a big production number out of these things, like it really mattered to him anyway, she thought to herself. It was his way of either getting attention or making a point. She didn't know which one he was going for right at the moment.

"Hmmm, I'll admit," Jenna calmly said, "their methods are extreme; and when they do damage like this, they should be made accountable for it. But you can't fault them for passionately embracing their beliefs."

"Bullshit! I can, and do. Their god is a fraud, an excuse for everything they do, or everything that happens to them. If something good happens, they say it's a blessing from god. If something bad happens, god's punishing them.

"What I especially can't stand is that bullshit about how if you're not saved, you'll burn in Hell, forever! And the only way to get saved is to ask Jesus Christ into your heart, and then you obey his will.

"So, I ask you, what do they say when one of their fellow lunatics goes out and gets drunk or sleeps around?"

"Well, they..."

"I'll tell you what they say. 'He's not living in the spirit.' What the hell's that supposed to mean, 'He's not living in the spirit'? It's just a freakin' lot of nonsense, that's what it is.

"But you know what the best evidence is that they're full of shit, don't you?"

Jenna studied him for a moment. His eyes burned with hate, and his fists were clenched. He looked like a man ready to do battle. She said, "No, I don't know."

"You're lookin' at it!"

"What do you mean, Joe?"

"Me. I'm the proof. They always talk about how their imaginary god is the creator of everything and how he cares about each of us…"

"Yeah, so."

"Their god didn't create me! I was born in a test tube and planted in dear, old mommy's womb. There was no act of creation, or divine intervention. There was just some doctor, an egg cell, and some sperm that some asshole spunked into a cup. Stick it in the blender and presto! Out comes Joe. Hell, for all I know, I might have some siblings stored away in a cryogenic state in a laboratory somewhere.

"So, you see, this bullshit of theirs with tearin' up some clinic to protect babies that some imagined god cares about is just crazy. These whackos need to get a dose of reality. They need to pull their collective heads out of their dungholes and smell the god damned roses!"

Jenna thought about what he said for a moment. She really couldn't argue with him. From where she stood, this business about Jesus of Nazareth being the Savior of the world was far fetched. True, he was a great moral teacher and spiritual master, but son of God? No, she had to draw the line there.

"Well, Joe, I have to agree with you about Jesus not being the savior," she said. "And their view of god is perverted, but each of us is still a creature that exists in three realms, a reflection of the divine spirit that is the universe."

"Oh, yeah? And just what might those three realms be, hmm?" he said with a twinkle in his eyes.

Jenna pulled a chair up next to his and sat down. She'd explained this to him a dozen times before, and each time he'd laughed. But, she figured, if he heard it enough, he may just accept it one day.

"It's very simple," she began. "Each of us occupies the physical, intellectual, and spiritual dimensions simultaneously. The physical needs are, well, the most basic. To survive, we must eat, rest, and have shelter from the elements. So from the beginning, this was humanity's primary concern, just like all creatures. And as we evolved, our intelligence grew, too, which brings us to the second realm: intellectual.

"The intellectual realm involves our ability to reason, to think, and to be aware of our own existence. You know, mankind has always had these abilities. But it wasn't until our technology evolved sufficiently to where we didn't live every moment just to survive that we were able to fully appreciate our intellectual abilities. See what I mean?"

"Uh huh," Joe said.

"Now, the last realm is spiritual," she continued. "When our intellect freed us to a point from the fight just to survive, then, well, we were better able to explore spiritual things. This realm involves that which cannot be examined with our natural senses. That is why early man left us only things like, well, crude tools. Because his was a fight for survival, he had little knowledge of the spiritual, and no time to devote to it.

"But later, after our technology advanced enough, we were able to explore the spiritual. And through the ages, mankind has attempted to express the spiritual through a variety of religions, but it all boils down to one simple truth."

"And what might this truth be, oh learned one?" Joe said with a smile.

"That all things, whether animal, vegetable, or mineral, are bound together by one permeating, allencompassing spiritual consciousness. And this force drives the universe through its natural, evolutionary course."

Joe was stymied for a moment. Then he chuckled. "And that includes someone like me, eh? I am part of this spiritual force of yours, bound together with the rest of creation through eternity. But how can that be if I was created in a lab? How does this force know that I am part of it?" He laughed.

"Joe, just by your presence," she said lightly. "Your being here makes you part of the universe, and it doesn't matter how you got here. It's like, um, well, a swimming pool. The people in the pool are part of the pool; when someone jumps in, they become part of the pool, too. See?"

"Yeah," Joe answered, snickering. "I see. You're as nutty as those Christian whackos!" He started laughing uproariously.

"Joe, that's awful!" she exclaimed as she slapped him on the thigh. "You're such a brat!"

Jenna got up and headed for the kitchen. Calling back to Joe, she asked, "Would you like some breakfast?"

Still chuckling, he replied, "Yeah, I'll have a couple eggs and some toast…and coffee."

"All right, hon."

Jenna took three eggs out of the refrigerator. She studied them carefully as, one by one, she cracked them and let the contents of each slide out of the shell and into the recesses of the egg tray.

These would have been chickens, she thought to herself, living organisms, and part of the cosmic community with as much purpose to their existence as hers. Instead, she was going to cook them and eat them. Life feeds on death, and she and Joe were about to consume creatures that never were. She put the tray into the microwave oven and turned it on.

While the eggs cooked, she popped some bread into the toaster and poured two cups of coffee. She remembered that Joe liked cream in his; so, she added some. After the cream was poured, she marveled at the white trails left behind as the cool creamer plunged into the hot coffee, and how they disappeared as she blended the two with a spoon.

The microwave dinged, signaling that the eggs were done. She stepped over to it and opened the door. The aroma of fresh cooked eggs stimulated her senses, bringing back memories of her mother's breakfasts. She called Joe as she spooned the eggs on to the plates and set the toast next to the eggs.

While she waited for Joe, Jenna looked at the white blotches of egg on the plates. She was always amazed at how perfectly round and domelike the yolks were.

She remembered the little baby chicks she'd often encountered on her grandfather's farm. They were soft and warm, and made these little peep, peep sounds. She'd always loved the way that the chicks would bunch together in a corner of the box when they slept. They continuously climbed over, around, and through each other, searching for the warmest spot.

For a moment, she thought she felt something move inside her abdomen. Inexplicable anxiety clouded her mind, and she no longer wanted to eat the eggs.

THE WORD

The auditorium was filled to capacity. People from all walks of life were in attendance. Even in this benevolent gathering, however, there was still a sense of distrust, a feeling of suspicion. As Jenna looked around the hall, she was disturbed to see that the different races had segregated themselves into pockets of autonomy. The African Americans gathered with other Africans. American Indians filled the seats on the left. Those of Asian descent occupied the front right. The descendents of Arabs filled the back rows, while the Indians, as in India, gathered in the rows between the Asians and the Arabs. The European Americans filled the center.

Here and there, a small pockets had crossed these arbitrary lines of separation: a few Asians seated with the Europeans, or Europeans with the Africans, for example. But for the most part, the races were segregated. All told, there must have been about fifteen hundred present.

They'd all come to hear the great Dr. James Emerson: Professor of Biblical Studies, and Utopian Scholar. He'd written several books and articles, and also served on the staff of a prominent New Age magazine as a contributing editor. Dr. Emerson was regarded by many as an authority on the common roots of the world's religions. He'd traveled the globe, visiting primitive tribal cultures, major religious centers, and isolated monasteries.

Jenna was really excited about having this opportunity to hear Dr. Emerson in person. Roxanne, who'd personally met him a couple of years ago, was so impressed with him that she couldn't say enough about the man.

Jenna had read several of his articles. She was most impressed with his concept of Single Source Spirituality, which is to say that all of the world's various religious systems and traditions evolved from a common root that recognized only one spiritual force in the universe.

As proof, he pointed to the apparent similarities between the monotheistic religions and the more primitive cultures, especially the creation myths. He claimed that, of all the advanced cultures of antiquity, only the Israelites maintained this truth, although through the millennia they themselves turned from the One True Spirit to a Creator God who was divorced from creation. Then, the Christians took it another step by giving this god paternal characteristics. And, of course, the Muslims continued to foster this error, although they, at least, freed humankind from automatic damnation.

Before the two had arrived, Roxanne said that it would be a very enlightening, uplifting evening. Jenna cast her eye towards Roxanne who was seated next to her. Roxanne's sandy hair, streaked with gray, brushed her shoulders as she turned her head. Her brown eyes sparkled as the corners of her mouth pulled up in to a slight smile, and her hands rested comfortably on her lap. Their eyes met for a second; and Roxanne patted Jenna's leg as if to reassure her. Jenna wondered if Roxanne was aware of the same suspicious spirit hanging over the room that she felt.

The lights in the hall dimmed, and a hushed silence came over the crowd. A single spotlight directed their attention to one side of the stage. A man walked out of the wing and in to the light. It followed him as he meandered to the center of the stage. He was a tall man, well over six feet, and a tad on the heavy side. His dark skin, broad nose, and short, tightly curled gray hair was indicative of his African heritage. His posture as he moved was tall and absolute, like a pine in the forest. Jenna recognized him from the pictures on his books: Dr. James Emerson.

At the center of the stage, Dr. Emerson turned to face the audience. He stared out into the hall, and in a booming voice, shouted, "Somebody turn up the house lights! I can't see my brothers and sisters! And turn off that spotlight!"

At his command, the house lights came on and the spotlight dimmed to nothing. He studied the faces in the audience for a few seconds, making eye contact as he searched the hall. He looked even more impressive from the front. His face was round with wire rimmed spectacles perched on his nose. Broad shoulders topped his barrel chest.

He took a handkerchief from a breast pocket and daubed his brow saying, "Whew! That light sure was hot!" The crowd chuckled in response, but quieted again as his piercing gaze roamed the audience.

With his hands behind his back, Dr. Emerson began his presentation. "I like being able to see who I'm talking to. Makes no difference if it's one or one thousand. I like to see 'em. I like to make eye contact with 'em. That way…I can tell if they're payin' attention to what I'm sayin'!"

With his arms at his sides, he began to pace the length of the stage, but he always kept his gaze out there, fixed on someone. "You see, brothers and sisters, I'm a man of few words. When I've got somethin' to say, I want to be heard, 'cause if it's not worth sayin', well, I'm not gonna say it. Plain and simple."

He paused at one end of the stage for a moment and rubbed his hands together before continuing. "Now! You're prob'ly wonderin' to yourselves, 'If he's a man of few words, why's he up there ramblin' on like the village idiot?'"

Chuckles rose from the crowd at that question.

"It's like this, my friends. Before I speak to a crowd of my fellow cosmic citizens such as yourselves, I like for them to know where I'm commin' from. I want you to know what it is…that I am all about."

Jenna noticed that many seated around her, including Roxanne, nodded their agreement at his confession.

For the next five or ten minutes, Dr. Emerson gave a brief history of his life. He was fiftyfive years old, and grew up in Georgia. His parents were simple, honest people. His father had worked in a chemical plant, on the line. His mother had held a part time position as a waitress. He had two brothers and one sister. He was raised in the Southern Baptist church, where he was baptized when he was eight.

While in college, though, he became disenchanted with his religion for a couple of reasons. First, in a Black Studies course he'd taken, he was taught that Christianity was the white man's religion, forced upon the conquered peoples of the world as Imperialist Europe spread like a cancer around the globe. Second, as he experienced new ideas and cultures, he decided that, for a religion that was supposed to be based on the Grace of God, those Baptists sure were a bunch of legalists, and Christians as a whole were hypocrites.

While a senior, he was introduced to a group who espoused a new way. One where people were in harmony with others and nature. One where there was no fear of a tyrannical, allpowerful, creator god. Heaven was where one's spirit resided, and Hell was nonexistent.

He attended some of their gatherings and discovered that he found the one thing missing from his life: inner peace. He could be free to be who he was. And love…it abounded for all who were willing to partake of it.

Ever since then, he'd put his knowledge of history and religion together with his spiritual yearning. He traveled far and wide trying to make sense of the multitude of religions that filled the world. It was his quest, his life's purpose.

Now, he stood before this crowd who eagerly waited for him to bring them some message, some truth that eluded them. Jenna was mesmerized by his presence. He was a dynamic speaker, forceful and convincing. She looked and saw that those around her were just as electrified as she. Jenna glanced at Roxanne's beaming face. When Dr.

Emerson finished his account of the journey to his awakening, the whole audience stood and applauded wildly. From the mass of people, a chant rose, shaking the building: "Emerson, Emerson, Emerson,…!"

Dr. Emerson raised his hand, and the crowd fell silent. Those standing sat back down. He looked out over the audience as he had that first time, making eye contact with individuals throughout the hall. Someone had wheeled a table out to him with a pitcher of ice water and a glass. He calmly filled the glass and took a long drink from it. After setting the glass down, he returned to center stage and stood motionless for a few seconds.

"Now, brothers and sisters, now that I have your attention…" He chuckled to himself. "…I want to tell you a story. And since Christmas will soon be upon us, I want to tell you a Christmas story."

Some yeah's and Go, brother's went up from the audience. Many people nodded in agreement.

"Two thousand years ago, my friends, a child was born. He was the son of simple folk, like you and me. He would grow up to be a carpenter by trade; but in reality, brothers and sisters, he was so much more. This simple man…this honest man…this compassionate man…would bring a new message. And his message would one day be carried to all nations!" Dr. Emerson paused and looked out over the congregation. "Jesus of Nazareth, my friends, may well be the single most influential man that ever walked the Earth. Let me hear an 'amen'!"

From around the auditorium, various individuals and groups responded as asked. Many others clapped their hands and nodded in agreement.

After the accolades died away, Dr. Emerson continued. He began by shouting, "Hold on, brothers and sisters! Hold on. While a message did spread, I'm here to tell you that it was a perverted message. His simple message of love and compassion was corrupted. They took his teachings, his example, and turned him in to something he was not.

"They said he was the son of God…Well, my friends, we are all children of God." He began to pace the stage, talking excitedly and gesturing with his hands. "Each and every one of us has locked within the potential to realize our spiritual fulfillment...just as he did! For Jesus said 'I and the Father are one.'

"Now, just who is this Father? What was Jesus really trying to say...when he said that he and the Father were one?" He stopped and put a finger to his lips as if thinking. "Orthodox Christians will tell you, with a straight face no less, that what he meant was that he and God are the same, that God...in all his magnificence...in all his benevolence...in all his omnipotence...in all his omniscience...saw fit to become a man, like you, my friend..." He pointed to someone up front, but Jenna couldn't see who it was. "...to save us from ourselves!"

Dr. Emerson stopped and laughed for a second. Some in the audience snickered right along with him. "Oh, my friends, those poor Christians...they done been duped! What I mean to say is this: why would an allpowerful, allknowing, supreme being have to lower himself to our level...to fix somethin' that he done messed up?" He shrugged. "Doesn't sound too impressive to me. What about you?"

Negative responses were shouted out as the audience thunderously concurred.

After the noise died away, Dr. Emerson calmly said, "No brothers and sisters. When Jesus talked about the Father he wasn't talkin' about some bearded guy in the sky."

He strode back to center stage. "You see, Jesus was a Jew. And Judaism is patriarchal. That is to say, the man called all the shots. Therefore, their god was a man. Pure and simple!"

He stopped and looked out into the crowd. Seeing all the baffled faces, he knew that he wasn't connecting. Jenna herself was at a loss.

"Let me put it to you this way" He put his hands together as if praying. "Now, most of us, when we talk about spiritual things, we refer to the Goddess, or the Eternal Mother, or Mother Earth...Am I correct?"

It was a rhetorical question, but some answers were yelled out anyway.

He just shook his head and continued. "We are all part of a greater One, which encompasses everything. The rocks, the trees, the water, the earth, all living creatures, all the stars, all the planets, the whole universe. All of these things are connected, are interrelated, are dependent upon each other." He paused. "There is no god that created these things...or is separate from them. Rather, there is one spiritual force that causes all things to take shape, to have substance, to exist...You and I call this the Mother, or the Goddess. Others have called it the Atman or Brahman. Well, Jesus called it the Father...because of the patriarchal system he grew up in." He looked around.

A murmur of understanding rose up from the crowd, and many nodded.

"So there's Jesus...talkin' about the Father. And how do I know that he was referrin' to the universal spiritual force that we know as the Goddess? Because of somethin' else he said that those misguided Christians got all fouled up."

By this time, he was standing next to the table. So, he paused to drink some water. "You see, brothers and sisters, one day...some men from the local religious establishment were givin' Jesus the third degree...And they asked him, 'Where is this Kingdom of Heaven you keep talkin about?'"

He paused. "Now, I'd like to have been inside of his head when they asked him that question. Could you just imagine what was goin' through his mind: 'Ignorant fools, why are they wastin' my time?'" He paused again. "But Jesus, he was cool about it. He looked 'em in the eye and said, 'The Kingdom of Heaven is within you.' Let me hear an amen!"

Once more, the congregation responded as asked.

After the applause died down, Dr. Emerson declared, "The Kingdom of Heaven is within you...and you...and you...and you..." He continued this for about a half a minute, pointing at a different person each time. "What a revelation! But those Christians...they were blinded, brothers and sisters. So, for two thousand years, my friends, they spread that myth of theirs, robbing millions of the eternal joy and inner peace that you only find...when you achieve unity with the One.

"Jesus said that the One is like a vine, and each of us is a branch." He began to pace the stage once more, keeping his eyes fixed on the audience, hitting each point like a drum. "If we abide in the vine...and the vine abides in us...then we will bear much fruit...for apart from the vine, apart from the One...we can do nothing! For you see, brothers and sisters, the universe is the vine...and like a branch grows from the vine...so we too, my friends...have arisen from the cosmos!"

Again, a thunderous applause, accompanied by stomping and chanting, arose from the audience. Dr. Emerson allowed this to go on for several minutes as he carefully gauged the impact of his words on the people. A feeling of complete satisfaction came over him as he realized that he had indeed reached them.

Dr. Emerson raised his hand to quiet the eager crowd, which took at least a minute. Then he continued. "Yes, brothers and sisters, from the Cosmos, from the Great and Eternal Mother, we have risen like...like the branch on the vine: that same vine that is the Universe." He paused and wiped the sweat from his brow. "And for a branch to bear fruit, it must remain connected to the vine.

"Now, brothers and sisters, Jesus recognized this truth when he said that no branch can bear fruit unless it remains in the vine. And a branch that doesn't bear fruit is cut off and cast into the fire...lest its rot spread to the rest of the vine. Jesus knew that for each of us to bear fruit...we must remain connected with the Universe. Each of us must become one with the Eternal Mother. It's the only way!

"Humanity, brothers and sisters, is like a field waiting to be cultivated...and like that field, it needs a farmer. Jesus used this analogy many times when he said, 'The harvest is plentiful, but the workers are few. Therefore, ask the lord of the harvest to send out workers into his fields.' That, my friends, is the real message of Jesus. Not to save humanity from sin...but to help the multitudes find their humanity.

"So, brothers and sisters, let us be the harvesters that Jesus wanted us to be…going forth into the fields of humanity…leading people to realize their full potential as human beings!"

He stood center stage once more, with arms triumphantly held high. The audience jumped to its feet, cheering wildly. Jenna felt weak in the knees. Chills ran up and down her spine, and her skin crawled. She looked at Roxanne who was standing on her chair, stomping her feet, and shouting some unintelligible chant. The room was filled with electricity. The congregation surged forward in one huge mass, enveloping Dr. Emerson who'd jumped down from the stage. Fifteen hundred people, fifteen hundred spirits, joined together in harmony, united with the great, eternal One. Jenna felt she'd found Nirvana.

The rest of the night was spent in joyful revelry. A partition opening to an adjoining room was pushed aside revealing tables laden with food and drink. Festive music filled the hall as the people danced, sang, and celebrated. Dr. Emerson thrilled everyone as he joined the band on the mandolin, proving himself to be an accomplished musician. Jenna threw herself into the festivities with wild abandon until, at around 3:00 AM, she slumped down in a corner with several other exhausted revelers and fell asleep.

Jenna reluctantly woke some time later as someone was shaking her. She looked up through tired eyes and saw the blurry outline of someone she didn't recognize saying, "Wake up, Jenna. We have to go." She stretched and rubbed her eyes. She shook her head. This time, when she looked up, she recognized Roxanne, hair a mess, clothes rumpled, standing over her with a broad grin across her face.

"What time is it?" Jenna murmured.

"It's about eight thirty," Roxanne softly answered.

"Oh, god," Jenna moaned. "I feel like I've been run over."

"I bet! You really let your hair down last night." Roxanne extended her hand to help Jenna up.

"Thanks," Jenna said as she pulled herself off of the floor. She remained motionless for a few seconds as she regained her composure.

Then, she slowly looked around the hall. The place was trashed. Garbage was strewn all around. The chairs had all been pushed to one side, helterskelter. Bodies, some clothed, some not, cluttered the floor. Jenna wondered how anyone could sleep in that condition on the hard floor. She turned to Roxanne whose face still had that same, warm smile.

"C'mon," Roxanne directed. "Let's get going."

"But what abou…"

"Leave it. They'll wake up soon enough, and the cleaning service will take care of the mess."

They stepped carefully over and around the sleeping forms lying on the floor. On their way, Jenna made one startling observation. The races were no longer segregated as they had been the night before. Amazingly, it had become homogenous. Africans lying with Europeans. Asians next to Africans. Arabs alongside Europeans. Native Americans sleeping with Africans. Yes, Jenna observed with satisfaction, they had come together, in a real sense.

Jenna stumbled as they left the building. The sunlight blinded her for an instant and she almost fell. Roxanne helped steady her as the two walked to the car. The air was cold against Jenna's face, and she began to shiver despite the coat she wore. Neither of them said a word as they crossed the parking lot. When they reached the car, Jenna got into the passenger's seat. Roxanne walked to the other side, opened the door, and got in. Roxanne flipped a switch on the console and a light next to it lit up.

"Are you all in?" she asked. "You better buckle up."

"Oh, right," Jenna said. "Thanks." She pulled the belt out and struggled with it for a few seconds. When she'd gotten it fastened, she sat back and sighed.

Roxanne pushed on the accelerator. As she did, the motor began to hum, the sound increasing in intensity as the car picked up speed. The ride down to the main road was along an unpaved track that violently jostled Jenna around with every bump and hole they hit.

"Can we turn the heat up?" Jenna weakly asked. "It's freezing in here."

"Sure can!" Roxanne reached over and touched a button on the console. Warm air began to blow out of the vents on each side of the passenger compartment. "How's that?"

"Better."

For the next several minutes, Jenna stared out the window as they rode along up hill and down. Most of the leaves had fallen, but she could still see them clearly in her mind's eye. The barren trees slipped by quickly while the hum of the motor droned steadily on. The dream came to her mind, rearing up like a serpent out of the murky waters. She cringed thinking about it. It had come to her three times, now, the last more real than the either of the first two. She began to move restlessly in her seat, tugging on the harness and nervously tapping her fingers on the door handle.

"Is something bothering you?" Roxanne inquired.

Jenna looked at Roxanne. Her brown eyes shifted from the road to Jenna and back again. Her brow was arched in such a way as to convey sympathy.

Jenna looked down and nervously asked, "Do you ever have dreams?"

Roxanne chuckled. "Of course. We all dream."

"No," Jenna firmly declared. "I mean dream, like recurring images that haunt you in your sleep."

Roxanne's expression changed from one of sympathy to curiosity. "Tell me about this dream."

Jenna turned towards Roxanne, as much as the harness would allow. She began to recount the vision as it had unfolded in her sleep. She described the parched earth, the dried up creek, and the whirlwind. She told of the thirst that drove her on as she painfully trudged forward with perspiration dripping down her face and her sweatsoaked shirt sticking to her back. She verbalized the scene as she gazed upon the mansion, describing in detail the building, the multitude, the winged beast, and the man with the blood stained face. She recalled how, as the man was coming for her, she suddenly found herself in her room with an unseen entity pulling at her, tearing her from the security of her warm bed.

When she'd finished, Roxanne was smiling and nodding her head. "Yes! Yes!" Roxanne exclaimed.

Puzzled, Jenna looked at her and asked, "What do you mean?"

"Don't you see, Jenna? Don't you know what's been happening?"

"No, no I don't."

Roxanne, wide eyed and beaming, looked Jenna squarely in the eyes. "You've been touched by the Word!"

"What are you talking about…the word?" Jenna said in disbelief.

"It's very rare…only a few people ever experience it. In the primitive cultures, such people were known as shamans. They had walked in the spirit world, and the people looked upon them almost like gods themselves. No one was their equal, or held so much influence. Their counterparts in the West would have been, oh, the great poets, gifted musicians, and philosophers. You know, people whose words have touched our lives, enriching the human experience."

Jenna knew a little about Shamanism, but she didn't understand where Roxanne was coming from. "Well…what does that have to do with this dream?"

"Oh, Jenna," she cooed. "Let me explain. The Shamans were individuals who managed to tap into the spiritual essence of the One. Whether it was by design or pure chance, they succeeded in contacting the Eternal Spirit, and maintaining that contact. Like I said, few people ever experience it, even fewer are able to hold on to it."

"So, what does that have to do with me?"

"My poor child. Are you so blind? You have touched the One; or, more precisely, She has touched you."

Jenna thought she began to understand. "So, what you're saying is that the Great Mother has been entering into my subconscious, trying to tell me something? But what does it mean?"

Roxanne chuckled. "Well, Jenna. That you have to figure out for yourself...Umm, being in the desert could mean that you will be required to spend time in depravation...and the mansion may signify a reward you'll receive upon completion of this trial. Being pulled from your bed could possibly show you the sacrifices you'll have to make to achieve this goal...and how difficult the decision will be. The man? Well, I don't know. You'll just have to meditate on it. If you are sincere and commit yourself to Truth, the Mother's wisdom will shine in your being."

"Wow," Jenna sighed. "That's incredible."

The rest of the trip was made in silence. Jenna continued to look out the window as the countryside sped by. Her thoughts were not on nature, though. Rather, she was considering what Roxanne had said. Before, the dream had frightened her; but now, she was excited. The notion that she had somehow communed with the very essence of the Cosmos uplifted her own spirit. And the possibility that she was chosen by the Great Mother caused her heart to leap. The past twentyfour hours had truly been enlightening. She had found Nirvana, she was sure.

THE WORD OF GOD

The cold rain, driven by a strong Autumn wind, beat against the kitchen window. Jenna looked out through the glass, her view obscured by the beads of water that covered the pane like blisters. It was a dreary day. The sky was dark with clouds, and the wind made a haunting moan as it whooshed down the street and around adjacent buildings.

She turned from the window and sighed. The kitchen was filled with the rich, wonderful aroma of fresh baked bread. Two loaves were done and another was in the oven. Jenna loved to bake. It was a creative process that occupied her mind with something other than her troubles.

"Homemade bread?" Joe asked as he came into the kitchen, stopping long enough to inhale a great quantity of the sweet smelling air.

"Yes," Jenna replied as he came over and caressed her cheek. Then he kissed her.

"Smells wonderful," he said.

"Thank you." She took his hand and gently squeezed it.

"What's the occasion?" he asked.

"Oh, there is none," she said. "I just felt like baking. Thought I'd take a loaf down to Hank, if you don't mind."

"Mind? Why would I mind? He's a nice, old geezer. He hasn't been making passes at you as he?"

"No," she answered in surprise. "And yes, he is a nice man."

"How is the old guy?" Joe asked.

"Well, I saw him a few days ago at the pharmacy," Jenna said. "And I gave him a ride home. And I saw him once after that. It seems he's got some lung problem. Alveolar protein-something. I don't remember. Anyway, I thought I'd check on him, and take him some bread."

"All right," Joe said. "But remember, we're going out tonight. So, don't stay too long."

"I won't," she said.

Joe kissed her again. "I'm going to go do some more work on the AKAGI project."

"Okay," she said as he left the room.

Jenna sat down at the kitchen counter and picked up her cup of tea. She began to think about Hank. He was a good man, and a good friend. He was a talker and enjoyed telling anyone who'd listen about how things used to be. Jenna was immediately drawn to him because he seemed so much like her grandfather.

Over the years, she'd learned a great deal about Hank, who was by no means reluctant to share his life's story. He was originally from Reading, Pennsylvania, and had joined the Marines at age nineteen. He saw action in Vietnam, the Gulf, and the Balkans. After thirty years of proud service, he had reluctantly retired.

After his retirement, Hank found that there wasn't much use for a combat veteran in the civilian world; but, eventually, he found a position with Pennsylvania Department of Corrections as an instructor at one of their juvenile penal camps, or boot camps as they were so fondly called.

Hank was perfectly suited for this kind of work. Thirty years in the Corps had given him a kind of sixth sense when it came to dealing with people. And having completed two tours as a Drill Instructor at Paris Island, he had first hand experience at riding herd over young people not much older than the ones he would encounter during his tenure with the Department of Corrections. Besides, Hank loved kids and always felt that with the proper guidance, all children could grow to be mature, responsible, productive adults. Even now, he volunteered at a local youth center, which Jenna found especially unselfish.

Jenna could remember Hank saying, "Train a child in the way he should go, and when he is old he will not turn from it."

Hank had been married, once. His wife of forty-eight years had been killed in an auto accident in 2018. Together, they'd produced three children: two boys and a girl. The youngest, Chuck, lived nearby in Trenton, N.J. The oldest, Henry, Jr., lived in New York City. The middle child, Paula, Hank never talked about too much. He would just say she'd been lost, and move on to another topic.

Jenna enjoyed Hank's company. He told some good stories, and she was never sure if he was pulling her leg or not. He also had a genuine concern about others, which was rare considering that most people who say they do have some angle they're trying to work.

The bread timer began to buzz. Jenna got up and went to the oven. The oven light came on as she opened the door. She was greeted by a wave of heat followed by the rich aroma of fresh-baked bread. The top of the bread was a nice golden brown. She put on oven mitts and removed the bread pan, closing the door with one elbow.

Jenna wrapped up one loaf in a clean towel. She carried it into the study where Joe was working. "I'm going to take this down to Hank," she said as she bent down and kissed him.

"Where's mine?" he asked.

"You're not an invalid," she said with a smile.

Jenna left the apartment and walked down the stairs to the first floor. She went to Hank's apartment and rang the doorbell. She waited several minutes before Hank said through the intercom, "Yes?" He coughed. "Who is it?"

"It's me," Jenna said. "I brought you some homemade bread." She waited as she heard Hank inside fiddling with the door. Then it opened.

"Jenna," Hank said, smiling. "Come in, come in."

She stepped in and he closed the door behind her. The apartment was cluttered with books and photo albums strewn around the room. Empty and partially filled boxes sat next to the sofa and below the mantle. "You're not moving, Hank?" Jenna asked, surprised to see the mess.

He looked around the room and chuckled. "Goodness, no, Jenna," he said. He coughed. "You'll have to forgive the mess. I haven't felt up to cleaning. And the boxes? Well, I'm not immortal. I just thought I'd put some things in order, for the grandchildren, you know."

She smiled. "Of course," she said.

"Where are my manners," he said. "Please, won't you have a seat. And I can take that."

She handed him the bread. Jenna seated herself on the sofa and began to thumb through a stack of photographs that sat on the coffee table. They all seemed to be from his days in the service. She didn't know what to make of them. Most showed Hank posing with a group of men, often in camouflage, sometimes with their faces painted, occasionally in kakhi. She even came across one with Hank in dress blues standing with a woman that Jenna recognized as his wife. She heard his footsteps and looked up in time to see him set a glass on the table in front of her.

"Ginger ale's all I got," he said as he sat down next to her. "I hope that's okay."

"It's fine, Hank," she said. "Thank you."

"I know you didn't come down here just to bring me a loaf of bread," he said. "Not that I don't appreciate it."

She looked at the old man. Despite the weary look on his face, his eyes twinkled mischievously. "Well, Hank," she said, "I did want to check on you. The bread was just a way to get you to open your door."

He slapped her leg and said, "I knew it. Just like a woman to employ her feminine guile to infiltrate a man's domain." He chuckled. "Very resourceful, my dear."

"Why, thank you," she said.

Hank began to cough. The fit grew into a long ordeal as he doubled over, trying to find his breath. His face grew red and agitated. Jenna put her arm around the old man to comfort him. The attack only lasted a minute, but it seemed longer.

"Oh, my god, Hank," she said. "Are you all right."

He rested for a moment. "Yes," he said. "That was a good one. It must be almost time for my medicine."

"What are you taking?" she asked.

"Cough suppressant," he said.

She looked at him. Pain and sadness peered back at her through clouded eyes, and she wondered what had happened to the man she once knew. "Hank, how have you been?" she asked. "You seem off lately. Is it your lungs? What are they doing for that?"

"There's nothing they can do, Jen," he said.

She took his hand. It was cold and trembly. "What do you mean? I thought they could do a lavage, flush it out?"

"Well, yes," he said. "Ordinarily, they could; but they said I was too old, that I wouldn't survive."

"Oh, I don't believe it," Jenna said in a huff.

"It's all right, Jen," he said. "I'll be fine as long as I watch myself. But what about you?"

"I'm fine," she said.

He looked at her, his brow furled. Disbelief stared at her from his dark eyes. "Are you pregnant?" he asked.

Jenna nearly lost her ginger ale. How did he know? Then she remembered meeting him at the pharmacy when she picked up the home pregnancy test. He must have seen it and put the facts together. "Well," she started to say. But she looked at him and hesitated. He was so much like her grandfather had been, and she could never lie to her grandfather. "Yes, Hank. I am."

"Ha!" he said triumphantly. "I knew it. Boy or girl?"

She didn't know what to say. "Well, I...I don't know."

"Good," he said. "Just as well. Better not to know. All this sex-selection they're doing any more is unnatural. It throws the whole natural order out of balance. God never intended us to have such knowledge or ability. Only He has the wisdom needed to control such power. Man is a devilish creature and would be better off without such knowledge."

"Well, Hank," Jenna said, "I have to agree on that…"

"You got names picked out?" he asked.

"Well, no," she said.

"Patrick," he said, "or Patricia. I've always liked those names. They're Latin. They mean 'noble'."

"Really?" she said.

"Yeah," he said. "Hey, I bet Joe's excited, isn't he?"

His questioning piqued Jenna. It was obvious to her that her pregnancy distracted him from whatever situation was troubling him, but he would never understand the end dictated for this pregnancy. It was not a subject that she wanted to dwell on. Eleven more weeks and it would be over. "Hank," she said, "I really don't want to talk about this."

"Oh, I see," he said. Dissapointment crossed his face like the dark shadow of a storm cloud.

The two sat in silence for a few minutes. It was an awkward time. Jenna didn't know what to say. He was only being excited for her, she realized. She was afraid that she had offended the old man, which was the last thing that she wanted to do.

Hank picked up his glass and took a long drink of the ginger ale. Then he sat the glass back on the coffee table. "I had a dream the other night," he said.

"Really?" she said. "Tell me about it." Jenna was relieved to hear him speak. She hadn't closed him off after all.

"Well," he said, "I was in a hospital bed, hooked up to all sorts of wires and tubes. And these people, all dressed in black, are standing around me. No expression, no speaking, they're just standing there, staring at me like vultures at a road kill. Then a figure comes in. He's dressed in black, too, and he takes hold of one of the tubes running from my arm. Then he pinches the tube between his fingers and the dream slowly fades away. And just before it winked out, my alarm went off, and I woke up."

"That's strange," Jenna said. "I wonder what it was about."

"I don't know," Hank said. "I think it was Carl Jung who said that dreams are our subconscious trying to tell us something through symbolic images. So, maybe I'm afraid of something."

"Like what?"

"I don't know. Death, maybe. I never really thought about it. I've cheated death so many times, maybe he's finally found a way to get at me." He looked at her intently. "What about you? You have any strange dreams lately you want to share?"

She eyed him for a moment. The twinkle was back in his eye. "Well," she said, "I did have one a couple of weeks ago that's still on my mind."

"Well, lets hear it," he said.

"All right," Jenna said. She made herself comfortable the sofa. "Let's see. I was walking in this desert. It was very quiet, except for a hot breeze blowing on my face. Suddenly, a huge mansion appeared before me. There was a huge crowd gathered around it, and a beast that looked like a lion, except with wings, was flying above it. As I approached the mansion, I saw a man in the midst of the crowd. He looked haggard, but gentle; and his robe was blood red. He reached his hand out to me and started to speak; but before any words came out, I found myself back in my own bed. Something was trying to pull me out, and I couldn't fight it off. Then, I woke up."

"Incredible," Hank said. "A dream within a dream."

"Yeah," she said. "What do you make of it?"

He thought for a moment. "Well, the man in the crowd sounds like the figure of Jesus Christ."

"What do you mean?" Jenna asked. She was familiar with Jesus and the attributes that Christians conferred upon him. But she had never envisioned him in the way that Hank was suggesting.

Hank reached down on the floor beside him and retrieved a book. He opened it to the back and leafed through the pages. Then, he leaned over and showed Jenna the text. He pointed to it as he read, "'And he is clothed with a robe dipped in blood, and his name is called the Word of God.' Revelation, Chapter 19, Verse 13."

Jenna searched her mind. Where had she heard that before—the Word of God? Then, she remembered. Roxanne had used a similar phrase when she said that Jenna had been 'touched by the Word.' Jenna was delighted. Hank's passage confirmed what Roxanne had said.

"You know," she said, "a friend of mine said a similar thing."

"Oh really?" Hank said. "Is she a Christian?"

"No," Jenna said. "But she has studied these things for a lot of years. She's very knowledgeable."

"Uh huh," he muttered.

"So, the Christ is synonymous with the Word?" she said. "I've heard that before."

"It is a common belief for Christians the world over," Hank said.

"I remember my grandfather talking about it," Jenna said. "He used to say something about the Word being God and becoming flesh."

"In the beginning was the Word, and the Word was with God, and the Word was God," Hank said. "And the Word became flesh and dwelt among us so that we might behold his glory."

"Yes. That's it," Jenna said. "'The word became flesh that we might behold his glory.' My friend said that I was touched by the Word."

"Touched?" said Hank. "Perhaps. I believe that He was definitely trying to tell you something."

"What do you suppose it could be?"

"I really can't say, Jen. It could be almost anything."

"Yes, I suppose it could," she said, disappointed "So, what about the part where I'm being pulled from the bed? What do you think that means?"

"Well, it could be a warning," he said. "Or maybe you're experiencing some doubt about something, and this was your subconscious manifesting that doubt, as Mr. Jung might say. I don't know. It may not mean anything."

"Well, I think there's a message in it somewhere," she said. "I just have to find it."

Hank looked at her and, taking her hand, said, "Jenna, I want to thank you for visiting, and for the bread. But right now I'm feeling very tired."

"Oh," she said. "Well, I'd better leave so you can rest."

"I hate to chase you off," he said.

"Oh, don't worry about it," she said. "I should get back up stairs anyway. I told Joe I wouldn't be gone long." Jenna got up and helped Hank to his feet. They walked together to the door.

"Thanks again for the bread," he said.

"It was no problem," she said. "I'll see you later."

"Let's hope so," he said as he opened the door.

Jenna gave him a kiss on the cheek and walked out into the hallway. She heard the door close behind her. She took the elevator to her floor and soon reached her apartment.

Joe was sprawled out on the recliner watching a football game. He had a beer in one hand, and a bowl of chips was nested between his legs. "How's the old man?" he asked.

She went to him and bent down to give him a kiss. "He seems to be in good spirits," she said. She sat down on the sofa and grabbed a handful of chips from the bowl.

"Well, that's good," Joe said, between chips.

"I just worry about him," she said. I wish there was something I could do."

"Hell, Jen," Joe said. "What more could you do short of having him move in? You're probably the only one in the building who gives a damn about the guy, let alone know his name. I think you're already doing plenty."

"Yeah," she said. "I guess you're right."

"Sure I am."

"I'm going into the kitchen," Jenna said. "You need anything?"

Joe shook the beer can. He handed it to her and said, "One dead soldier. Better bring me another, please."

"All right, hon."

Jenna got up and went into the kitchen. She opened the refrigerator and took out a can of beer. Then, she started brewing a cup of tea. While the tea brewed, she took the beer to Joe, for which he thanked her. Then, she returned to the kitchen.

She leaned back against the counter and considered her position. She was in the thirteenth week, with eleven to go. Nausea still dogged her, and her clothes were becoming harder to squeeze into. Her breasts were sore, and she was irritable. All in all, there was nothing good that she could say about the situation except that it wouldn't last forever. In eleven weeks, the fetus would be removed and her life would return to normal.

The light on the brew machine came on, signaling that the tea was ready. Jenna poured the contents into a cup and set the carafe back on the hot plate. She stirred in a teaspoon of sugar. Carefully, she tested its flavor lest she burn her lip. It was just right.

Jenna placed the cup on a saucer. She carried the tea into the living area and set it on the coffee table. Joe was busy munching on a mouthful of chips. The chair was filled with crumbs. She sat down on the sofa. A commercial was on the television.

"Who's winning?" she asked

"Pittsburgh, if you can imagine that," he said with a huff.

"Too bad," she said. Jenna knew he had money on Detroit.

She grabbed some chips from his bowl. She ate one and grimaced—too salty. She sipped some tea, which helped. At least it took the salty taste from her mouth.

As she sat there, Jenna began to feel ill. The nausea rose up like the tide at the beach, engulfing everything in its path. "You'll have to excuse me," she said.

"You okay?" he asked with a mouthful of chips.

"I'll be fine," she said, as she hurried into the bathroom.

A minute later, Jenna knelt at the toilet and discharged the contents of her stomach into it, followed by the inevitable dry heaves. She flushed the toilet and weakly sank to the floor. She was drained by the experience, as she always was. The bitter taste that lingered in her mouth made her angry. It didn't have to be this way, she thought bitterly. She could have been free of it a month ago. But no, she had to try and cash in on her misfortune. Now she was paying the price for betraying the Mother. There was no way out, either, since she had taken partial payment for the fetus and ASAMAR had invested in her health maintenance.

She sat on the floor for a long time when Joe called, "Jen, are you all right?"

"Yeah," she called back. "I'll be out in a minute."

Jenna started to get up from the floor; but as she rose to her feet, she felt a new sensation. It felt odd, like something moving inside her abdomen. And she new that her ordeal was far from over.

PAULA

Jenna sat by herself in the power plant's cafeteria restlessly making figures in the soup she'd purchased. All around her, coworkers she hardly knew were talking, laughing, or reading. One group of men seated near by, in particular, were boisterously discussing football. They were no better than a bunch of monkeys jockeying for position in the group, she thought to herself. Mindless jabbering, she thought. Men get excited over the stupidest things.

She put a spoonful of the soup in her mouth, burning her tongue. Her face convulsed from the searing pain, and a little of the hot liquid dribbled down her chin and onto the table. The loud exchanges were beginning to get on her nerves, and she thought she would scream if they all didn't just shut up! But the endless chatter continued and there was nothing that could be done. She put the spoon down and stared out the window.

She was in the sixteenth week of gestation. So far, the nausea and vomiting she'd experienced during the first few weeks had been the worst part. Of course, the sore breasts were an annoyance as well. Now, however, Jenna was beginning to feel the movements of the nameless monstrosity growing inside her as it shifted and turned within her womb. It wasn't often or really noticeable; but when she did notice it, she would become angry. She cursed herself for letting it go on this long. She just wanted to be done with it, but she had another nine weeks to go.

Jenna was scheduled to have the fetus removed during the week of February 24, which would be the twentyfourth week. She wished she'd never agreed to wait so long. She was beginning to feel like a whale, although she hadn't really put on much weight yet. Nonetheless, she was self-conscious. She could feel every eye upon her when she entered a room. She didn't care to go into areas of the plant where she had to wear protective clothing because it was necessary to change alongside coworkers who would certainly become painfully aware of her condition.

What probably hurt the most, though, was Joe. He didn't seem interested in her anymore; they hadn't made love for the past month. She found him the other day lying naked on the bed, wearing the virtual reality visor with a glass in one hand and his erect penis in the other. The sight of him masturbating like that was stupefying. Jenna was speechless; and, saddened, she left the room. He was supportive enough in other ways, she guessed; but still, it made her feel less than human and undesirable.

"Hi, Jenna! Is anyone sitting here?"

She looked up into the glowing visage of Sharon Fordyce. Sharon was in her fifth month of the pregnancy. She'd put on a considerable amount of weight, but that didn't seem to dull her spirits. A broad smile graced her chubby face, and her eyes glittered with excitement.

Jenna remained silent for a moment and then said, "No. No one's sitting there."

"Great," Sharon cheerfully said. She set her tray on the table across from Jenna, then pulled the chair out. She sat down and swept her long, blonde hair back over her shoulders.

"You're really starting to show, Sharon," Jenna bluntly pointed out. It made her curious about how she would feel when she reached the twentieth week and took on the proportions of a small whale. "Is it uncomfortable?"

Sharon laughed. "Only when I sit, or stand, or try to sleep. She sighed and picked up a fork. "Seriously, though. It is irritating at times. But I wouldn't give it up for anything! You have no idea how it feels. It's as if, well, I can't really find the words!"

Jenna didn't say anything. Sharon was wrong, though. She did know how it feels. She was well aware of the misery that came with pregnancy.

Despite her own apathy, however, Jenna couldn't help but be happy for Sharon. She watched as Sharon dumped some dressing on the salad and mixed it in. A slice of cucumber fell from the salad plate and on to the tray. Sharon speared it with her fork and eagerly gobbled it up.

"Mmm, oh, I love cucumbers. Don't you?" Sharon asked as she chewed.

"They're all right," Jenna replied somberly. Then, she rested her head in one hand and began to play in the soup again.

There was general silence between the two for several seconds. Then, Sharon said quietly, "Hey, guess what I heard."

"What," Jenna answered without looking up.

"Manny Santiago, from Operating? He's getting married, again."

Jenna lifted her head. "Manny Santiago? Isn't he already married?"

"Yes. He's married to Hillary…You know, over in data processing."

"Wow. I didn't know they were getting divorced."

"Well, that's just it…they're not," Sharon declared.

"Oh, you've got to be kidding," Jenna said in disbelief. "Isn't that, oh, what's the word…"

"Bigamy!"

"Yeah that's it: bigamy!" Jenna leaned closer "Have you talked to Hillary?"

"Yes. She says she's happy about it, but I think she's just fooling herself."

Jenna sat back and shook her head. "That's incredible. I never would have guessed that Hillary goes either way."

"Well, I don't think she does, or didn't used to, anyway." Sharon looked around to make sure no one else could hear. "I think Manny's talked her into it. You know he's propositioned just about every woman that works here."

Jenna thought for a moment. It was true that Manny Santiago was a womanizer who took great pleasure in controlling others of the female persuasion. Nothing would please him more than getting two women in bed with him at the same time. Then, he could play the part of the conductor leading the orchestra in erotic crescendos of lustful pleasure.

Why Hillary stayed with Manny, Jenna never knew. Whenever she would see them together, he was always subtly putting Hillary down. Of course, Hillary wasn't the sharpest person in the world either. Maybe his mocking went unnoticed, or maybe there was something more to their relationship than what others observed.

"Hey. Enough about them. I've got something I want to show you." Sharon opened up a folder and pulled out two pictures. "These were taken a couple of days ago," she said as she handed them to Jenna.

Jenna hesitantly took the pictures from Sharon and held one in each hand. Shifting her eyes from one to the other, she wondered if the images were real.

"They were taken by my obstetrician," Sharon proudly noted. "I can't get over how clear they are!"

Jenna couldn't either. She held two images of what appeared to be a baby curled up as if asleep: one frontal view and one profile. The images were grainy but discernable, and the color enhancement gave them a painted look. Its eyes appeared to be closed, like it was sleeping, and one hand was resting on its head with the other pulled into its chest. Jenna regarded them skeptically and handed them back to Sharon.

"Aren't those good?" Sharon asked.

"What are they?" Jenna inquired.

"They're my baby, Jenna. What else did you think?"

"Oh," she said stupidly. "Well, considering that you haven't had it yet, yeah, I suppose they're good. How'd they get images like that?"

"They're ultrasound images."

"Really? I didn't think that they could get such detailed images with an ultrasound," Jenna proclaimed.

Gazing lovingly at the photos, Sharon said, "A computer enhances the image. I don't understand how it works, but it makes beautiful pictures."

"Yeah, those…those are nice, Sharon," Jenna said as she tried to put the images out of her mind.

"And Sean is so excited. You know what he did?"

"No, Sharon. I don't. What did he do?"

"He built the crib…all by himself! Can you believe it?"

"Boy, that's great," Jenna said, unimpressed. "All by himself, huh?"

"Yes. Well, of course, it was a kit," Sharon pointed out apologetically. "But he did put it together himself."

Sharon put the pictures back into the folder. She looked at Jenna for a moment. "Jenna, are you okay? You don't seem like yourself."

Jenna smiled and said, "Yeah, I'm fine. My mind's just on other things right now."

"Well, I hope everything's alright."

"Well, don't worry. It will be." Jenna glanced at the clock on the wall. "You'll have to excuse me now, Sharon. I really have to go."

"Oh, all right," Sharon said. "I'll see you later, then."

Jenna picked up her tray and left the table without saying another word. She walked over to the waste receptacle and dumped the unfinished soup along with the other trash into the chute. Where it let out, she didn't know, or care for that matter. She placed the tray, along with the eating utensils and dishes, on the conveyor belt and watched as the conveyor slowly transported the items through a hole in the wall.

That afternoon, Jenna made a tour of the reactor containment building. The radiation fields she entered generally didn't go higher than fifty millirem per hour; but, during the tour, she managed to pick up twentytwo millirem, which wasn't really significant. Federal regulations limited a pregnant woman to only five hundred millirem during the gestation period. This was done to protect the developing fetus from damage due to radiation exposure. Cells that reproduced rapidly were among the most susceptible to damage from ionizing radiation.

If Jenna had considered the fetus within her womb to be a baby, she might have been concerned. But, as it was, the little sucker could fry for all she cared. It was just an inconvenience, like a boil or a wart, albeit a profitable one.

After the tour, while changing back into her regular clothes, some woman Jenna hardly knew made a comment about her putting on a little weight. Jenna glared at the woman, saying nothing. She resented what the woman had said and the way they stared at her. It was demeaning. The woman's grin melted away, and she backed off into a corner, completely cowed.

That remark, though, really angered Jenna. It was just the sort of thing that she didn't want to have to put up with in the first place. She quickly finished dressing and stormed back to her office.

By the time she went home, Jenna was in a much better mood. That afternoon, she started thinking about Christmas, which was only a week away. She and Joe had been invited to a Christmas Eve party at a mutual friend's residence. She also remembered what Dr. Emerson had said at the seminar about Jesus. How did it go? "If we abide in the One, and the One abides in us, we can do all things. For apart from the Mother, we can do nothing." That one truth warmed her spirit and eased her mind.

Jesus truly was divinely inspired, a shooting star that landed here on Earth to show humanity a new way. How sad, she thought, that for thousands of years the real essence of his teachings had been perverted.

On the drive home, Jenna relaxed in the driver's seat. She could feel the vibrations from the tires rolling along the road and the hum of the motor. The sensation was hypnotic, and soon, she was daydreaming.

Jenna's mind conjured up the dream of the mansion in the desert. It had come to her a fourth time, now. Although that time, it wasn't so frightening. Since Roxanne had given her impression of it, which had been supported by Hank's assertion, Jenna anticipated the dream. She'd spent many of her meditation periods pondering the dream in an attempt to discern its true meaning. If it were indeed a revelation of some sort, then she must unlock whatever secrets lay within it.

Roxanne had once told her that a dream is correctly interpreted when the experience of it causes the dreamer to alter his life in some profound, meaningful way. She pondered the dream all the way home, going over it again and again, searching for some detail, some key that she may have overlooked. It was all for naught, though.

Before Jenna knew it, she was on her street a couple of blocks from home. She guided the car around her building and into the garage. After placing it on the charging stabs, she switched the power off and got out. Tired from her day, she decided to take the elevator rather than the stairs.

Once on the elevator, she began to think about Henry Philips. She hadn't seen him for a couple of days. Come to think of it, she hadn't seen him for quite a while. She began to wonder if he was all right. She remembered a story he once told her about how he'd fallen into a pig-pen when he was a boy; and ever since then, his father called him pig-let. The thought of a young Hank, lying in the mud, surrounded by grunting and squealing hogs made her laugh.

She undid her coat and brushed her hair back with one hand. She got off the elevator on her floor and walked quickly down to her apartment. When she entered, Jenna didn't immediately see Joe; but she heard some activity in kitchen. She threw her coat on a hanger and wrestled to get her boots off. Then, she went into the kitchen. Joe had just taken a casserole dish out of the oven and he was still holding it.

Joe smiled when he saw her and said, "Hi, Jen. I thought I heard you come in." He put the dish on the counter and walked over to her.

With his arms around her, Joe gave her a friendly smack on the lips and a quick hug. "So, how was your day?"

"As well as could be expected," she replied.

Sensing that she was preoccupied with something, he asked, "Anything you want to talk about?"

"No, nothing I care to discuss right at the moment." She lifted the cover from the dish, allowing the steam to rise and the aroma to fill her senses. "Broccoli and garlic cheese. It smells delicious."

"Why, thank you. I know it's one of your favorites."

"So, what did you do all day, hon'?" she asked.

"Teleconferencing with Akagi and the contractor building the headquarters. They finally agreed to use composite materials," he noted proudly. "Except for the framing structure. That will still be steel."

Composite materials were essentially garbage turned into bricks, plaster, fiberboard, and a host of other things. It was a technique first used in Europe. Instead of burying or burning the waste, it was sorted, compressed, super heated, and chemically treated to produce a light, strong, fire resistant, inexpensive material. Composites were extremely versatile and could be used in place of concrete, plastic, aluminum, and many other substances.

Jenna thought composites were beneficial because of their low impact on the environment. Instead of mining new ore, digging up more sand and gravel, or consuming more petroleum, humans made use of their own waste. Joe liked them because he held stock in one of the industry's leaders.

"That's great, Joe." She hugged him, and smiling said, "I'm so proud of you."

"Why don't you go change while I get dinner on the table," he insisted.

"All right." She gave him a quick peck on the cheek and started for the bedroom.

She turned the light on as she entered the bedroom. She didn't notice anything unusual, although she did wonder if Joe had been visiting his electronic friend today. Realizing it would only anger her, Jenna put the thought out of her mind. She opened a bureau drawer and looked through it for something comfortable. She pulled a royal blue sweat suit with the Philadelphia Flyers emblem emblazoned on the chest.

She stepped out of the jump suit she'd worn all day and studied herself in the mirror for a moment. Her figure was still there, although it appeared to her that her stomach had a slight pouch to it. She shook her head and sighed. Scratching her head, she thought to herself, oh well, only two more months. She donned the sweat suit and rummaged through the closet for a pair of walking shoes. Not finding the shoes, she put her slippers on and went back into the living area.

Joe was already seated with his elbows resting on the table and his hands clasped together. Soft music was playing and the lights were dim. As she walked over, she saw that, along with the broccoli, some sort of baked fish, dinner rolls, and a bottle of wine graced the table. Jenna took her chair and said, "Mmm, this looks wonderful, Joe."

For the next few minutes, they silently filled their plates. Joe took the bottle of wine and filled each of their glasses. Jenna took one of the warm dinner rolls and broke it open. Steam from the roll wafted up into the air, and the aroma of fresh baked bread filled her senses. True, it wasn't really fresh baked. Rather, it came from the freezer section; and all one had to do was to pop it in the oven to bake. She patted a little of the hard spread on the roll and watched as it melted into the fibers of the bread.

She put the roll on her plate and reached over to touch Joe's hand. "You're so good to me, Joe. I'm really lucky to have you."

"I know, Jen." He picked up the wine glass to make a toast. "To us!"

"To us," she answered.

The conversation during dinner was generally light, as it always was. Joe talked about the Akagi project, which got old after a while. Jenna brought up the Christmas Eve party they'd been invited to. Joe said he was looking forward to it. He made some off the cuff remark about the religious aspect of it being a bunch of bullshit, but it did make a good reason to get reacquainted with old friends or visit family.

Then, the conversation took a sudden turn when Joe said, "You know, this whole business with Christmas is really far fetched, anyway. After all, the Christians stole…excuse me, borrowed the event from the pagans in Northern Europe. There they were, celebrating the Winter Solstice, minding their own business when along come the Christians who seized upon an opportunity to increase their numbers and fill their coffers. So they wrapped up their savior in the pagan's celebration, and turned it into his supposed birthday." He paused for a moment. Then, leaning towards Jenna, elbows straddling his plate, continued, "I can well imagine that the pagans, who enjoyed a good party, just naturally took to it. Yeah, the Christians really pulled the old baitandswitch on the heathen masses. Hey! They even maintained some of the pagan trappings like the tree and mistletoe!"

"You know, you're right, Joe," Jenna said. "And it isn't just Christmas either. They did the same thing with Easter. Took a perfectly good celebration and tailored it to their own purposes."

"Yeah, that's right," he agreed. "I never thought of that before. On the one hand, they say that the day marks the resurrection of their savior; and on the other, they still keep the eggs and the bunny: both pagan symbols of fertility."

"That's right, Joe."

A few minutes later, Joe said, "By the way. Do you know a Paula Philips?"

Jenna searched her memory, but the name didn't ring a bell. Puzzled, she replied, "No, I'm afraid not."

Joe put his fork down and cleared his throat. "Well, she called this afternoon. Said she was Hank's daughter?"

"Oh, Hank's daughter. All right."

"Anyway," he continued "she said to have you call her this evening, sometime. The number's on the recall list."

"Mmm, I wondered what she wants." Jenna remembered Hank mentioning a Paula. Of course, he never talked about his immediate family very much, either. Maybe something happened to Hank. She was worried, now. They both finished dinner in silence.

After they'd cleared the dishes from the table and cleaned up the kitchen, Jenna went to the vidphone. She punched up the recall list and located Paula Philip's number. She selected the number and touched the dial button. The phone rang three times before someone answered.

"Good evening." The face on the screen was long and thin, with smooth skin, a petite nose, and blue eyes accented by a touch of eyeliner."

"Hi," Jenna said. "I'm Jenna Kelemen. Could I please speak to Paula Philips?"

The woman at the other end smiled revealing white, perfect teeth. "I'm Paula. I'm so glad you were able to get back to me so soon."

"Well, when Joe said you were Hank's daughter, I figured it was important. How is Hank? I haven't seen him for a while, now."

The woman's smile melted, and her face became serious. "Yes, that's why I had to get hold of you. My father died recently…"

"Oh," Jenna sadly interjected. "I'm so sorry. How did it happen?"

"Well," Paula said, "I really don't care to go into that right now, you understand. Anyway, he left something that he wanted you to have. So, I'd like to set up a meeting where I can give it to you."

Curious as to the item, Jenna asked, "What is it?"

"It's a book," she snapped. "Now, if we can arrange something, I'll bring it to you, all right?"

"Yeah, sure," Jenna replied. She could see that the woman was obviously not in a good mood. Talking further, they decided to meet for lunch on Saturday at a restaurant on Delaware Avenue, which was on the other side of town from where Jenna lived.

After getting off the phone, Joe asked her what that was all about. She told him about Hank's dying and leaving her some book. They both were curious about it. Joe thought that maybe it was some old, rare edition of one of the classics. He speculated on how much it might be worth. Jenna, though, felt that the book probably had some sentimental value; and Hank wanted to pass it on to someone who could appreciate it.

Either way, she would be glad to have it. Knowing that Hank thought enough about her to leave her something, even some trinket, brought a warm, satisfied feeling to her spirit. She knew that in some special way she had made a difference in someone's life.

Just an Old Book

The air in the restaurant's lobby felt cool to Jenna. She shivered briefly as a chill ran up her back, and she contemplated putting her coat back on. That would never do, though. While the coat she'd worn was more than adequate for the current cold spell that had descended upon Southeastern Pennsylvania, it was much too bulky to wear inside for any length of time. No, she thought, the coat would not be appropriate. It would only serve to add to the discomfort of meeting Paula Philips.

Not that meeting strangers was normally a cause for alarm. On the contrary. She enjoyed new people; it made life interesting. Today, however, was different. This encounter would see the transfer of a dead man's personal property from a woman who seemed none too pleased to be turning the item over.

Jenna pushed the thought out of her mind. Reflecting on the imminent rendezvous merely agitated the anxiety already gnawing at her.

She turned her attention to admiring the colorful decorations that adorned the lobby. The restaurant owners had obviously spared no expense in embellishing their establishment in tinsel, garlands, and other accessories of the holiday season. A large, magnificent tree gleaming with bright, colorful lights and ornaments filled one corner of the room. The chairs, lamps, and tables had been beautifully trimmed in red and green ribbon. A small nativity scene was perched upon the mantle. In the artificial fireplace below, plastic logs glowed red where the hot embers were supposed to be. Garlands hung from the ceiling, and a sprig of mistletoe dangled above the doorway into the main dining area.

The place was beginning to fill up now with last minute Christmas shoppers. The constant drone of conversations going on around her pierced Jenna's brain. The sounds blurred like a needle with thread in tow going through a piece of cloth over and over and over again until, at last, it was impossible to distinguish between individual turns of the thread. She sat back and checked the time. It was 12:05 PM; Paula was five minutes late. Nothing to be alarmed about, she hoped.

Jenna turned her attention back to the fireplace. Warmth emanated from it which seemed odd since there was no real fire burning there, just a red glow whose shade constantly changed. There must be something behind the artificial logs causing that effect, she thought. She intently watched the fluctuating radiance of the counterfeit fire. There seemed to be no pattern, at least none that she could detect. The undulating flicker of light was hypnotic; and, very soon, she lost all sense of reality. All of her attention was fixed on that one place.

Eventually, the feeling of someone staring at her broke her trance. She turned, and standing not more than ten feet away was a woman. The woman did not appear to be much older than Jenna. She had taken her coat off, revealing a trim and shapely figure. Her face, framed by thick, black curls, was smooth and winsome. Her eyes were blue. Then, when their eyes met, Jenna realized who the woman was: Paula Philips. Almost simultaneously, Paula smiled and walked over with an outstretched hand.

"Good afternoon," Paula cheerfully said. "You must be Jenna. I'm Paula Philips."

Jenna, looking up, accepted her hand. Paula barely stood above her, and Jenna guessed that she couldn't be much over five feet tall. "Hello, Paula. It's so nice to meet you." Jenna rose to her feet. Paula was considerably shorter than herself.

With her head leaning back, Paula said, "Sorry I'm late. There was an accident, and my bus had to make a detour."

"Oh, that's all right. I haven't been waiting all that long. Besides, it gave me time to admire the lovely decorations." She motioned around the room.

Paula looked around. "Yes, they are beautiful." She turned back to Jenna. "Now, are you ready to eat? I'm famished!"

Paula turned and walked over to the hostess and said something that Jenna couldn't hear. The hostess nodded her head. Paula turned back towards Jenna and motioned her over. When Jenna was next to her, Paula said, "They're checking our table now."

Jenna nodded her acknowledgement. Otherwise, she remained quiet.

Soon, the hostess returned and said, "Right this way, please." She picked up two menus as she led the two women into the main dining area.

Paula and Jenna followed closely. The rich aromas invaded Jenna's senses as they passed other patrons seated with plates of food in front of them. All around them the festive overture of people enjoying their lunches filled the air. Jenna's stomach let out an obnoxious gurgle that she was sure everyone had heard; but, much to her relief, no one gave her a second glance.

At last they were at a table near the front of the dining room in a corner far from where they'd entered. Jenna looked back over their route. The way the place was laid out had caused them to take a serpentine path winding around booths and tables.

The hostess turned to face them and said, "Here is your table." As Paula and Jenna seated themselves, she handed the menus to them and added, "Your server will be Kyle. Enjoy your stay." With that, she was gone.

Jenna opened up her menu and said, "You know, I've never eaten here before."

"Never?" Paula asked in amazement. "Well, I think you'll be very happy. Their lunch menu is one of the best."

"Mmm, it does look good," she replied as she examined the menu. The lunch menu included a wide selection of soups, sandwiches, and burgers. One section was devoted to Mexican cuisine, although Jenna questioned its authenticity. About a half dozen entrees were also featured.

A young, clean cut man who Jenna guessed was about twenty years old came over to them. "Hello," he said with a warm smile. "I'm Kyle, your server. Are you ready to order?"

Jenna looked up from her menu. "Um, I think I'd like a few more minutes, please." She glanced at Paula. From the way Paula was eyeing him, Jenna thought Paula was going to order the Kyle special.

Paula smiled, revealing a perfect set of teeth. "I would like a few more also."

"All right, then. Can I bring you something to drink while you look over the menu?"

"Iced tea, please," Paula directed.

"Well, um, I'll have some sparkling water, please," Jenna said.

"That's one iced tea and one mineral water." He looked at Jenna and asked, "Would you like anything in the sparkling water?"

"No, thank you."

Paula admiringly watched as Kyle hurried off. She leaned towards Jenna and said under her breath, "He's got a tight ass! I'd like to butter those buns."

Jenna chuckled. Not that she found Paula's comment amusing. She just didn't want to be...unfriendly. He was an attractive man though; she'd allow Paula that much. But to refer to another person like a slab of meat just wasn't her style.

Kyle returned with their drinks and set them on the table. "Now, are you ready to order?"

Paula spoke up first. "I'll have the turkey club with, uh, what is today's soup?"

"French onion, or clam chowder."

"French onion."

"Very good ma'am." He looked at Jenna. "And for you?"

"I'd like the fruit plate."

Kyle straightened up and looked at the ledger. "Okay. That's one turkey club with French onion soup, and one fruit plate."

They both nodded, indicating their agreement.

"Very well," he said. "We'll have this right out to you." He scurried away toward the kitchen.

Once again, Paula closely observed his derriere as he left the table. Jenna just laughed to herself. Paula could probably be this guy's grandmother, she was certain. If Paula was sixty and he, twenty, it would work out. There used to be a name for someone like her; but Jenna couldn't recall it, although she'd heard Hank use it on more than one occasion.

Paula straightened up and folded her hands on the table. "So, Jenna, my father often spoke of you."

"Oh, really?" Jenna said.

"Yes, he did." Paula took a drink of tea. "You know, he thought the world of you. Of course, he was getting senile."

That remark struck Jenna as being insensitive, especially from his own daughter. She studied Paula's face, trying to read the woman's mood. Paula's eyes, despite their sparkle, were cold and indifferent, like cubes of ice; and her lips were taut, forming two painted, red lines below her nose.

Paula picked up the glass again and took a big swig of the tea. The ice made a clinking sound as she jostled the glass, and her Adam's apple momentarily disturbed an otherwise smooth, graceful neck. She had a businesslike air about her that Jenna couldn't help but notice. Why on Earth the woman wanted to go through this charade just to give Jenna a book was without explanation.

"Well, I cared about your father very much," Jenna said. "He was one of the kindest men I've ever known."

Paula chuckled. "Is that what you thought about my father? The kindest man you ever knew? My dear, if that was your opinion of my father, then you didn't know the real Henry Philips."

She leaned closer and shook a finger at Jenna as she spoke. "Let me tell you…Hank Philips was probably the most manipulative man ever to walk the face of the Earth. My life growing up in his household was a living Hell. He used to call me 'Missy'…God, I hated that!" She paused for a drink of tea. "Nothing I did was ever good enough for him. He controlled us like…well, like a rider controls a horse."

Jenna was stymied by Paula's assault upon her own father's character. True, she'd hardly known Hank, when you got right down to it. But she couldn't fathom the indignity Paula had heaped upon him. What would make a woman speak out so against her own father? Jenna didn't have an answer.

Paula sat back in the chair. She began to speak again, randomly gesturing as she spoke. "You know, my father spent thirty years in the Marines; and he dragged us with him from one post to the next, in the States and overseas. We must have lived in a dozen different places when I was growing up. I never had any friends…I never had a real life.

"I can remember one time, when he was in the Balkans during the NATO intervention, hoping and praying that he'd come home safe. Now, I look back on that and wonder, 'Why?' He was ruining my life…I was just too stupid to know it."

Jenna felt completely taken aback. Astonished, she said, "Oh, god. You must really have hated him."

"Hate isn't the word I'd use." Paula took another swig of tea. "Indifferent perhaps, but not hate. I didn't even realize how he'd screwed up my life until I started seeing a psychiatrist because of the depression that haunted me."

About this time, Kyle brought over a tray loaded down with their lunch. "Here we are…one turkey club with French onion soup," he noted as he set the food before Paula. "And one fruit plate." He set the plate in front of Jenna and asked, "Can I get you anything else?"

"No, we're fine," Paula declared.

Jenna smiled and nodded in agreement.

Paula carefully looked through the sandwich, saying softly, "You can never be sure of what they'll put in these." Satisfied that it was safe for consumption, she opened a pouch of oyster crackers and poured its contents into the soup. Jenna watched as Paula carefully dunked each cracker under the surface with the soupspoon she'd been provided.

Jenna forked through the fruit on her plate. It contained quite a variety, especially considering the time of year. Of course, that was reflected in the price. The plate had cantaloupe, pineapple, banana slices, pears, grapes, orange wedges, and some sort of melon that she didn't recognize.

"Oh!" Paula exclaimed, her mouth full with a string of lettuce hanging out. "This sandwich is excellent. How's the fruit?"

"Delicious," Jenna answered between bites.

"So, Paula," Jenna began, "Are you from around here?"

"Goodness, no," she said with a mouthful of sandwich. "I live in Baltimore. I just came up for the funeral. My older brother, Sid, lives here, though; and my younger brother, Frank, lives in New York."

After swallowing, Jenna asked, "Paula, why did you want to meet me like this? I mean, you could have just mailed the book to me?"

Paula smiled. "Why, my dear, I wanted to meet the girl who stole Daddy's heart." She took a large bite from the sandwich.

"Paula, if you don't mind me asking," Jenna said, "How did Hank, I mean your father, die? The last time I saw him, he seemed fine, except for a lung condition; but it didn't sound like he'd die from it."

Paula let the spoon rest in the soup. Looking directly at Jenna, she bluntly said, "He was put to sleep."

Jenna was flabbergasted. "You mean, killed?"

"No, I mean put to sleep," she declared. "It was the best way...for him as well as the family."

"But...how? Why?"

Paula put the spoon down again, only this time more forcefully. "The doctor recommended it," she said in an annoyed tone. "You see, Daddy was too old to qualify for the surgery, and my brothers didn't want to watch him waste away. They felt it was undignified, not that it mattered to me.

"Anyway, the doctor felt that the best thing to do was to just let him die painlessly, with some dignity. I mean our father had already lived a full, productive life. He'd raised a family, been a military hero, and buried one wife. What more could we ask of him? Now, please. Let me finish my lunch."

Jenna sat in silence. Her stomach had become ill, and she couldn't finish. She couldn't even look at Paula. She just rested her head in her hands, elbows on the table; staring into the distance, she thought about what Paula had just revealed. Hank didn't die naturally; he'd been put to rest. She couldn't believe that Hank would willingly go like that; he was only eightytwo. He was too vibrant, too alive. Instead, his end came prematurely, almost like suicide: a doctorassisted suicide.

No, she thought, that doesn't properly describe the circumstances surrounding his death. She came up with a more descriptive phrase: doctorinsisted suicide. Yes, she thought sadly, the doctor had insisted upon it.

Why would the children agree to such a thing? She had no answer. To put someone out of their misery when there was no other hope was humane, even compassionate. Yet, to kill a man when there was a treatment available that could restore his health seemed cruel and monstrous. Was it done out of genuine concern for him, or could convenience have been the real reason for the act?

Suicide was not illegal, and doctor assisted suicide was accepted as part of the daytoday business of health care. If his family and doctor had convinced Hank that death was the only, correct choice, then they'd done nothing illegal.

Yet somehow, Jenna found it morally reprehensible. Whatever perceived offense Hank had committed, real or imagined, against his family, did it really warrant this action? She watched as Paula stuffed the last bite of sandwich into her mouth and licked her fingers clean. Whether or not Hank was guilty of some atrocity, Jenna thought, Paula must be pleased with the way she'd managed to direct her father's demise.

Paula wiped her hands on a napkin. Looking at Jenna, she said, "You're not going to finish?"

"No," Jenna replied. "I've lost my appetite."

The corners of Paula's lips turned up into a cruel, conceited smile. "Now, let's get to the business at hand. When my father died, he didn't have much to leave behind: a small bank account, some insurance, a box of letters, a closet full of military memorabilia, and some boxes of assorted junk. But among these things, we found a small box that contained a note with your name and phone number. The note said that what was in the box was to go to you."

Jenna tried to suppress her bewilderment. "What is it?"

Paula reached into her coat pocket and produced a small box. She tossed the box over to Jenna. "A book."

Jenna's hands trembled as she carefully opened the box. On top was the note Paula had mentioned. The content of the box was wrapped in tissue paper. Jenna took it out of the box and cautiously unfolded the wrapping.

What she found was a small, pocketsized book bound in leather. One cover was plated with some sort of metal that was stamped with some lettering. The cover was worn and corroded, and she couldn't make out the words. She opened the front cover and found an inscription on the inner sleeve that said, "To Hank with love, Joanne".

"Paula," she said, "This is from your mother to your father, isn't it? I can't take this."

"No," Paula snapped, "he wanted you to have it. Besides, none of us want it."

Jenna turned to the title page. It was a bible: a King James Bible. Jenna had never seen one before. As she thumbed through it, she discovered that it was written in lofty tones. A poetic English. She felt the texture of the pages. The paper was thin and delicate. She closed the cover, rewrapped it, and put it back in the box.

"Oh, Paula, this will be a family heirloom one day. I couldn't possibly take."

"You have to take it. Besides, it's just an old book. It's not worth anything."

What a cold woman, Jenna thought to herself. Not worth anything? Maybe not in dollars; but sentimentally, it would be priceless. She wondered if the rest of Hank's children were as unfeeling as this one. No, they couldn't be.

"Well, if you insist," Jenna said. "I guess I'll have to keep it."

"I insist," Paula replied.

Kyle returned to the table. "Can I get you ladies anything else?"

"No, nothing else," Paula answered.

He started to put the tab down when Paula took it from him. She smiled at Jenna. "Lunch is on me, dear."

Jenna was stunned. "Thank you."

The two left the restaurant and parted without a word.

Jenna walked somberly down the street, holding the box in her right hand. It was 1:10 PM. The sun was past its apex now, and the shadows grew longer with each step. As she swung her arm, Jenna could feel the small book sliding around inside the box.

Why had Hank left it to her? Obviously, it had great sentimental value for him. It would have been better left to his children, but maybe his children weren't interested in family heirlooms.

Her hands were beginning to grow numb in the cold air. She'd neglected to bring her gloves. So, she thrust her hands into her coat pockets. The right hand still grasping the box fit tightly into the pocket, and she thought that she might tear a seam.

After she got into her car and began the drive home, her mind drifted back to Iowa and memories of a tall, lean man scratching a life out of the land. Sometimes it seemed to Jenna that her grandfather watered his fields with the sweat from his own brow, working so hard, from sunup to sundown. Yet, he always had time for her, even if it meant taking her with him out into the fields.

She could remember going to church with him, a place her mother had rarely frequented. The exact name of the church was long forgotten, but she was sure that it was Methodist. In her mind's eye, she could see the minister in his pulpit: a softspoken man, eloquently proclaiming the unity of mankind. "All are brothers," he would say, "whether we be Jew or Gentile, Muslim or Hindu, Buddhist or Christian. Each of us praying to his or her God, and really the same God. For as Jesus said, 'A house divided against itself will surely fall'…we must join together, all across this great world, if we are to endure!"

She parked in front of the apartment building and slowly got out of the car. She took a minute to reflect on the building before going in. She trembled as a chill migrated up her back. Whether from the cold December air or from loneliness, she didn't know. She looked at the building for a long moment. Somehow, the place seemed empty and less friendly.

No longer would she encounter Hank in the elevator or the laundry room. Playing a round of spades or hearts with him would never happen again. She felt an emptiness in her heart, a void that hadn't been there before; and she began to quietly sob.

FORMED IN THE BELLY

As Jenna entered the apartment building, she was overcome by a sudden wave of bereavement. The hallway was strangely quiet and dark. She stopped at what had been Hank's apartment and lingered at the door for a few minutes.

Had Hank been mercifully killed, or brutally murdered? Jenna found that to be a profound question as she slowly walked from the parking garage to her apartment. Suicide was honorable; she knew that the Japanese had been infamous for their willingness to take their own lives rather than risk dishonoring the family. Suicide in the U.S. had been illegal at one time, which was rather stupid, she thought. If a person succeeded, what could the authorities do? And if the attempt failed, what would they do? It was a ridiculous question.

This wasn't really a suicide, though, was it? Jenna recalled accounts she'd read where some Indian tribes in North America would send their elderly out into the forest to await death. To the first European settlers with their Christian paradigm, this practice seemed barbaric, even inhumane. They just didn't understand the Indian's way.

It was not cruel to leave an aged father or mother alone in the forest to meet their end. To the Indian, a person was not one unto himself. Rather, he was part of the greater whole. Man came from the Earth; She gave birth to him. Jenna recalled a song of thanksgiving from the Pawnee Indians. Mother Earth lies with us and gives of her fruitfulness to us. She gives Her power to us, and we give thanks to Her. So, rather than a cruel death, it was more like dying in the arms of one's own mother. There was honor in it.

But Hank hadn't been left in the wilderness to die, either. He'd been put to death. Jenna could vaguely recall stories about the fight to legalize physicianassisted suicide. Many felt that terminally ill patients or individuals in great physical pain should not have to be made to continue in their suffering. Some felt that it was a Constitutional right to end one's life if that person chose not to endure their affliction.

Humanity and compassion had been the watchwords of the Right to Die proponents, and they carried their slogans like swords with which to smite any adversary who dared to oppose their flag. "Which has more compassion?" they'd cry, "To mercifully end a man's torment, or to let him linger in pain on the threshold of death?" An easy question, Jenna thought. Why, to end his suffering, of course.

She recalled her own grandfather and how he'd died from prostate cancer. He could have chosen suicide, but he didn't. He endured to the end, despite his suffering.

In his last months, she could remember her grandfather saying, "The Lord will deliver me in my suffering. He speaks to me in my affliction." It was as if, even in his pain, he found strength from some unseen source. He delighted in it because he felt that some higher power, some Supreme Being, had a purpose for his suffering. What that purpose may be, he did not know. He only knew that the purpose, whatever it may be, would serve to glorify his unseen god; and, therefore, he was serving his god. There was honor in it.

In the end, though, it wasn't cancer that took her grandfather, nor suicide. Ironically, it was the lack of medical attention that had killed him. The Establishment had refused to treat him because he was old and had nothing left to contribute.

But Hank was altogether different. He wasn't really suffering, or in great pain either. Yes, he was having trouble breathing; but there was a treatment available that would have restored his vitality. Why, then,

Jenna wondered, was Hank "put to sleep," as Paula had said? Jenna mulled this question over for some time. She could think of no answer, no reason. Hank's only fault, she decided, was that he was old, frail, and unwanted, if his daughter's testimony was any indication.

Hank had lived into his eighties. He'd raised a family. For thirty years, he'd dedicated his life to the security of his nation. But when he could give no more, when his society determined that the cost of maintaining his quality of life was not justified by the benefit, then the humane and compassionate solution had been administered.

Jenna slowly turned from the door and walked to the elevator. She wiped the tears from her eyes as she reached for the elevator's up button. The doors slid open and she got in. She leaned against the wall as she tried to regain her composure. Joe mustn't see me like this, she thought, as she wiped the tears from her face with a crumpled up napkin she'd stuffed in her pocket back at the restaurant. By the time the doors opened, she'd stopped crying. Jenna blew her nose on the napkin and tossed it in a trashcan just outside of the elevator.

Jenna quietly entered the apartment. Classical music, Chopin, she thought, softly filled the room, but Joe was nowhere to be seen. She took off the heavy coat and slipped out of her shoes. She went into the kitchen. Opening the refrigerator, she took out a bottle of peach flavored soda water. The bottle gurgled as the water filled the glass, and bubbles rose up in the glass like tiny jewels. She was about to take a drink when she felt someone's hands on her waist.

"I didn't hear you come in," Joe purred as Jenna turned around to face him. "So, how was…Wait a minute. Have you been crying?"

As hard as she wiped the tears, Jenna guessed that she couldn't eliminate the redness in her eyes. "Oh, yeah, a little. But I'm okay now."

"Well, I hope so," he said. "Anyway, how was lunch?"

"It was fine."

"And the meeting? What was this Paula like?"

Jenna hesitated. She recalled the indifferent, spiteful attitude that Paula showed concerning her own father. She remembered the bitterness with which Paula had recounted her life growing up with him. "She's a bitch." she said at last.

Joe stepped back and said, "Jesus christ, Jen. I don't think I've ever heard you come down on someone so hard before. She must really be wicked."

"Wicked witch is more like it." She folded her arms and, looking at the floor, shook her head. Then, she looked at Joe. "I've never met anyone so vindictive before. She makes Saddam Hussein look like the good fairy!"

"Damn! She is wicked, isn't she." he agreed. "But, why? What's she done to deserve your wrath?"

Jenna ignored the question. Joe wouldn't understand. He was probably incapable of understanding. She didn't want to talk about it right now anyway. She picked up the glass and headed for the living area, with Joe following closely behind.

"Common, Jen," he called out to her. "What did she do? Did she slap you? Did she accuse you of boppin' her dad? Did she give you a ration of shit because dad left you something she wanted? Jesus christ, Jen. What the fuck?"

Jenna set the glass on the coffee table and plopped down on the sofa. As she sank into the cushion she crossed her legs and looked intently at Joe who was still standing. Finally, he sat down next to her.

"They killed him," she said.

"What?" he asked stupidly.

"Didn't you hear me? I said, they killed him!"

Joe looked thoroughly confused. "Wait a minute," he said. "Are you saying that they killed their own father?"

"Yes. That's exactly what I'm saying."

Joe sat back and stared off into the distance as Jenna drank some water. They'd remained silent for several minutes when, curious, he asked, "Why did they kill him?"

Jenna gazed at him rather coldly. She didn't feel like putting up with any of his twisted notions right at the moment. As a matter of fact, she thought that he looked genuinely concerned, if that were possible.

"I don't know why, Joe," she quietly said. "I just know that he's dead...and he didn't die of natural causes."

"Well, what did she say? She must have given some cause."

Jenna turned to him. "Do you really want to know what she said? Do you? She said they had him put to sleep!"

Once more, silence filled the room. She looked at Joe. She could see that he was thinking. Joe had to choose his next words carefully. She knew that Joe had a unique take on the sanctity of life. As far as he was concerned, there was no fundamental right to life. The sanctity of human life was just more excess baggage left over from the Christian era, which had hampered the advancement of humanity for two thousand years. The thought of human life having some special significance sickened him. Life could be hatched in a lab and grown in a test tube, if he was any proof.

To Joe, individuals were nothing more than a resource to be used by society as it saw fit. As long as a person could contribute, then society had an obligation to keep that individual healthy and happy; but, once they could no longer meaningfully participate, then they had to be dealt with. The aged and the handicapped must not be allowed to inhibit the progress of society, he thought. They must step aside, if not voluntarily, then by force.

Children were often referred to as a resource. Jenna had heard this before from him. He believed this appropriate since a society's continuance depended upon the quality of its children. If a society produced a low quality offspring, then it was doomed. Likewise, superior offspring often assured the longevity of a society. He often said that the quality of the children was influenced by more than the gene pool, but eliminating the deadwood certainly didn't hurt.

"You know, Jenna," he said at last, "he was an old man. He'd lived a long, productive life. His time had just come. That's all."

Jenna was becoming tearyeyed again. "Yeah…well, maybe. But it's still sad, the way he died, I mean."

"Really? And why's that?"

"Oh, I don't know," she sighed. "There just doesn't seem to be any dignity in it. How's a man's spirit supposed to find serenity if someone else takes his life?"

"So, where's this book the old guy left you?" he asked to change the subject.

Jenna wiped her eyes and, gesturing towards the door, said, "It's in my coat pocket."

"Well, let's see it," he insisted.

Jenna got up and walked over to the door where she'd discarded her coat. The first pocket she checked was empty, but she located the small box in the other one. Showing this book to Joe wasn't her idea of a good time. As a confirmed atheist, he always cast a doubtful eye upon anything religious.

He was especially intolerant of all things Jewish or Christian, in which she at least partially concurred. She firmly held to the New Age philosophy, and anything that separated the creator from the creation was heresy in her eyes. Joe, however, went beyond simple objection; he hated them.

With box in hand, Jenna went back to the sofa and sat down. For several moments, she remained silent, holding the box on her lap.

"Well, c'mon," he urged. "Open it."

Jenna looked at him. His eyes had a curious spark to them and he was almost salivating. She removed the lid from the box and took the note out. She hadn't really looked at it at the restaurant, but the paper appeared to have a message written on it.

"What's that?" Joe asked.

She stuffed the paper into one of her pockets and said, "It's just a note telling his family to see that I get this."

Joe accepted the explanation without a word.

Jenna removed the package from the box. She set the box on the coffee table, out of the way. Then, she carefully unwrapped the tissue paper that concealed the content. Holding the book in one hand, she placed the paper in the box.

"It's awfully small," Joe noted. "And I can't read...hold on a second. Is that a metal plate on the cover?"

"Yes, it is," she replied as she ran her fingers over the plate, feeling where the engraved title had once been obvious to read.

"What is it?"

"It's a Bible."

"Oh, you've gotta be shittin' me!" He snatched the book from her hand.

"Hey! Be careful with it!"

"Don't worry," he reassured her. "I just want to look at it."

Despite his reassuring words, she only managed to fume over his obtrusion.

Joe examined the outside of the book for a few seconds and whistled. "Damn! Real leather...and steel plated to boot, too." He opened to the title page and laughed. "Incredible! You weren't kidding; this really is a Bible."

"Well, did you think I was lying?"

Through his laughter, he snorted, "No...no. I just can't believe that some dead, old fart would leave anyone a book of fairy tales. Oh, shit." He wiped the tears from his eyes. "This is a real museum piece," he declared as he began to laugh again.

Jenna was starting to get angry. "Just shut up! And give that back!"

Regaining control, he said, "All right, all right...I just want to look at it."

"Okay. That's better. Be careful; the pages are really thin!"

"Now, let's see what we can find." He leafed through a few pages before he stopped. With a grin, he looked at Jenna. "Listen to this. 'And the Lord God caused a deep sleep to fall upon Adam, and he slept; and he took one of his ribs, and closed up the flesh instead thereof. And the rib, which the Lord God had taken from man, made he a woman and brought her unto the man. And Adam said, This is now bone of my bones, and flesh of my flesh...Therefore shall a man leave his father and mother, and shall cleave unto his wife: and they shall become one flesh.'"

Joe commenced to laugh uproariously, and Jenna thought he would surely split a side. He howled for several minutes. When he finally regained his composure, he said, "Jesus christ! Whoever wrote this bull sure was pulling the wool over someone's eyes." He chuckled for a moment. "Of course, I must agree with this part about a man leaving his mother and father and...What's this word? Cleaving? Yeah! Cleaving to his wife...and the two becoming one flesh. I never did have much patience with homosexuals.

"I get so damned tired of all those whackos telling me that I'm the one who's sick, that I'm homophobic. Well, let me tell you...When I see one of them playin' bob the bologna with one of their queer friends, then they can start preachin' to me about bein' homophobic!"

Jenna looked a Joe intently. There was a certain fire in his eyes. She'd seen that look before. It wasn't anger that burned. Fanaticism was a better name for it. Joe didn't hold to very many convictions; but, those he did, he passionately embraced. To him, homosexuality was in the same vein as Christianity: a cultural evil that would destroy society as he knew it.

"Now, let's see what else there is." Once more Joe leafed through the pages. He stopped and let out a loud burst of laughter. "Oh, listen to this! 'For Thou hast possessed my reins; thou hast covered me in my mother's womb. I will praise Thee for I am fearfully and wonderfully made. Marvelous are Thy works; and that my soul knoweth right well!'" Once more, he began howling.

While he was doubled over in laughter, Jenna grabbed the book from him. What he had just read caught her attention, and she wanted to be sure she heard it correctly. So, she briefly perused the page he was on until she found the spot he'd been reading. It was "Psalm 139", starting at verse 13. She quickly read up to the point where he'd left off. Then, she began reading in earnest. "My substance was not hid from Thee, when I was made in secret, And curiously wrought in the lowest parts of the earth. Thine eyes did see my substance, yet being unperfect; And in Thy Book all my members written, which in continuance were fashioned, when as yet there was not one of them. How precious…"

"Hey, give that back!" she yelled, as Joe snatched the book out of her hands.

"No!" he barked. "I wasn't done yet!" He thumbed through many more pages before he stopped again. "Listen to this. 'The words of Jeremiah, the son of Hilkiah, of the priests that were in Anathoth in the land of Benjamin…The word of the Lord came unto me…' Yeah, right. '…Before I formed thee in the belly, I knew thee…'"

Joe started to laugh again, this time more hysterically than any time before. He howled for several minutes, while Jenna looked on in amazement. What was so funny?

After he calmed down, Joe said, "Before he formed me in the belly, he knew me. What a bunch of shit! Impossible! Well, I'll give the asshole that wrote this one thing: he had a good imagination! After reading that shit, though, I gotta go take one." He tossed the book onto the sofa next to Jenna and got up. On the way out, he lifted a leg and broke wind as if he were making a final statement about the book.

Jenna picked up the book. It was opened to "The Book of Jeremiah". She began reading it when, very soon, she realized that this was where Joe had been reading. Verse 5 said, "Before I formed thee in the belly I knew thee, And before thou camest forth out of the womb I sanctified thee, and I ordained thee a prophet unto the nations." Jenna closed the book. She could not go on.

What did it mean, "Before I formed thee in the belly, I knew thee"? And what was the significance of that first passage, "Thou hast covered me in my mother's womb"? At first glance, it seemed that the writer was referring to a preborn baby; but that couldn't be. Why would anyone write such a thing? What kind of person would dream up such a riddle? And that's exactly what it was to her: a riddle.

Many of the stories, or myths, that had been written or passed down through the generations were metaphors conjured up by ancient mystics to explain events that could not be understood in a physical or intellectual sense. They were ascribed to the spiritual realm. Jenna knew that much. But these passages weren't just stories that sought to rationalize the world. These were messages to individuals from someone, or something.

Jenna had no formal knowledge of Old Testament scripture to go on. The strange language didn't help, either. Perhaps Roxanne could shed some light on this, Jenna thought; but, until she could bring this puzzle to Roxanne, Jenna would spend many fretful hours trying to unlock its mystery.

Jenna rested her head back on the sofa and thought about Hank. She remembered the note he'd left. She became curious since she hadn't read it yet. With Joe was still in the bathroom, she could read it without interruption.

Fishing around in her pocket, Jenna found the note and pulled it out. It was badly crumpled by now; but her name, address, and phone number were still legible. She carefully unfolded it so as not to tear the paper. After the note was opened, she smoothed it out as best as she could on the coffee table. Then, she picked it up and held it in the light.

The writing, in pencil, was light and smudged. From the scrawls on the page, it was obvious that an elderly person had written the note. With some effort, Jenna began to decipher the message.

The note began with several lines describing how much Jenna had meant to the old man during the past few years. It revealed that the Bible was a gift from his wife while he was in Vietnam; the steel plate on the cover was meant to stop a bullet if carried in the left, breast pocket. Because of his fondness for her, he wanted to leave her something, a small remembrance that his own children would surely not miss. So, he left the Bible for her as a reminder of the relationship that had developed between them. The note ended with a simple thank you.

Jenna sobbed quietly to herself as she crumpled the note in one hand. Somewhere, deep within her soul, she felt as if another small piece of her being had been consumed by the unforgiving Spirit that is the Universe. Something moved within her abdomen, drawing her attention as it shifted its position. For a brief moment, she was reminded that, soon, another part of her being would be consumed as well.

THE TRUTH

Jenna anxiously waited in Roxanne's small, East Side apartment that was situated on the fifth floor of an old, converted mill overlooking the river. The front room had about two hundred square feet of floor space with walls that rose twelve feet to the ceiling. Two high, narrow windows looked out over the river. The room was modestly furnished with two wicker chairs and matching couch, a wicker table, and several beanbags grouped in one corner. A thick, beige carpet covered the floor; and a beautiful, floral tapestry brightened the otherwise drab, ivory colored walls. A little stove and an equally dwarfed refrigerator occupied a tiny nook on one side of the room that served as the kitchen. The bedroom was in the smaller, adjoining room; the bathroom was off the bedroom.

The fetus growing in Jenna's womb was in the twentieth week of gestation. Jenna could feel it quite regularly now as it moved around; even Joe said he felt it kick him while they lay together in bed.

She'd put on about twelve pounds so far, and her stomach was beginning to become obviously bloated. Several weeks earlier, Jenna had started buying bargain bin clothes that were several sizes too large; and she led everyone to believe that she was putting on weight. Despite all of this, she maintained a strict exercise and meditation regimen because she was determined to recover as quickly as possible from the inconvenience she was enduring.

For the greater part of the pregnancy, she had scornfully viewed the fetus growing inside her womb as an interloper. In her mind, she had often pictured it as a terrible monster, waiting to devour her life. Jenna had despised the thing, wishing it had never happened, looking forward to the day when it would finally be removed. The money that ASAMAR was paying her only partly compensated for the aggravation.

When she started to feel the movement in her abdomen, though, Jenna's attitude began to change. In some way, the fetus had touched her being. The thing seemed to take on a life of its own: a part of her, yet separate. Her hate of it had diminished, only to be replaced by doubt. Jenna began to wonder if she really was doing the right thing.

But since she had first read those lines from the Bible that Hank had left her, and gone back to reread them, she was beginning to question the reality of the situation. Was it really possible that something so small could be woven into the conscious fabric of the Universe? Part of her said, "No!" But the seeds of doubt had been planted, none the less.

She sat in one of the wicker chairs while Roxanne was busy getting them some tea. Jenna noticed a small, simple shrine set up in one corner of the room. The shrine consisted of a twotiered stand with a statue of the Buddha on the top tier and a picture of Jesus the shepherd on the lower one. Both levels were covered with small, white candles, some of which appeared to be new. The picture of Jesus hadn't been there the last time she visited, and it made her wonder.

As she waited, Jenna could hear the clinking of china from the nook located behind and to the left of her. Roxanne softly humming a tune that Jenna didn't recognize accompanied the rattling of the dishes. It was a peaceful strain, filled with joy and contentment. Jenna rested her head on the back of the chair and closed her eyes.

"Here we are," Roxanne cheerfully said, as she set the cups on the table.

Jenna opened her eyes in time to see Roxanne take the other chair. Her face was glowing with bright eyes and a broad, gracious smile. She had her hair pulled back in a ponytail, revealing a sharp, widow's peak.

Jenna picked up the cup from the table. It felt hot in her hands. She started to take a sip, but the extreme heat radiating from the brew caused her to stop.

"Careful. It's hot," Roxanne warned.

"Yes, thank you." Jenna noticed the exquisite pattern on the side of the cup. "These are beautiful. Where did you find them?"

Roxanne smiled as she set her cup down on the table. "A friend sent them to me…from China."

"Oh," Jenna said. Curiosity getting the best of her, she said, "That's a beautiful picture of Jesus; I don't think it was there the last time I was here."

Roxanne glanced at the small shrine and chuckled softly. She sighed and said, "No, I don't believe it was. Of course, I only put it there recently, after the gathering we attended, the one with Dr. Emerson?"

"Yes," Jenna agreed, "he did speak eloquently about Jesus. Very profound. His thoughts must have greatly impressed you."

Roxanne smiled. "Oh, yes…very much. I had always recognized Jesus as a gifted spiritualist. But to even consider that his vision was of a global scale. Well, it's just astounding. I don't know of any other person who could have put forward such a suggestion."

"I don't quite follow you," Jenna said.

Roxanne smiled and shook her head. Leaning forward, she said, "The Great Commission."

"The great what?"

"Commission. Where Jesus instructs his followers to go out and make disciples of all nations?"

"Oh, the Great Commission," Jenna replied. "But what does that have to do with Dr. Emerson?"

"Weren't you listening? Don't you have ears to hear?" Roxanne put the cup down and began to gesture liberally as she spoke excitedly. "Dr. Emerson believes that Jesus was the greatest spiritual master that ever lived, and part of his greatness lies with his desire to teach others in the ways of the Shaman.

"You know, in most cultures, the secrets of Shamanism were held by only a few and not generally shared. Those who had the knowledge would have been the medicine man, the witch doctor, the priestess, or the seer passing their craft down along family lines. And the result? A spiritually starved people who depended on a small minority for guidance.

"But somewhere, though, Dr. Emerson believes that Jesus gained an understanding of this, probably during his forty days in the wilderness. But anyway, he desired to teach all men and women the way to eternal life, the kingdom of god. Hence the Great Commission, 'Go and make disciples of all nations, teaching them the ways that I have taught you.' Do you remember Ramakrishna?"

Jenna searched her memory. "Ah, yes. Wasn't he one of the great mystic sages of the Hindu tradition?"

"Yes, exactly," Roxanne affirmed. "He taught that everyone would attain Godconsciousness, in his or her own time. There are no exceptions.

"Jesus knew this to be true, and his desire was to help others realize their true nature. Unfortunately, he was killed before things really got started, and that allowed his message to be perverted by the early Christians."

"Amazing," Jenna said. She took a sip of tea and sat quietly.

Roxanne blew on the surface of the tea, causing the steam rising from it to form curly wisps of vapor that dispersed away from her lips. She put the cup to her mouth and, sensing the tea was cool enough, delicately sipped a little of the opaque liquid. Then, she set the cup down on the table and said, "Now, what can I do for you, Jenna? From the way you sounded on the phone, I'm sure this isn't just a social call. Is it about that dream? Have you been having it often?"

Jenna shifted nervously in the chair. Roxanne was the most perceptive person she'd ever known. "Well, um, I have had the dream several times, now; but that's not why I called you. I've got this question that I've been puzzling over? And, well…"

"Yes?"

"Well, I just can't find a satisfactory explanation. And you're the only person I know who could possibly answer it for me."

"Okay," Roxanne said. "What's the question?"

Jenna took a gulp of the tea forgetting it was still hot. She grimaced as the searing liquid burned her mouth.

"Are you all right?" Roxanne inquired.

"Oh…yes," Jenna replied, as she fought back the tears.

After recovering, Jenna said, "Back to my question. You see, a friend of mine from work is going to have a baby…"

"Oh, really!" Roxanne exclaimed. "How wonderful."

"Yes, it is," Jenna declared. "I'm really happy for them. They've been trying to have a baby for years now.

"But it just got me wondering…" She paused and thoughtfully looked at the ceiling. "…at what point does a baby become part of the collective One? I mean, oh, are they…well, I don't know how to put it."

Roxanne smiled. "I think I know what you're trying to ask: Since a baby is not mature enough to fully understand its environment, let alone express itself intelligently, how does it define its own personhood? When does it enter into the Universal Consciousness?"

"Yes," Jenna said, "That's it. When does the baby become a person."

Roxanne took another sip of tea and set the cup down. "Well, let me see if I can explain." Her eyes searched the room as if she were looking for the answer in the walls or the furnishings. "While in the womb, the baby is still developing. It is quite incapable of even beginning to rationalize what is happening to it. Its existence in relation to the Greater One is only certain inasmuch as the mother's persona exists. *It* is because the mother is. The baby's not aware of the Consciousness.

"For the baby at this stage, the mother's womb is its universe. Therefore, it is subject to the mother's will in the same way that we are subject to the forces that control the universe: the Cosmic Consciousness, if you will."

Jenna considered Roxanne's explanation for a moment. "I don't understand."

Roxanne took another sip of tea and set the cup down. "Okay, let me try this. We exist because the universe exists. If our sun were to blow up tomorrow, destroying the Earth, it would do so because that is the conscious, evolutionary path of the Universe. Likewise, if the Great Mother induced an earthquake, or a hurricane, or some other natural disaster, many people would have their lives drastically altered. Some would lose their homes or their jobs. Others would lose loved ones, or die themselves. But the point is…we are powerless against it. We cannot even predict with great certainty when or where such an event will take place. We can only live through it and grow because of it, if we survive. In the same way, a child in the womb is subject to its mother's will."

"So, what you're saying then," Jenna replied, "is that while a baby is in the womb, the womb is that baby's universe. Because of that, it is at its mother's mercy, just like we are at the mercy of the Universal Mind."

"Yes, exactly. A good analogy would be this. Because of the centuries of the wanton ravaging of the environment, the Great Mother responds by causing earthquakes, floods, and droughts…all manners of things that humanity cannot control. She sends these visitations to warn us of the irreparable harm we have done, and to demonstrate Her power. It's almost as if She would vomit us up if She could, because She rejects us. In a similar manner, a woman's body will occasionally reject a child through a miscarriage if it has some terrible abnormality."

"Mmm, I don't know." Jenna was perplexed. "What does that have to do with when a baby becomes a person?"

Roxanne lovingly gazed at her and spoke with a motherly tone. "My dear, a child in the womb is only part of the Collective Consciousness if its mother chooses to infuse it with part of her own consciousness. If the baby is unwanted, then the mother's self will not, cannot, acknowledge its reality. It becomes like a spiritual deserted island, so to speak.

And it will not begin to gain consciousness until after it is born and becomes separate from its mother's body. And even then, the individual is not truly human until he or she has achieved unity with the One."

"I see," Jenna said. "But, what about an elective abortion? Those aren't miscarriages."

"Yes, that is true. The miscarriage is a physical rejection of the fetus. Abortion goes much deeper; it reaches into the very consciousness of the woman. It is an emotional, even spiritual, rejection; and in such cases, the child is better off having never been born since the mother rejects it to begin with. It may grow up to adulthood, but it would carry many emotional scars.

"The thing you have to remember is that if the mother spurns the child from the beginning, then it has no stake in the Universal Mind whatsoever. Consequently, the Universe has no stake in it either. All life comes from the Mother."

Jenna thought for a moment. "So, what you're saying is that while in the womb, there is no consciousness or force directing the development of the child?"

"Yes. Beyond the mother's own life force, that is." She paused and searched the room again. "You see, while developing, the child is part of the mother, just as I said. Therefore, there is no Power external to the mother directly at work, here. Indirectly, perhaps, by nurturing the mother. But directly? No."

"I see," Jenna said. "Um, I have something that I want your opinion on."

"All right."

Jenna fished around in her one of the pockets of her coat, which hung on the back of her chair. Roxanne sipped her tea as Jenna pulled out a small book.

"I found some passages in this Bible that maybe you could help me understand."

"Oh," Roxanne uttered, unprepared. "All right. Let's hear what you found."

Jenna paged through the book until she came to "Psalm 139". Roxanne listened intently while Jenna read verses thirteen through sixteen.

When she'd finished, Roxanne said, "Yes, very interesting…"

"Wait," Jenna interrupted. "There's more."

She then turned to "The Book of Jeremiah" and read verses one through five of the first chapter. As she read, Roxanne sat quietly taking in every word, trying to sift through the meaning.

When Jenna stopped reading, Roxanne asked, "Do you have more?"

"Yes, one more," Jenna declared.

She thumbed through the pages again until she came to the last passage. It was in "Matthew", chapter nineteen. She carefully read verses thirteen and fourteen. "'Then were brought unto him…' That's Jesus."

"Yes, I figured that," Roxanne said.

"Oh, okay," Jenna said. Then she continued, "'…little children that He should put His hands on them and pray; and the disciples rebuked them. But Jesus said, 'Suffer little children, and forbid them not, to come unto me; for of such is the kingdom of heaven.'"

After she'd finished, she closed the book and rested it on her lap.

Before Roxanne could comment, Jenna said, "In that first passage I read, it sounds to me like whoever wrote that was addressing some entity other than his mother: some external, directing force or consciousness. And the second passage, well, it sounds like an external consciousness preordained that this man would speak for it."

"Yes, but that's from a Jewish text, isn't it?" Roxanne complained.

"Well, what about what Jesus said? Isn't he saying that we aren't to stop the children from realizing their full potential and becoming one with the Universal Consciousness?

"It seems to me that after reading these first two passages that the Greater One does have an interest in the unborn children. I mean, if one man says that he was formed in the womb by the One, and the other man says that he was called by the One even before conception, what else can there be?

"And Jesus himself says not to inhibit the children from achieving their full spiritual maturity. If we take them from the womb before they are ready, aren't we interfering with their own spiritual evolution? Who knows how the fabric of the universe has been altered because one child was aborted?"

Roxanne gathered her thoughts and said, "Yes, well, those things are according to the JudeoChristian tradition. Other traditions…"

"Hold on," Jenna interrupted. "Now, you, along with every great spiritual teacher that I've read or heard, have said that each of the world's religions holds some element of truth, some piece of the Conscious puzzle. A short while ago, you spoke of Ramakrishna; didn't he say that all spiritual ideals are expressions of the same Divine Reality? Does that include Christianity and Judaism, or not?"

"Well, of course. But…"

"But what? It seems to me that what I've stumbled on reveals some profound truth: that the Universal Consciousness does include the unborn. What difference does it make if these writers understood this Consciousness to be external to creation, they still perceived this fact.

"And since we know that all of creation, the entire universe, is bound together by a permeating, real spiritual consciousness, then why shouldn't a developing baby in the womb be just as much a part of the Whole as you or I?" She sighed and said, "I'm just trying to find the truth."

Roxanne, who had been quietly and patiently listening, smiled. "Truth…what is truth? Throughout eternity, many have searched for truth. But it is an elusive thing, truth is. So, most fail in their quest. Oh, some do find it, I suppose: Jesus, Gandhi, Jung, Mohammed, and Confucius, to name a few. But most don't.

"Truth is found only at the highest level of consciousness. It is like a river that flows through the Universal Mind. Where it is shallow, it runs swiftly; in the deep part, there is calm. The deepest truths are where we find peace and serenity. And like a river, it is always changing. Each place on the river is unique.

"Every life that lives, whether it is human or not, has its own truth which resides within that life. And each life's truth flows into the great river of universal truth like a tributary into an earthly river. My truth is not the same as yours, any more than the writers' of those passages truth is my truth."

Jenna considered these things for a few moments. "So, what you're saying, then, is that what these men wrote apply only to their own lives."

"Yes."

"But if the One transcends all things, why doesn't a revelation or truth given to one individual apply to all?"

"Because the universe is eternal, ever changing," Roxanne answered. "A given moment is never the same as the previous one or the next. You see, within that moment, something has changed."

"But we're not talking about a physical reality," Jenna declared. "Consciousness transcends the physical. Isn't there some ethical standard that can guide us along through our journey?

"I mean, compared to the entire universe, our world is so insignificant. The magnitude of the Universe's spiritual consciousness must be so great that it is constant when compared to the relatively short period that humans have existed on the Earth."

Roxanne sat back and sighed. "Well, Jenna, I don't know. You'll just have to meditate on that one. I think you'll find the answer."

"Yeah, I hope so." Jenna glanced at her watch. "Wow, look at the time. I've got to go."

"Well, if you must," Roxanne said, as she stood up.

Jenna got up and slipped on her coat. "Thanks for the tea; it was delicious. Next time you write your friend, see if she'll send me a set of those cups, would you?"

"Okay," Roxanne said, as they moved to the door. "I will."

Roxanne opened the door for Jenna; but before she left, Roxanne said, "Jenna, can I ask you something?"

"Well, yeah. I guess so."

"Are you pregnant, Jenna?"

Jenna was stunned. How did Roxanne know? Only Hank had ever asked her that before. She thought she'd managed to cleverly conceal her condition thus far, but Roxanne must have seen through the facade.

Her first thought was to deny it. Then, she considered ignoring the question altogether. Finally, though, she realized that there was no point in hiding it from Roxanne. So, she simply said, "Yes."

Roxanne thoughtfully looked at Jenna. "Jenna, I hope I've helped you in your search."

"I think you did," she replied. In reality, she felt more confused than ever. She turned and started down the hallway.

On the way home, Jenna relived the conversation she'd had with Roxanne. It seemed that there were no simple answers. If the fetus growing in her womb was just part of her body as Roxanne had said, then there was no moral obligation whatsoever to bring it into the world. It drew its identity from her. It was part of the Whole because she was part of the Whole. Since she rejected it, then it was not real.

On the other hand, she thought about what was written in those passages she'd read. From those it seemed that the One did have a part to play in the fetus' development. The fetus was included as an entity in the greater scheme of the Universe, contributing to the collective whole as much as anything else. It did have a part to play. The One even went so far as to predetermine that certain individuals would achieve a higher level of consciousness.

However, she could draw no conclusions from this day. Roxanne seemed lost when Jenna had started reading the passages, and even tried to dismiss them. It was as if Roxanne was trying to deny the truth because it didn't fit into her paradigm, but Jenna couldn't accept that. Roxanne was too strong and too selfassured. Jenna began to consider that she was being too inflexible. Like Roxanne said, "Truth...what is truth?"

Earthworms

As the thing growing inside her abdomen forcefully made its presence known, Jenna tossed the book she'd been reading onto the coffee table in frustration. "Stop it!" she exclaimed in a whisper as she stared down at the rounded, swollen form that at one time had been a firm, flat stomach.

Jenna had to stop for a moment each time the fetus noticeably shifted its position, that was becoming quite frequent. The movement was another unmistakable reminder that there was something more there than just extraneous tissue or a clump of immature flesh growing in her womb. It was alive.

"Is something wrong, Jen?" Joe asked from his workstation.

Jenna turned to look at him. Joe's eyes turned to narrow, dark slits under his worried, wrinkled brow; he sat in his chair as if ready to spring into action at a moment's notice.

"No, Joe," she sighed, as she shook her head. "Nothing's wrong. Nothing you can do anything about, anyway," she finished under her breath as she turned back around.

Jenna struggled as she reached over to take the book from the coffee table. The size of her stomach combined with the amply cushioned sofa made this difficult. Each shift of her body, each attempt at relocating her form, demanded what seemed to be a superhuman effort. She swore to herself under her breath.

After Jenna had retrieved the book, she sank back in the cushions and tried to relax. Two more weeks, she thought to herself. Two more weeks and it would all be over. The fetus would be removed, and things would get back to normal. No more wearing bargainbin, oversized clothes. No more pretending to be overeating. No more lying. And, most importantly, no more signs and symptoms of pregnancy.

For a moment, she considered her body. Overall, it had fared pretty well. Aside from the obvious changes in her abdomen, Jenna had done an admirable job in maintaining herself. She continued to exercise regularly and eat properly. Yes, she anticipated no problem in returning to her preordeal condition.

A couple of weeks ago, she'd had something of a scare. One morning, during the twentieth week, Jenna had noticed an abnormal amount of vaginal discharge. The secretion was yellowish and very thick, and she was afraid that she had contracted an infection.

After talking to Ms. Zambezi later that day Jenna's concern was alleviated. Ms. Zambezi indicated that Jenna was experiencing a condition called leukorrhea. It was caused by the increased blood flow to the skin and muscles around the vagina. There was nothing to worry about. It did clear up after several days, much to Jenna's relief.

Emotionally and spiritually, though, she was in turmoil. Was the developing fetus a person or not? And if it was, what right did she have in aborting it? Roxanne's explanation had been unsatisfactory, although Jenna found that Sharon's reaction to her own pregnancy did appear to support at least some of what Roxanne had said.

Sharon obviously wanted the child and, therefore, nurtured the unborn baby through her own consciousness. She gave meaning to the child. It existed because she existed, just as Roxanne had proclaimed.

But still, the Psalmist and Jeremiah both declared that the One had known them while yet in the womb, and even before then. If that were true, who was she to deny the unborn the right to achieve its potential as a person? Didn't Jesus say not to hinder the children from coming unto him?

Jenna glanced down at the book she held in her right hand: <u>A Fundamental Guide to Theosophy</u>. Theosophy, neither a religion nor a science, was really a combination of the two. It was a philosophy of the highest order, and its goal? To know God by acquiring knowledge of God in three ways: the study of tangible facts; the discovery of the individual consciousness' relationship to its source, or the One; and the construction of a plausible explanation of life and its meaning by way of reasoning. She had been exploring Theosophy with the hope that in it lay a more definite answer, something to balance with what she already knew. In the end, this was not the case.

Thus far, she had learned that Theosophy seemed to assert that reality existed only in the individual consciousness, or soul, as it evolved through the cyclic processes of life and death, or reincarnation. This evolutionary process took the individual through higher and higher planes of consciousness until it returned to the One from which it was spawned.

Theosophy espoused that the soul is the self, and that life exists only inasmuch as the soul exists. The soul, or the self, begins as a spark in the Universal Mind, or God. Therefore, the individual is God; but first, the soul must mature before it can take its place in the collective mind of God.

The body is a reflection of the self. It merely acts as the vessel through which the soul can interact with the physical world, which itself is a reflection of the universal mind. As the soul progresses on its evolutionary track, it becomes capable of greater and greater aspirations. To ensure that the soul can achieve its full potential for its present stage, the body evolves with it. A stunted soul would find itself clothed in a frail vessel, while the more mature soul would be given a strong body with a sound mind.

When the body is no longer capable of fulfilling the needs of the soul, the body dies; and the soul returns to the astral plane. There, its experiences and knowledge gained while in the body combine with those that it already possessed. If sufficient wisdom has been gained, the soul evolves to the next plane from where the process repeats itself.

Jenna had found all of this drivel concerning pantheistic evolution interesting but inconsequential. She did not believe in reincarnation. Her holistic philosophy had no room for myths about climbing some ladder to achieve godhood. Rather, she accepted herself and everything around her as already part of God. Some just didn't realize it yet, and others were on higher levels of realization than the rest.

One thing in her study of Theosophy did raise her brow, though. Theosophy taught that as the body matures, the soul enters into it until, at last, the body becomes saturated and can accommodate no more. A newborn baby is not yet capable of accepting the full self. So, as the infant grows into childhood and the child to adolescence, and the adolescent to adulthood, the body becomes in possession of an ever-increasing part of the soul. Throughout this growth process, the soul accumulates a veritable treasure chest of experience and wisdom to add to the rest. She found that concept particularly enlightening since, as many have said, each religion holds some element of truth. Perhaps this was Theosophy's.

This, however, opened up several other questions. When does the soul begin to enter the body: during conception, sometime after conception, or at birth? Wouldn't theosophical reasoning indicate that development while in the womb is part of the experience sought after? After all, even a fetus possesses a brain, no matter how rudimentary in the beginning. What happens to the soul that would have entered that body if it was aborted while in the womb? It has gained nothing; so, it can't evolve. Does it remain in its astral plane? If so, for how long? And what would happen to her own soul if she robs another of its opportunity for further development? How would that affect her own evolution, not that she believed in reincarnation?

Jenna sighed and closed the book. She tossed it over onto the coffee table, making a loud thump that reverberated around the room for much too long. As she closed her eyes, she could hear Joe behind her as he worked diligently on some project that he hadn't yet divulged to her.

A buzz at the door woke Jenna from her thoughts. She turned to look at Joe. "Joe," she said with a whining nasal tone, "can you get that?"

He looked at her out of the corner of his eye. "Yeah, I'll get it," he muttered, as rose from his chair and dropped the lightpen onto the desk.

Joe walked over to the door and activated the monitor. "Can I help you?" he asked.

Jenna faintly heard a woman's voice answer, "Yes. Is Jenna home?"

Joe, pointing to the monitor, looked over at Jenna as if seeking direction. Jenna stared blankly at the image for a moment but then brightened up when she realized it was Roxanne. Jenna nodded to Joe.

"Yeah, she's here," he pointedly said.

"Would you tell her Roxanne would like to see her, please?"

"C'mon up," he invited. Joe touched a spot on the access panel, admitting Roxanne into the building. Then he deactivated the monitor.

By now, Jenna had managed to pull herself up from the sofa. "Did you let her in?" she asked Joe as they met near the kitchen.

"Yes, I let her in," he replied as they passed. "I'll be in the bedroom; I don't want to hear you two cackling."

Fine, she thought to herself. I don't want you around either if that's the way you're going to be.

Jenna opened the door and stepped out into the hallway. The air was stuffy since ventilation in the hall had malfunctioned the day before, and it hit her like walking into a wall. Beads of perspiration were beginning to form on her brow as she watched down the hall to where the elevator doors remained closed. The lift's pulsating floor lights indicated that one of the cars was approaching her floor. She leaned back against the doorjamb and sighed. The dense atmosphere was thick with odors she didn't care to think about.

After a few moments, the elevator stopped and the doors effortlessly slid open. Roxanne stepped into the dimly lit hall and smiled when she recognized Jenna's still form leaning against the doorway. A man of African heritage followed her. Jenna stood up when she saw that the man was Dr. Emerson.

Roxanne approached her with a big grin and arms outstretched. "Jenna, my child, it's so good to see you!" She hugged Jenna and kissed her on the cheek.

With Roxanne still holding her hands, Jenna smiled back and said, "It's good to see you, too."

Roxanne looked at Dr. Emerson. "Jenna, I believe you know James…I mean, Dr. Emerson."

Dr. Emerson chuckled and extended a hand. "James is fine. And how have you been Jenna?"

Jenna stood mesmerized for a moment. "Oh…I'm fine. Ah, won't you come in?"

"Yes," Roxanne cheerfully replied. "That would be nice."

"Certainly," Dr. Emerson answered.

Jenna stood to one side and let Roxanne and Dr. Emerson go in. Their visit was curious. It wasn't like Roxanne to just drop in unannounced, especially with a noted theologian in tow.

Jenna studied Roxanne as they walked towards the living area. Something was different. Her hair color. Roxanne had colored her hair. It was red, now almost the same shade as Jenna's.

As Roxanne seated herself in the sofa, Dr. Emerson sat down beside her. Jenna asked, "Can I get either of you anything?"

"Nothing for me, thank you," Dr. Emerson declared.

"No, dear. I'm fine. Please…sit down." Roxanne patted the cushion next to the one she occupied.

"Theosophy?" Roxanne said.

Jenna glanced at the coffee table as she sat down, realizing she had left that book there. "Yes," she sighed, somewhat embarrassed. "I was just…"

"Looking for answers?" Dr. Emerson finished. "Yes, I understand, Sister. Sometimes we are forced to search for even the most obvious answers to the most basic questions."

Roxanne picked up the book and leafed through the pages. "But Theosophy?" She shook her head. "I just never subscribed to it. The thought of living through multiple lifetimes to achieve what we know we already possess seems so unnecessary and, well, dangerous. I mean, this philosophy creates a hierarchy where some are better than others...because of some supposed spiritual evolution." She ended on a sarcastic note and looked at James.

He smirked and said, "I would have to agree with you on that, Roxie."

Jenna took the book from Roxanne; and, running an index finger down its spine, said, "Yes, well, I found a lot of it to be, well, rather far fetched." She set the book down on the coffee table again and turned back to Roxanne.

Roxanne placed a hand on Jenna's knee. There was an expression of genuine concern in her voice. "Enough of this theosophical rubbish. What about you, Jenna, how have you been? Are you getting along okay?"

"Yes, I'm fine," Jenna answered. "Aside from the normal pregnancy pains."

Roxanne smiled as if relieved. "Good, good." She took in a deep breath. "You know, I've been thinking a great deal about the conversation we had a couple of weeks ago. It's troubled me ever since, and, well, I called James."

Jenna glanced at Dr. Emerson.

Roxanne shifted. "I'm sorry, my dear; but I feel that I have done you a great disservice."

Jenna leaned closer. "How do you mean."

"After you left my flat, I began to realize that you'd come to me with a matter of great importance. I just didn't know how important, or personal, it was until you had to leave." She looked at Jenna as if look-ing for some sign of forgiveness.

"Don't be too hard on yourself," Jenna said. "I wasn't totally honest with you to begin with. I should've told you I was pregnant."

"No, no," Roxanne answered, shaking her head. "I should have been more sensitive." After a short pause, she nobly asserted, "So I've brought James along. Maybe he can help you."

Jenna turned her eyes to Dr. Emerson. He gazed at her like a school-teacher out to educate the ignorant masses: determined, selfassured. Jenna wondered just how much he really knew.

"Roxanne tells me that you're pregnant," he began. "I understand that you are concerned about the child's relationship with the One."

"Something like that," Jenna said. "But…I guess what I really want to know is when does an individual achieve personhood?"

Dr. Emerson cleared his throat. "Some would say that we become persons when we are born, simply because we exist physically. Yet, oth-ers propose that personhood begins when we are able to rationalize and communicate our thoughts. In other words, it is not enough to simply exist. Rather, we must know that we exist.

"But, these ideas, noble as they may be, are only partially correct. You see, since all things exist as one, true personhood is not achieved until we come to that realization, until we become as one with our Mother. Then and only then will She accept us completely."

Jenna scratched her head. "So you're saying that we are not persons until we achieve unity with the One?"

"Yes, exactly," he agreed, smiling, eyes gleaming. "In the universal sense, that is. When our consciousness comes to the realization that there is no duality, then can we throw off the cloak of darkness that hides the Truth. Otherwise, we are still creatures spawned by the Uni-verse, destined to suffer in the realm between good…and evil. There must be a rebirth, so to speak."

Jenna was puzzled by his assertion. "What do you mean, rebirth?"

Dr. Emerson smiled as his eyes twinkled. "My dear, you have provided the clue."

"I did?" Jenna asked, wondering what sort of guessing game she was about to play.

"Yes, you did." Dr. Emerson took out a pack of gum and offered a piece to the ladies. Then he took a stick, carefully unwrapped it, and put it in his mouth. After chewing for a second, he continued, "Roxanne tells me that you had referred to a Biblical passage where Jesus tells his disciples to let the children come to him?"

"Yes." Jenna began to listen more intently.

"He finishes by saying that the Kingdom of Heaven consists of ones like them. And there is another place, in John's Gospel, where he tells a man that he must be reborn to enter the Kingdom."

"And the Kingdom of Heaven is another way of saying, 'I am one with God'," Roxanne interjected.

"Exactly," he confirmed.

Jenna wrinkled her brow as she puzzled over the concept of rebirth. "But how is a person reborn?" she pointedly asked.

"To be reborn, one must become like the child," Dr. Emerson replied confidently. "For as Jesus said, the Kingdom of Heaven is made of ones like them."

Jenna thought for a moment and shook her head in frustration. "I don't understand. Why is it so important to be like a child, other than because children see the world on simple terms, through a child's eyes?"

"Yes!" he exclaimed. "That's exactly it. Children do see the world in simple terms. Their minds are not so cluttered with all the worries that we as adults experience. Because of that, they are more in tune with the natural order. If it weren't for their immature minds, they would be able to grasp the truth and soar with the spirit of the One."

"Yes, I can see that," she said. "A child's mind is not littered with excess baggage. It has no obstacles to get in its way...and if it were learned enough, it could achieve unity." Jenna smiled broadly with the warmth that came from inside. In some way, she felt liberated.

"Oh, yes, Jenna," Roxanne responded encouragingly, as she took Jenna's hands. "To be born, to mature, and then return to a childlike state…with all the years of wisdom and insight that one can gain in a lifetime. That is what it means to be reborn!"

Dr. Emerson broke in. "And only through this rebirth, this return to innocence, can we ever experience complete and…and utter joy and contentment…as we surrender ourselves completely to the Universal Mind. Our very lives must become the conscious, everlasting testimony of Reality by Reality—I and the Father are one." Dr. Emerson paused, taking a deep breath. He looked at Jenna. Her faced glowed with realization as her mind opened up.

"Imagine how that must feel," he continued, his voice filled with electricity, "to be at such a level of consciousness. Why, it must be like…like, well, an earthworm. Yes, an earthworm. To be so simple…and to be able to commune with the Earth Mother on such a basic level…your whole existence based on Her, and in Her.

"And you see, that's how that unborn child is, in your womb," Roxanne added. "Its existence is based on you. Without you, there would be no child. *It* is because you are."

"Yes, I can see that," Jenna remarked, as a sense of understanding came into her being. "But when does life itself begin? I mean, at what point…"

"Yes, yes," Dr. Emerson said, anticipating her question. "In what terms can we define life."

"Yes, how do we define it?"

Dr. Emerson chuckled. He looked at Roxanne and then Jenna. "That question has eluded the greatest minds the world has known. In a sense, everything is alive, inasmuch as all creation is alive through the One.

"You see, Jenna, there is never really a beginning to life. Life is perpetual. The Earth lives and gives birth to Her children. The sperm and the egg are alive before they have their fateful union. After they join, The Tibetan Book of the Dead says that a human being, or an animal, has been conceived. So, a new life begins and grows until its birth, at which time another life begins.

"Life is a continuum, woven into the tapestry of the Universal Consciousness like a thread in a fine Persian rug. Up close, as you and I are, and it has little significance. But step back, and behold its majesty!"

Jenna considered this for a moment. "But if one thread becomes damaged or loose, the whole rug loses its beauty and may even unravel."

"Well, I suppose it would," Dr. Emerson noted. "But I am speaking metaphorically, of course."

"Oh, so then what you're saying is that, on an individual basis, each life is worthless." Jenna was beginning to doubt him.

"No, that's not it." Dr. Emerson leaned towards her. "A life has value inasmuch as it harmonizes with the Universe. Otherwise, it is like a piano string that is out of tune: the chord is ruined. Don't misunderstand me though. Every life has at least some value."

"Even an unborn child?" Jenna asked.

Dr. Emerson stopped for a moment. An inquisitive expression moved across his face like the shadow of a cloud across the Earth. After a pause, he said, "Consider the earthworm again. How does it compare to an infant? When a baby is born, what is it? What are its capabilities?"

"Well, it's an immature human," Jenna replied, "and not really capable of much at all, is it?"

"Exactly," Dr. Emerson agreed. "At birth, and for several months after, an infant is incapable of doing anything other eating, sleeping, and dirtying its diaper. It is a prisoner of its undeveloped mental capacity, only able to respond to various external and internal stimuli as they are applied."

"Yes," Jenna agreed. "And your point?"

Dr. Emerson had smiled again. "The earthworm is the same, Jenna. It eats, and it defecates." He paused. "That's all it does.

"And think about its brain, if you can call it a brain. Really nothing more than a junction point for a rudimentary nervous system. Why, even with this simple brain, and I use the term loosely, a worm still knows when it's in danger. Have you ever tried to catch one when it's still part-way in its hole?"

"No, I can't…"

"If you slap a baby, or prick it with a pin, it screams. If it's hungry, it cries. If its diaper becomes soiled, it wails. And these are all it can do. It doesn't know why it feels these things; it only knows that it does. And why? Because all an infant can do is respond to its environment. When you really think about it, a baby is no more developed than the earthworm. Yet, an earthworm is more in harmony with the Blessed Mother than any human who ever walked upon Her. It does Her no harm. It takes no more than it gives back. Its very existence enriches her soil.

Have you ever been fishing, Jenna?" he asked.

"Yes, but it's been a few years."

"And what did you use for bait?"

"Well, worms, I suppose."

"Did you feel any anguish over placing the worm on the hook?"

"Well, no."

"Then, if you feel no remorse over having sent an earthworm to its death, why are you pining over the existence of something that we both agree is less than a common earthworm?"

Jenna thought for a moment. "I don't know, Dr. Emerson. I just don't."

"Don't you see, Sister? Are you so blind? You are the Mother, and the unborn is like that earthworm. You have the power to choose, and you must decide for yourself what the relevance of that unborn child is to your existence. If you seek earnestly, and faithfully, the Light will reveal all things to you."

Roxanne and Dr. Emerson stayed awhile longer to visit. Nothing else was said about Jenna's pregnancy or the relationship of the fetus to the Universe. All the while, and even after they left, Jenna continued to mull over what had transpired. A lot of it made sense. The rebirth. Returning to a simpler frame of mind. The Kingdom of Heaven made up of childlike minds, filled with innocence. Even what Dr. Emerson had said about there really being no beginning to life was a compelling argument.

Yet, what he had said about the earthworm Jenna found disturbing. Perhaps she still held on to some misguided notion that humanity was superior to all the other creatures. It still made her wonder. Was Dr. Emerson suggesting that something as simple as an earthworm had more right to exist than most people, let alone a fetus? If this was based on simplicity of form, or mind, then why would a fetus be denied that right? After all, an unborn child, especially in the first few weeks, is about as simple in mind and body as a creature can get.

Of course, an earthworm will always be an earthworm; whereas an unborn child only has potential.

Spilled Beer

Jenna stared at the soup that sat before her like she was in a trance. The steam rose from it, forming curly, translucent wisps of vapor below her chin that dissipated with each exhalation of air from her nostrils. She took the spoon that she held in one hand and dipped it in the broth, causing ripples to form along the surface. Slowly, she moved the spoon in a figure eight pattern, watching as the soup's contents rose to the surface and then plunged to the bottom.

Joe's homemade vegetable soup was excellent. He used only the finest herbs and spices, and the freshest vegetables. The ingredients were carefully, even lovingly, combined in the morning and allowed to simmer in a crock pot all day. What resulted was a stew with the most delightful aroma and heavenly flavor. Add his homemade cornbread, and it was one of the finest meals around.

Unfortunately, Jenna's appetite was not what one might call ravenous. If anything, it was nonexistent. Ordinarily, she loved his soup and would eagerly have seconds and sometimes thirds. Today, though, it was all she could do to sit at the table. She felt a chill as Joe's steely eyes looked upon her while she pointlessly stirred the soup.

At last, Joe said, "Is something wrong, Jen? You've hardly touched your soup."

Jenna glanced up at him. His eyebrows were lifted slightly, and his mouth was pulled almost into a frown. He appeared genuinely concerned. She just wasn't sure if he was concerned for her or for his soup. "It's just hot, Joe. That's all."

"Oh." Satisfied with her answer, he returned to his meal.

Jenna watched him for a moment longer and then returned to her ritualistic agitation of the soup. It smelled wonderful. Finally, she took a spoonful, with Joe looking on approvingly, and ate it.

It tasted as good as she'd expected. But, after a few more spoonfuls her stomach soured and she thought that she would be sick. "Excuse me, please," she said as she rose from the table.

"Are you all right, Jen?" Joe asked.

"I think I'm going to be sick," she said as she left the room, not waiting for a response from Joe, lest she lose the contents of her stomach on the carpet.

Jenna knelt at the toilet, waiting for the fated event to occur. She felt like she should be praying, but to what god should she pray? And what should she ask for? As she paused, her stomach churned, and she could feel the pressure building up within the pit of her belly.

As she readied her self for the inevitable moment, she suddenly despised the thing inside her with a hatred she hadn't felt for some time. This was *its* fault, she was certain. She had never been sick like this before until the pregnancy. Any more, she hardly ever kept her food down, or so it seemed, although the first twelve weeks had been the worst.

This was the twenty-fourth week of gestation. Tomorrow, she was to have the fetus removed. It had been a long twenty-four weeks. In that time, Jenna had experienced cramps, weight gain, morning sickness, sore breasts, fatigue, itchy stomach, and a host of other symptoms of pregnancy. And throughout the experience, she'd moved from disdain to indifference to tolerance. Now she was feeling doubt.

During those five months something had changed inside her.

Something had profoundly touched her. Perhaps it was the way the fetus moved around and kicked. Sometimes, she would laugh to herself when it did that. Maybe it was some physiological change that women go through during pregnancy. It was also conceivable that being around Sharon, who was also pregnant, had triggered some motherly reaction buried deep inside her. She recalled the ultrasound pictures that Sharon had shown her and how detailed they were. Possibly, the passages she'd read from the *Bible* had spoken to her in some profound, unseen way.

All of these factors had clouded her mind for many weeks now. And she still hadn't reached any definite conclusions. The only thing that she was certain of was that she didn't want a baby. A child just wasn't in her plans at the moment, and she'd already signed the contract with ASAMAR, receiving partial payment. So, she was bound by an agreement to give up the fetus. She was sure that others would benefit from her sacrifice. Wasn't that what the counselor had said? Who knew? Perhaps her fetus would be the one used to find a cure for AIDS. Besides, what was one less person in the great expanse of the Universal Consciousness?

After a few seconds passed, she finally threw up once, twice, then a third time, followed by the inevitable dry, heaving cough. The experience drained her; it always did.

The bitter taste of vomit was still strong in her mouth as she looked at herself in the mirror. Her face was red and streaked from the effort she'd just expended. Her body was bloated from the pregnancy, and she was sure that she was as big as a whale. Jenna wanted to cry.

She ran some cold water on a wash cloth and wiped her face. The cool, moist cloth against her warm face felt wonderful. She filled a cup with cold water and drank it, partially flushing the bitterness from her mouth; but the acrid flavor would taint her mouth for some time.

When she went back into the living room, Joe was still eating. As she passed him on her way to the kitchen, he asked, "Did you puke?"

She didn't answer. What did he think? Of course she puked.

Didn't he hear her? He had to have heard her. As she heaved up the contents of her stomach, she must have sounded like a lonely elephant, trumpeting for others of its species.

Once in the kitchen, Jenna filled a glass with ice. She opened the refrigerator and searched around for some club soda, but there was none to be found. She'd finished it earlier in the day. So, she filled the glass with tea instead and returned to the living room.

Joe was still eating as Jenna set the glass on the coffee table and sank down into the sofa. She could hear him slurping as he ate, but she pushed the sound out of her mind as she closed her eyes.

In her mind's eye, Jenna visualized herself standing naked atop a ridge in the noonday sun. The rays from that closest star were warm against her skin. A gentle breeze out of the northwest effortlessly brushed her hair against her cheek; and soft, billowy clouds randomly crossed the bright, blue sky.

The ridge itself was clear, although a line of trees circumscribed the crest, forming a living wall that seemed impregnable. A large deer walked out of the woods, grazing on the tender shoots of grass that were growing along the tree line. It looked up, revealing a magnificent rack of antlers, and spotted her. But it did not run away. The deer continued on its way, nibbling the grass along the edge of the woods as it followed the tree line.

Jenna lay back on the ground and rested her head on both hands. The ground felt cool, and the grass tickled her ribs. She looked up and saw a bird floating effortlessly among the clouds. It must be an eagle, she thought, although she couldn't be sure since the bird was silhouetted against the sky. She continued to watch as the bird glided along until it was just a speck on the horizon.

Then her attention was fixed on the clouds as they drifted by. She loved to picture the shapes they formed and often spent many lazy hours doing so. The first cloud she thought looked like an elephant, with big, billowy ears and a thick body. The next appeared to be a face. The bulbous nose, puffy cheeks, and white hair and beard made her think of Santa Claus. Another cloud, she decided, was a chubby, little boy kicking a ball. Several more clouds drifted by. As they did, her level of anxiety decreased. She became more relaxed and completely forgot about the recent sickness.

She spotted another cloud on the horizon. From a distance, she couldn't decide what it was; but as it grew bigger it began to take on a definite shape. She carefully studied the figure for a moment. There was a big head; a chubby body; and short, stubby legs and arms. The face had a small, button nose, and fat, little cheeks. She smiled and said to herself, "It's a baby."

Jenna opened her eyes with a start. Her pulse was racing, and she'd broken out in a cold sweat. Looking around the room, Joe was nowhere to be seen; but she could hear him in the kitchen. She took a deep breath and let it out slowly. A dull pressure from within her abdomen caused by the cervical plug made her uncomfortable; so, she adjusted her posture in an attempt to relieve the discomfort.

She picked up the glass that had been sitting on the coffee table and took a long drink of tea. After setting the glass back down, she rested her head on the back of the sofa and stared vacantly at the ceiling.

After a few minutes, Joe came in and sat down next to her. He put his hand on her knee and leaned over to kiss her. After the kiss, he said, "Are you okay, now?"

Jenna rubbed her face with one hand. "Yeah, I guess so."

Joe had been wonderful ever since she first revealed her secret and told him of her plan to abort it. He had been very supportive, as a matter of fact, and nowhere near as confrontational or patronizing as she'd feared he'd become.

After a few seconds, Joe asked, "Is there anything I can get you? Do you want something else to eat?"

"No," she softly replied, "not at the moment."

"Okay."

Joe picked up the remote and turned the television on. He was a big basketball enthusiast, and there was a double bill tonight: Philadelphia at Pittsburgh, and Mexico City at Chicago. The games were being played simultaneously; so, he'd have to make use of the split screen, which made following the play-by-play rather tricky. Joe claimed that he could do it, although Jenna never did believe him. The pre-game shows were almost over by this time.

"Games start in a few minutes," he noted as he got up. "I'm going to get some chips and a beer. Sure you don't want something?"

"Well, maybe a grapefruit."

"Great." He seemed happy to hear that she wanted something to eat. It must take away his guilt, she thought as he hurried off to the kitchen.

Jenna half-heartedly observed the last few minutes of the pre-game show. She liked to watch basketball, but the pre-game commentary she found boring. Two, sometimes three, individuals sitting in a booth somewhere, critiquing the teams as if what they said really mattered. Those guys must really have some inflated egos, she thought, like the game couldn't go on without them making their insipid remarks. She supposed, though, that a few of the commentators were genuine and reliable.

Joe came back into the room about five minutes later balancing a bowl filled with chips, a bottle of beer, and a smaller bowl. "Here you go," he said, as he handed the small bowl to Jenna. Then, he sat down next to her.

The bowl contained a grapefruit, already peeled and sectioned. Jenna thought that it was especially gracious of him to go through the extra effort of peeling and sectioning it. He could have missed the first few moments of the games. As it was, the Philadelphia-Pittsburgh game was just beginning as he sat down, and there was a slight delay at Chicago because a Mexican couple had run naked out on the floor, taunting the Chicago players.

Jenna bit into one of the sections of grapefruit. The sour taste made her grimace; but then, she remembered something her grandfather used to say, "The first bite locks your jaws; the second one opens them." She chuckled when she thought of it.

"What are you laughing at?" Joe seemed kind of annoyed at the interruption.

"Oh, just something my grandfather used to say." She popped the rest of the section into her mouth. Despite her grandfather's wise counsel, Jenna still winced when she tasted the fruit.

In the first few minutes of the game, Philadelphia had jumped ahead of Pittsburgh, ten to two, which made Joe extremely happy. He was a Philadelphia man, through and through. Meanwhile, the Chicago-Mexico City match had just tipped off with no score; Joe had money on Mexico City. Jenna didn't care too much about who won; it was the excitement that attracted her to the game.

Jenna finished eating the grapefruit and set the dish on the coffee table. By this time, Philadelphia was ahead, twenty-two to sixteen. Chicago was trouncing Mexico City. She didn't believe Joe would lose a lot of money if Mexico City lost; he generally limited his wagering to one hundred dollars a week, what he called pocket change. He didn't appear to be upset. Of course, it was still early in the game, and Mexico City was known for their late starts.

After an intense first period, Pittsburgh had come back to tie the game, twenty-eight to twenty-eight. Still in the first period, Mexico City remained behind Chicago, but they were beginning to show some life. During a commercial break from the Philadelphia-Pittsburgh game, Joe sat back on the sofa.

"Mexico City's not doing too well," Jenna said.

Grinning, Joe looked at her and said, "They'll come back. They're just toying with Chicago, looking for the weakness. They'll explode in the second period. Just wait and see." He took a drink from the bottle.

"Joe, do you ever want to have children?" she timidly asked. Her timing wasn't good, and she knew that she'd probably regret ever asking.

"Children? Yeah, someday. Hey! The game's coming back on." With that, he was back on the edge of the sofa, mechanically stuffing chips in his mouth.

Jenna felt relieved. She had asked the question before she knew what had come out. But, for obvious reasons, Joe hadn't really heard it. The question never registered. She relaxed and turned her attention back to the games again.

After a few minutes, Joe looked at Jenna and said, "Wait a minute. Did you just ask me if I ever wanted to have children?"

His question startled her. Jenna was certain that he'd forget all about it once the game came back on, but she was mistaken. "Uhm, well, yes. I did; but..."

"Hold it a second," he interrupted. "You're not thinking of allowing that fetus to mature so you can have a baby, are you? Because if you are, just remember that you've already agreed to give it up, and accepted a down payment."

"I know all that," she defensively declared. "And no, I'm not planning on keeping it. It's just, well, what I've been going through's got me wanting a baby. I'm not saying right now. But someday? Yes, definitely!"

He stammered around, trying to find the words. "Well, uh, and I want to have children, too, very much. We're just not ready, yet. That's all. And I don't want you to get in trouble over this."

"Don't worry, Joe. Come tomorrow, and it'll all be over." She leaned over and kissed him.

They silently sat together on the sofa for several minutes. Joe continued watching the games while Jenna held her glass in one hand and rhythmically rubbed the rim with a finger from the other.

She reflected on the circular motion her finger made as it followed the rim of the glass. The cycle of life made a similar pattern, she thought. Even though she knew that life was constantly evolving, one thing always remained the same: life takes from itself to produce new life. Living plants took in nutrients from the soil, carbon dioxide from the atmosphere, and energy from the sun to continue living. And as they did, seeds were produced which gave birth to new life. Herbivores fed off of living plants so that they might flourish, while carnivores ate the herbivores. Then, of course, you had the scavengers that feasted off of the remains of what the carnivores left behind, or else consumed what simply died.

Some might argue that plants really don't feed off of life; but that wasn't true, she felt. Although most plants didn't go out and kill their food, save for those like the Venus flytrap, they still benefited from what was once alive. The nutrients that they took from the earth were byproducts of decayed vegetable matter, as well as rotted animals. Where the first plants found these nutrients, she wasn't sure: some chemical process, perhaps.

Jenna considered these things as she tried to rationalize her decision. Even if the fetus was an entity deserving of life, the cycle demanded that it be available for other living organisms to benefit from its existence. It may well be true, she thought, that the fetus was as much a part of the Eternal Fabric of the Universe as, say, herself. Even so, she was only a part of the Fabric and not its essence. Ergo, the living for their own survival could claim the fetus. Thus would be the outcome for the fetus that she carried: to die, that others might live.

Still, though, Jenna wondered if there wasn't a flaw in her reasoning. Roxanne had said that a fetus was not a human being that had a place in the Consciousness of the Universe. The only place where it mattered was in the womb. If the woman chose to deny it, then it might as well have never existed. For, while in the womb, its life is derived from the woman, who gives it life.

Yet, at one time, at least two seekers of truth, possibly three, had the insight to declare a greater role for the unborn child than just that of extraneous tissue. Those people believed the place of an unborn, immature baby to be as a vital part of the Universal Mind. Had not Jesus said that the kingdom of heaven was made of ones such as them?

Of course, what were the musings of two or three men from a single religious tradition when placed against the whole backdrop of spiritual thought that the entire world had to offer? Jenna didn't have the answer. She knew of no other traditions that contained a similar testimony, although what Dr. Emerson had referred to concerning the *Tibetan Book of the Dead* was interesting. Of course, that piece of literature was concerned with reincarnation, which Jenna didn't accept. Since the Biblical references were the only witnesses of their kind, she decided that they should be looked upon skeptically.

Having made this conclusion, Jenna drank the last little bit of tea there was in the glass. She shook the ice that stuck to the bottom to loosen it. Then, she swallowed it. She stood up and said, "Can I get you anything, Joe?"

He was engrossed in the game.

"Joe," she repeated, as she nudged him.

He looked up, irritably. "What?"

"Can I get you anything?"

He had this stupid expression, like he didn't understand her.

Then, he shook the beer bottle. "You could bring me another beer?"

"Okay, Joe."

Jenna went into the kitchen. As she opened the refrigerator, she felt a movement in her abdomen. It'll be gone after tomorrow, she thought.

Jenna took a beer out but couldn't find the opener. "Hey, Joe," she yelled, "Do you know where the bottle opener is?"

"Yeah," he answered in kind, "it's on the counter, next to the fridge."

She looked around; and, sure enough, there it was. She opened the bottle and tossed the cap into one of the refuse bins.

On the way back to the living room, she felt the fetus move again. This time, it forcefully kicked, startling her and causing her to drop the bottle. The bottle made a loud thud when it hit the carpeted floor; and beer spilled out, forming a large wet spot on the floor as the carpet eagerly soaked the brew in.

Joe looked over just as Jenna hurried to pick it up. "Jesus christ, Jen! Don't waste the god-damned beer."

Only about a quarter of the contents were on the floor. She took the bottle to him and said, "Sorry about that...I'll get a towel and clean that up."

Joe took the bottle without saying a word.

Jenna got a towel and knelt on the floor to sop up the beer. The whole time, all she could think of was how wonderful it will be after tomorrow when everything would be back to normal.

HARVEST

Jenna checked the clock hanging on the wall at the other side of the room. It read 9:45 AM. Impatient, she looked towards the doors located to either side of the receptionist's counter hoping that, very soon, someone, anyone, would come for her. The anticipation was unbearable. She'd been waiting for this day since October.

Jenna had arrived at ASAMAR thirty minutes ago for her 9:30 appointment. Patients typically waited past their appointed hours to see the doctor. So this particular wait didn't come as a surprise to her. Then again, she wasn't really a patient, was she? She was more like a business associate. She'd been paid to provide a product, so to speak. She had something that they wanted. The fact they'd taken care of her medical needs during the past four months seemed inconsequential. A doctor was simply the middleman in a financial transaction.

Eighteen weeks ago, she'd first come to this place out of curiosity as much as anything else. She'd been prodded, probed, and violated. They'd told her that the fetus was in its sixth week of development. The counselor had outlined her options, and she'd agreed to allow the fetus to mature to the twentyfourth week for a mutually agreeable price. ASAMAR Corporation would take care of all expenses.

Now, it was the twentyfourth week; and she was more than ready to have this over and done with. For six months, Jenna had endured the agony of pregnancy. The physical toll on her body would be easy to recover from since she'd taken care to exercise regularly and maintain a proper diet. The psychological impact, though, had turned out to be more taxing than she'd ever envisioned.

Many waking moments were spent on trying to reconcile the numerous aspects of her dilemma. First, there was the apprehension over her possible condition. Then, the shock of verifying that she was pregnant was expected but costly, none the less. The uncertainty of Joe's reaction at every turn had drained her on more than one occasion.

However, the most demanding of all had been the debate over the morality of what Jenna was doing: was she taking a life or not? Sharon's pictures of her developing fetus were impressive but easily dismissed as an interpretation by the conscious mind. However, the Bible passages were not so easily ignored. Spiritual men of faith had written them, Jenna was sure. And, despite the patriarchal system that they adhered to, she knew that there must be an element of truth in what they'd said.

Roxanne's argument to the contrary was compelling but not one hundred percent convincing. Dr. Emerson, too, presented a forceful argument as well. Only after she'd convinced herself that the unborn was subject to the Cycle of Life was Jenna able to reconcile her intentions. But even then, Jenna's own reasoning had left her empty and unsatisfied.

While she considered these things, someone touched her arm. "Jenna?"

Jenna looked up. It was Mandisa Zambezi. "Oh, I'm sorry Ms. Zambezi," she said. "I must have been daydreaming." Ms. Zambezi smiled. "That's all right. A lot of people who come here do that." She gestured towards the door on the left side of the receptionist's counter. "If you'll follow me, we can get you prepped now."

Jenna followed Ms. Zambezi through the door, down a drab, narrow hallway, and into a small changing area. Ms. Zambezi took a clear, plastic bag and a folded gown from a cabinet and handed them to Jenna.

"You'll need to completely disrobe and put the gown on," Ms. Zambezi said. "Your other clothes and belongings can go in this bag. I'll have it waiting for you in the recovery room."

Jenna obediently followed her instructions. She removed her own clothing and carefully folded each article. Then she placed them in the bag and handed it to Ms. Zambezi. That done, she put the gown on. The gown was thin, and she felt a chill as Ms. Zambezi led her into another room.

The room was small and brightly lit. It smelled of antiseptic. The air felt cool on Jenna's skin, and she shivered underneath the flimsy gown. Light was provided by fluorescent lamps that lined the ceiling, reflecting dully off of the colorless, marbled, freshly waxed tile floor. The windowless walls were drab, making the room seem cold and impersonal.

There was little in the way of furnishing in the room itself. A sink with a shelf holding fresh linens occupied one corner, and a laundry hamper was conveniently located nearby. An examination table was located in the center of the room. Off to the side, along one wall, was a hospital bed.

One nurse wearing green scrubs was working at the counter. She turned. "Good morning, Ms. Zambezi," she said.

"Good morning, Anna," Ms. Zambezi said as she led Jenna toward the table. "Jenna, I'd like you to meet Anna Guiterez."

Jenna eyed the nurse. She was an Hispanic woman, a few inches shorter that Jenna. Her dark hair was cut short, framing a round face. And she looked back at Jenna through deep, thoughtful brown eyes. "Good morning," Jenna said.

"Hello," the nurse said, taking Jenna's hand.

"I trust that I can leave Jenna in your care?" Ms. Zambezi said.

The nurse glanced at Jenna and, with a smile, said, "Of course you can. I was just finishing the preparations for her."

"Good. You'll let me know as soon as she's finished."

"Yes. I will," Ms. Guiterez replied.

Ms. Zambezi took Jenna's hand and gave a reassuring squeeze. "Everything will be fine," she said. "It'll be over before you know it."

"God, I hope so," Jenna said.

Ms. Zambezi smiled. "It will be, and I'll be nearby if you need me."

"All right. Thank you," Jenna said.

Jenna watched as Ms. Zambezi left the room. She suddenly felt alone. Ms. Zambezi was the only friend she had in the place. She didn't know anyone else. Anna Guiterez looked friendly enough. But then again, she was supposed to.

"Would you please get on the table," Ms. Guiterez asked.

Jenna didn't answer. She instinctively got on the table and lay on her back. She placed her feet in the stirrups without thinking. It was as if she had been there before.

"Are you nervous, Jen?" Ms. Guiterez asked, placing one hand on Jenna's shoulder.

Jenna looked at her. "Yes," she said. "I am."

Ms. Guiterez smiled. "Well, don't be," she said as she pulled a screen across Jenna's abdomen. "It will be over before you know it."

Jenna watched in solitude as Ms. Guiterez prepared her for the procedure. She checked Jenna's blood pressure, pulse and temperature, making notes of each on a small, hand held computer.

"How long do these usually take?" Jenna asked.

"Oh, thirty minutes at most," Ms. Guiterez said as she put the instruments away. "Of course, that doesn't include cleaning you up. We'll have you in the recovery room in fortyfive minutes, I promise."

Thirty minutes, Jenna thought. It was the same time that Ms. Zambezi had quoted. It didn't seem like a very long time.

Ms. Guiterez moved to the other side of the screen, partially blocking Jenna's view of the nurse. Jenna felt a chill as the nurse lifted her gown to just above her abdomen. Then Jenna felt five small points of iciness on her abdomen and heard squishing sounds. "What are you doing?" Jenna asked.

"Placing the sensors so the doctor can see the path," Ms. Guiterez replied.

The nurse pulled a monitor around so she could see it.

The monitor was suspended from the ceiling by an articulated arm that could be manipulated into a variety of orientations. "What's that for?" Jenna asked.

Ms Guiterez looked at Jenna. "The sensors will generate an image that the doctor can view on this monitor. It aids him in guiding his instruments and extracting the tissue."

"Oh, I see," Jenna said. She felt so stupid. "Ms. Guiterez?"

"'Anna', dear," Ms. Guiterez said. "You can call me 'Anna'."

"All right, Anna," Jenna said, relieved. It was friendlier. "Please don't think I'm a fool for asking so many questions."

"Oh. Of course you're not, Jen," Anna said. "You're just nervous. I understand, and I don't mind. All the girls do that."

"Thank you, Anna."

"It's all right, dear."

"Anna?"

"Yes, Jenna?"

"Have you done many of these?"

Anna's eyes darted from side to side as if searching the room for answers written on the walls. "Well. Yes, I suppose I have."

"How many?" Jenna asked.

"Oh, I don't know," the nurse answered. "Hundreds I guess. What tape do you want?" the nurse asked.

"What?"

"What tape? To watch during the procedure?"

"Oh," Jenna muttered. "Um, 'the Rockies', I think."

"All right," the nurse said.

A man wearing green scrubs entered the room pushing a cart with a large vessel mounted on it. Cables and tubes protruded from one end, winding down to various objects located on shelves below the vessel.

The man rolled the cart to a spot along the far wall and began to attend to the vessel.

"What's that?" Jenna asked.

Anna stopped her preparations and looked toward the cart. "That's the incubator."

"The what?"

"The incubator, for the fetus."

"Oh," Jenna said. Of course. She knew that.

Jenna heard the door behind her open and close. The footsteps of two individuals were definitely discernable. She craned her neck to see two people, a man and a woman, walking toward her. They both wore green scrubs. The man was about fifty, slim, with a pleasant face. The woman was shorter than he, and younger, but plain looking.

"Good morning, Jenna," the man said. "I'm Dr. Loeffler. How are you feeling today?"

"Well, all right, I guess." She'd never met the doctor before, and didn't now what to say. "I just want to get this over with."

"Yes, I'm sure you do," he said with a smile. "Let's see. You're in your twentyfourth week, correct?"

"Yes, that's right," Jenna said.

"Hmm, that'll be no problem," he said. "Now, I'll give you a local anesthetic, so you shouldn't feel any pain. You will feel pressure, though. So, don't be alarmed. But if you do feel any pain, you let me know. All right?"

"Okay, doctor."

"We'll have you out of here in no time. Just relax."

"I'll try," she said.

"That'a girl," he said as he squeezed her hand.

He looked at Ms. Guiterez. "Is everything set?"

"Yes, Doctor. She checked out fine, although her B.P is a little high and her pulse fast."

"Well, that's to be expected," he said. "Just stay with her."

"Yes, Doctor."

Jenna watched him as he walked down the table. He stopped to check the positioning of the fetal sensors attached to her abdomen. He poked and prodded, and checked the monitor. Then he went to the end of the table, out of Jenna's sight.

Ms. Guiterez placed a visor over Jenna's eyes. "There you are, Jenna. Just relax and it will soon be over." Then Jenna felt a slight pressure as Ms. Guiterez inserted the earphones into her ears.

At first, it was silent and dark. Then the scenery and accompanying sound that she'd selected began to run through her mind. The view of the mountains was spectacular. It was almost like being there. The sun was setting to the West, and the horizon was a brilliant red. She could see several elk grazing on the slope across from her, and the gentle sound of the wind blowing through the trees was very calming.

The pinch of the needle as the local anesthetic was administered made her flinch. But soon, she lost all feeling in her pelvic region. She felt the pressure of the speculum as it opened her vagina and experienced a peculiar sensation that she was sure must have been the removal of the cervical plug. She was beginning to find it difficult to stay focussed on the image. She was growing restless.

Jenna closed her eyes. She visualized herself as an eagle soaring high above those same mountains. She looked down to see the land spread out beneath her. The trees formed a plush, green carpet, with a river cutting a meandering path through the forest. Jenna felt a pinch as the cervical block was administered; but, in her mind, it became a sudden, uprush of air lifting her higher above the trees. Soon, she was in a trancelike state.

Jenna was in a state of euphoria. Images danced through her subconscious mind as she guided herself into a higher plane of blissful reality. Soon she was in the desert. In the original dream, she'd only been able to observe, although the man in the crimson robe was beckoning to her. It was clear that he had a message for her, but she was not in control as she dreamed. Nonetheless, through many periods of quiet meditation, she had managed to guide herself to the point of being part of the multitude as they joyfully sang and danced. What they were singing, she didn't know. The words were of a strange tongue.

One thing was clear, though. The man in crimson was the key to the vision. The last time she meditated on the vision, Jenna had gotten close enough to look into his weary, hazel eyes that, despite the tired gaze, sparkled with life. He'd looked upon her with love and understanding, but he didn't speak. Now, in this present vision, she stood before him, trembling like a child.

Jenna stood before the man in crimson, eagerly waiting for the words he was sure to speak. She searched his face for some indication of his intentions, but there was none. His expression only revealed sorrow and pain.

At last, he reached out his opened hand and lamentably said, "Do not hinder the little children from coming to me."

Jenna frightfully awakened from the trance! In an instant, the dream flashed through her mind; and she suddenly knew its significance.

It wasn't her in a darkened room being pulled from her bed. Rather, it was the unborn baby being wrenched from the safety of the womb. The security broken by the unseen tormentor grabbing its leg. The inability to hold on to anything. The pointless fight. The silent scream. It all made sense. At that moment, she became painfully aware of the murderous deed being committed.

"No!" Jenna screamed, as she twisted her body on the table.

The sudden contortion of her pelvis caught the medical staff completely off guard. The doctor lost control of the instruments and almost fell off of the stool on which he was perched. "Hold her down, damn it!" he bellowed. "Sedate her, now!"

Ms. Guiterez threw herself over Jenna's chest as the assistant administered the sedative. All the while, Jenna kept repeating over and over, "Stop, don't kill it." After a few seconds, the sedative took effect; and she lulled into unconsciousness.

Jenna woke an hour later in the recovery room. She was already dressed, and there was a tightness in her crotch. She felt tired, but otherwise, okay. Ms. Zambezi was sitting beside her.

"You're awake," Ms. Zambezi said, cheerfully. "You had us worried."

"Wh…what happened?" Jenna asked, still weak from the ordeal.

Ms. Zambezi stroked Jenna's hair. "The delivery was terminal. The fetus didn't survive."

Jenna blinked and gazed at the ceiling. Suddenly, she remembered where she was and what had happened. Too late, she realized the gravity of the situation. She began to weep softly.

"Oh, now, everything will be fine," Ms. Zambezi said in a comforting tone. "There's no harm to yourself. The nurse has got you all cleaned up, with extra protection that should be more than enough to get you home. And I have a small box of some extra napkins, just in case.

"Now, you'll experience some bleeding for a day or two, but that's nothing to be alarmed about. If it continues, see your doctor. All right?"

Jenna didn't look at her. She didn't even hear half of what was said. She just nodded her agreement.

"Fine. Now, about your payment, since…"

"I…don't want your money," Jenna said. "I don't want it."

"Well, I don't know," Ms. Zambezi said. "I mean, we have an agreement."

"Forget it," Jenna muttered, as she slid off the table. "I gotta get out of here."

"Well, uh," Ms. Zambezi uttered, stupidly. "I guess we can mail you the balance."

Jenna didn't stop to acknowledge Ms. Zambezi.

She left the room and walked down the hallway, searching for the right door. After a few seconds, she found the door that opened into the reception area and went in. She didn't notice if anyone else was in there as she passed through. She really didn't care. All she wanted was to get out, to be far away from the threshing floor.

When Jenna walked out into the sunlight, she was beginning to feel lightheaded. She thought that the sensation was from the sedative they'd given her. Perhaps it wasn't completely worn off. She didn't bother to stay long enough to be sure. The only thing on her mind was to get far away from this nightmare.

Jenna recounted the dream with every step as she hurried back to the train station. In retrospect, the message was so obvious. Why hadn't she realized what it was trying to say? She felt so alone. Who was there to share her grief?

She began to sob. The tears distorted her vision as they filled her eyes, causing her to stumble. Anxiety, fear, and sorrow had overtaken her. She began to wish that she'd been the one to die, and not the baby. "It should have been me," she mumbled through the sobs, "It should've been me!"

Jenna began to run. She couldn't escape the dream. The terror it caused when she first experienced it haunted her. She knew what her baby must have gone through. She just wanted to find a place, to curl up, to die. The anxiety was killing her, and she could hardly breathe.

Through the pain and sorrow, she cried out, "Oh, God! Why…why?"

Eventually, Jenna found her way to the train station. As she stood, waiting for the train, her mind was awash with images of death and sorrow. She was no longer in control of her thoughts. The floodgates were opened, and her consciousness became inundated with torment and bitterness. She had allowed her child to be killed. She had denied its potential as a human being. And in denying it, she had denied her own bond with the Blessed Mother as giver of life. Jenna had sought to be in tune with the Mother; but, after one tragic moment, she had caused the One to turn Her face from her, leaving her alone, awash in her own misery.

At last, the train pulled up. Looking over her shoulder like someone being stalked, she pushed her way through the doors and hurried into the passenger car. No empty seats. She hurried down the aisle and passed quickly through a coupling enclosure into the next car. It was sparsely occupied. So, she threw herself into the first empty seat she found.

Her eyes felt as if they would explode. Jenna could hold it back no longer as the tears flowed freely while she sobbed uncontrollably.

"Do not hinder the little children from coming to me," he had said.

Her mind wandered back in time. Roxanne had been wrong, Jenna now knew. When she had said that an abortion was the manifestation of a woman's inability to accept the unborn child as her own, she had been mistaken. She had been wrong in saying that an unborn child has no place in the One unless the mother acknowledges it. Roxanne had misled her when she said that the Universal Mind did not have a hand in directing the growth of the unborn child. Roxanne had been wrong, and Jenna and her baby had paid the price.

By denying the child, Jenna had done more than disavow its existence; she had also refused her own. The act of abandoning her unborn child had not removed it from the Universal Mind. Rather, it had caused the One to turn away from Jenna. If her whole hope in life had been to emulate the Blessed Mother, then giving her baby over to the darkness had been a grave contradiction of that hope. And there was no more reason to live.

Jenna rested her head against the window. Wanting to escape, she struggled to regain control of her thoughts. She closed her eyes and eventually drifted off into another world as the rhythmic vibrations from the train lulled her into a fitful rest.

REQUIEM

Joe sat alone in the living room, carefully nursing the same bottle of beer he'd been drinking for the past hour. Since Jenna's death a week earlier, he had been reclusive, moody, even melancholy. His face was unshaven with several days growth, his hair was greasy and matted, and his clothes unkempt. He hadn't been out for days, now; and his work piled up, unfinished.

When he found out that Jenna was dead, Joe was watching a basketball game. The phone rang. He answered it. The call came from the Montgomery County Coroner's office. They called him because her identification listed him as the person to call in case of an emergency.

He was told that Jenna had died from traumatic hemorrhagic shock, which was a polite way of saying that she'd bled to death. The coroner's office indicated that the hemorrhaging occurred primarily due to a puncture in the wall of the uterus. There was some additional minor damage to the cervix and vagina, but the bleeding from those areas would have been superficial.

Why had it happened? They had no answer. She was found on a train. The conductor remembered that she appeared somewhat disoriented and listless when she boarded the train. He said that later she had fallen asleep. After several hours, someone noticed the blood.

The police believed that she may have been sexually assaulted by a religious cult that was known for its bizarre, brutal fertility rituals. Several women, dead from similar injuries, had been found in the area during the past five years. However, no definite connection could be made, and there were no suspects. It was all just a theory put forth by some criminologist in an attempt to explain a string of mysterious deaths having the same circumstances.

Joe was dazed by the news. He didn't know what to do or say. He told them where she was from and, after some searching, found her mother's phone number, which he passed along.

When he learned of her death, it was like a piece of himself had fallen away, like losing a leg. He no longer had that support, that crutch. His life had at that moment become empty. He was scared, despite the haughty boasts and cavalier facade.

Had he loved her? Yes, but not so much for who she was. Rather, he loved her for the way she made him feel.

All his life, there had always been a female figure who, in some way, kept him propped up. When he was young, it was his mother and, to an extent, his mother's domestic partner. In college, he went through two or three girlfriends whom he selected based on how they stroked his ego. After college, there was an older woman that worked at the corporation where he first was employed; and she used him as much as he used her. Finally, there was Jenna.

Joe liked to be in control, too. It gave him sense of stability. In many ways, Joe was an insecure man. What little bit of control he held over something, or someone, was an anchor for him. Whenever the storms of life, events that he couldn't direct came along and threatened to dash him against the rocks, or upset his plans, Joe found safety with that anchor: a constant, reassuring presence.

A tall, shapely woman wearing royal blue slacks and matching jacket with a ruffled, ivory blouse entered from the bedroom. Her pleasant face was framed with long, wavy auburn hair. She was carrying a rather sizable box, which Joe didn't offer to help her with. He thoughtlessly watched as she struggled to the door and knelt down to place the box on the floor.

He'd never met Jenna's mother before. They'd spoken on the phone several times, but he'd never seen her face to face. She was an attractive woman, he thought, for an older lady. In person, now, the similarities between Jenna and her mother became obvious. Joe had a fleeting vision of taking this lady into his arms and making love to her, but only for a moment.

The lady straightened up to her full height and gracefully walked over to Joe. She looked down at him, almost frowning, and said, "Well, I believe that's everything."

He didn't look up, only grunted. She had called a couple days ago about collecting Jenna's belongings, and she wondered why Joe hadn't attended the funeral. He made some lame excuse about not being able to leave home to go to Iowa because of business commitments, which she graciously accepted. Joe was never sure if she really bought his story. If she didn't, she never let on. He didn't care, anyway.

He glanced at the box sitting on the floor next to the door. One box. All this way for just one box. He could have mailed that much to her and saved them both an awkward encounter. What would he do with the rest of Jenna's things?

"The rest of her things," she continued, "you can do with as you please. None of it's worth anything to me."

"Yeah, fine…whatever." He took a swig of beer. He grimaced. The beer was getting warm and he knew that it was his last. He hated warm beer.

She sat down in the chair next to him and brushed back a lock of hair with a delicate hand. "Ah, I realize we don't know each other all that well…uhm, I mean, Jenna told me so much about you," she said, smiling, "but, well, I just want you to know…to me, you're like one of the family. She cared about you a great deal."

Joe slowly shifted his gaze from the floor to her. Her face had a pensive, sincere quality to it. He sighed and nodded. "Hmm, well, I can appreciate your sentiment, Ms. Blackwell…but I only wish I could return it."

He sat back in the sofa, allowing the cushions to embrace him. Looking off into the distance, he said, "I loved your daughter...very much; but I have to get on with my life, now. I just don't want any reminders. That's all. Understand?"

Her brown eyes darted around the room as they began to cloud up. She was hurt by what he'd just said; his cold words had cut like a stiletto thrown from across the room. She knew that Jenna's life growing up hadn't been everything it should have been, and she realized that the blame rested squarely on her shoulders. Joe was the last, and dearest, thing that Jenna had possessed. She only wanted to keep hold of this final piece of Jenna's existence.

Joe didn't notice the tears. He had turned his attention away from her. She looked too much like Jenna.

Wiping her eyes, she said, "Well...I understand." She blew her nose on a tissue she'd pulled from a pocket.

Joe took another swig of beer, as if she wasn't even there. She looked at him, wondering what Jenna had seen. He wasn't particularly attractive, nor was he very congenial. Perhaps he was correct after all. Maybe they should just part company and leave well enough alone.

After a few moments of silence, she said, "I suppose I should be going now."

He said nothing as she stood up.

She walked to the door and put her coat on. Looking down at the box, she was reminded of something. "By the way," she said, turning to Joe, "who is Hank Philips?"

He looked up and cocked his head. After several seconds, he said, "I don't...wait a minute. Yes. I remember him. Never met him, though. He was some old guy that Jenna'd latched on to. I think she used to spend time with him at the senior citizen's center. I'm surprised she never brought him home," he added sadly.

Jenna's mother smiled and looked at the box. She remembered how, when Jenna was growing up, she would bring home stray animals all of the time. Dogs, cats, injured birds. She'd even come home with a squirrel in a box, once. "Yes," she noted, "I'm surprised, too."

Jenna's mother picked up the box with some effort. Then, she realized that she couldn't open the door while holding the box. "Could you please open the door, Joe?" she asked.

He just sat there at first, looking rather stupid. "Sure," he muttered, at last. He got up and walked over.

As he opened the door, she said, "Joe, I hope you have a long and happy life. Take care."

Joe said nothing as she left the apartment. He watched her until she was at the elevator where she turned and waved. He returned the gesture; then, closed the door.

The apartment felt empty and utterly quiet. He was alone. Joe walked into the bedroom. Most of the boxes he'd put Jenna's belongings into sat undisturbed. Only a couple had been opened.

Noticing a small book lying on the bed, he picked it up and thumbed through the pages. It was the book that Hank Philips had left for Jenna. Joe gently ran a finger over the worn, steel-plated cover. Then, he sank to the floor, sobbing.

About the Author

Al currently works in the training field as an instructional technologist. He has a B.S. in Psychology. He served honorably in the U.S. Navy for 6 years. Al is divorced, and has two daughters. There is nothing remarkable about him, except that he continues to pursue a dream.

0-595-22346-X

CPSIA information can be obtained
at www.ICGtesting.com
Printed in the USA
FSOW01n1936260117
30050FS